PENGUIN CLASSICS

THE KISS AND OTHER STORIES

ANTON PAVLOVICH CHEKHOV, the son of a former serf, was born in 1860 in Taganrog, a port on the sea of Azov. He received a classical education at the Taganrog Secondary School, then in 1879 he went to Moscow, where he entered the medical faculty of the university, graduating in 1884. During his university years he supported his family by contributing humorous stories and sketches to magazines. He published his first volume of stories, *Motley Stories*, in 1886 and a year later his second volume, *In the Twilight*, for which he was awarded the Pushkin Prize by the Russian Academy. His most famous stories were written after his return from the convict island of Sakhalin, which he visited in 1890. For five years he lived on his small country estate near Moscow, but when his health began to fail he moved to the Crimea. After 1900, the rest of his life was spent at Yalta, where he met Tolstoy and Gorky. He wrote very few stories during the last years of his life, devoting most of his time to a thorough revision of his stories for a collected edition of his works, published in 1901, and to the writing of his great plays. In 1901 Chekhov married Olga Knipper, an actress of the Moscow Art Theatre. He died of consumption in 1904.

•

RONALD WILKS studied Russian language and literature at Trinity College, Cambridge, and later Russian literature at London University, where he received his Ph.D. in 1972. He has also translated 'The Little Demon' by Sologub, and, for the Penguin Classics, *My Childhood*, *My Apprenticeship* and *My Universities* by Gorky, *Diary of a Madman* by Gogol and three other volumes of stories by Chekhov, *The Party and Other Stories*, *The Duel and Other Stories* and *The Fiancée and Other Stories*.

CHEKHOV

THE KISS

AND OTHER STORIES

Translated with an Introduction
by Ronald Wilks

PENGUIN BOOKS

PENGUIN BOOKS

Published by the Penguin Group
Penguin Books Ltd, 27 Wrights Lane, London W8 5TZ, England
Viking Penguin, a division of Penguin Books USA Inc.
375 Hudson Street, New York, New York 10014, USA
Penguin Books Australia Ltd, Ringwood, Victoria, Australia
Penguin Books Canada Ltd, 2801 John Street, Markham, Ontario, Canada L3R 1B4
Penguin Books (NZ) Ltd, 182–190 Wairau Road, Auckland 10, New Zealand

Penguin Books Ltd, Registered Offices: Harmondsworth, Middlesex, England

This translation first published 1982
7 9 10 8

Printed in England by Clays Ltd, St Ives plc
Filmset in Monophoto Bembo

In memory of my father

R.W.

Contents

[illegible]

[illegible] stories in [illegible] as a story [illegible] with [illegible] three [illegible] magazine [illegible] are [illegible] of the [illegible] and [illegible] so [illegible] much [illegible]

[illegible] markably [illegible] a major [illegible] physical [illegible] lack of [illegible] revolution [illegible] for [illegible] with [illegible]

Introduction

The ten stories in this selection were written when Chekhov had reached his maturity as a short story writer, between 1887 and 1902. If they are compared with his earlier feuilletons, sketches and very short stories – of two or three pages – which he had turned out by the dozen for weekly magazines, it is astonishing to see how far he had progressed in this genre in a comparatively short time. In 1885 Dmitry Grigorovich, one of the first Russian writers to show the dark side of peasant life, together with the literary editor of the journal *New Times*, Alexei Suvorin, had begged Chekhov not to squander his talents on short sketches but to take up 'serious literary work'. Chekhov himself had not attached much importance to his early, very short stories nor to some of his mature work; in 1890 he wrote amusingly to one of the Tchaikovsky family that he had 'drawn up an honours list' of contemporary Russian talent, according first place to Tolstoy, second to Tchaikovsky, third to the painter Repin, leaving himself ninety-eighth.

The remarkable advance is displayed in these stories and shows Chekhov as a master stylist and a probing analyst (he himself had often admitted that his medical training had helped greatly in his explorations of the human psyche), unmasking the mediocrity, lack of ideals, and spiritual and physical inertia of his generation. In a biting letter of 1892 to Suvorin he accused his contemporaries – and writers in particular – of complete lack of ideals and purpose: 'We have no politics, we don't believe in revolution, God doesn't exist ... the man who wants nothing, hopes for nothing and fears nothing can never be an artist.' But it would be quite wrong to regard him as a moralist, castigating his generation with a sombre didacticism, or even as a writer 'with a message': he always made it emphatically clear that he never wished himself to be regarded as such. In these grim pictures of peasant life, in these telling portraits of men and women enmeshed in trivialities, in the finely observed, suffocating atmosphere of provincial towns with their pompous officials, frustrated, self-seeking wives and spineless husbands, Chekhov does not expound any system of morality but leaves the reader to draw what conclusion he will: Chekhov observes and suggests, but rarely judges.

'The Kiss' was first published in 1887. Chekhov had asked a friend – a retired artillery officer – to read his description of a brigade on the move. The officer was astounded by the amazing accuracy of detail and acuteness of observation, remarking that he found it difficult to believe that the story had been written by a civilian and not by a 'hardened soldier'.

According to Chekhov's brother Mikhail, elements of the story recall the period when Anton took a holiday in the small town of Voskresensk, where an artillery battalion was stationed.

The 'hero' of 'The Kiss' is an unprepossessing young army officer, Ryabovich (the surname suggests a 'pock-marked' or 'pitted' complexion and is an example of how meticulous Chekhov was in selecting apt and descriptive names for his characters); he is short, stooping, very shy and obviously most unattractive to women. When his brigade stops for the night in a small village, he is invited, together with his fellow-officers, to take tea with a retired general, who lives on an estate not far from the village. Embarrassingly timid and withdrawn, and fully conscious of his own insignificance, Ryabovich takes no part in the general merriment and dancing at the general's house and eventually wanders off on his own. First he finds himself in the billiard-room, where he declines an invitation to join in the game. Trying to return to the ballroom, he loses his way in the huge house and enters a room which is quite dark. Evidently a young lady had a rendezvous with a lover in that room and by mistake kisses Ryabovich in the dark: she is horrified and Ryabovich rushes off towards a chink of light in the door. After this incident, nothing at all eventful takes place in the story, the rest of which is devoted to a subtle psychological analysis of the tremendous effect the 'mistaken' kiss has on Ryabovich, who plainly has no experience of women and whose entire being has been aroused.

He feels his whole life has been transformed and anxiously tries to discover, without success, who the young lady was. He surveys the young ladies at dinner and attempts to build up an image in his mind, merging features from several different possibilities into one composite ideal person. This idealization is sharply contrasted with the earthy, hearty attitude of his fellow-officers: there is the dashing Lobytko, who can 'sniff out' women like a setter and whose own rather salacious and probably fictitious account of a mysterious encounter on a train caps the few words Ryabovich can find to say about his experience in the darkened room. Later in 'The Kiss', a brigadier makes uninhibited comments to the officers about affairs, and Chekhov makes mention of the 'sexual sallies' carried out by the officers when they go rampaging in the village.

Gradually, however, Ryabovich's euphoria gives way to the grim realization that the kiss had not been intended for him and that he had built up the whole incident into something quite unwarranted by the facts of the matter. His habitual feelings of isolation and frustration return and he withdraws into his shell again.

Not long afterwards, the brigade happens to stay overnight again in the same village and the general sends an invitation once more, chiefly for form's sake and not from any real desire to entertain the rowdy, hard-drinking officers. By then Ryabovich's dream has been shattered, he has no inclination to accept. Earlier in the story, nature had appeared joyful, with the sweet fragrance of blossoming trees, singing nightingales; but now Ryabovich's surroundings seem to echo his innermost feelings of desolation and despair. Although it might be termed the pathetic fallacy, this mirroring of a character's mood in nature, which is coloured by his whole outlook, is characteristic of Chekhov and is achieved so subtly that it never appears as any contrived seeking after effect. Chekhov brilliantly conveys this mood of despair and utter hopelessness:

> He went down to the river, where he could see the general's bathing-hut and towels hanging over the rail on the little bridge . . . He looked down at the water . . . 'How stupid, how very stupid!' Ryabovich thought as he looked at the fast-flowing water. Now, when he hoped for nothing, that adventure of the kiss, his impatience, his vague longings and disillusionment appeared in a new light . . . And the whole world, the whole of life, struck Ryabovich

as a meaningless, futile joke. As he turned his eyes from the water to the sky, he remembered how fate had accidentally caressed him – in the guise of an unknown woman. He recalled the dreams and visions of that summer and his life seemed terribly empty, miserable, colourless . . .

Clearly, an experience which his fellow-officers would surely have shrugged off as a joke has had a deeply traumatic effect on him and colours his whole outlook.

'The Kiss' is a fine portrayal of a great emotional upheaval: by some cruel quirk of fate, an accidental kiss, destined for a luckier person, sets in motion a whole turmoil of longings in the mind of an unloved, insignificant little officer, which for a brief while had given him a new lease of life. Inevitably, the sad realization dawns on him that he would never know who had kissed him and, worse, that he would never be loved. The apparently meaningless routine of army life fully echoes Ryabovich's own return to a dreary, monotonous existence. Life is ruthless and that happiness, which he had fleetingly glimpsed, has turned out to be a sad deception.

'Peasants' was first published in 1897 and the censors immediately took a strong objection to the 'too black a picture it paints of peasant life'. Indeed, so true to life were the descriptions of the downtrodden, exploited peasants that the censorship committee looked upon the story as a documentary article and cut out several passages, including an entire chapter which, in their view, would lead readers to believe that the clergy and provincial civil servants were directly responsible for the unfair imposition of taxes and confiscation of property from peasants in arrears with rent, etc. Some of the most 'offensive' passages, portraying the drunkenness, irreligion and general depravity of the villagers, were toned down when they were published in Suvorin's edition.

Chekhov, in a letter to his brother Mikhail, states that the fire in the story was based on an actual occurrence at Melikhovo, his country estate, two years previously, and Mikhail Chekhov wrote, most revealingly: 'These five years in Melikhovo were not wasted by Anton. They laid their special imprint on his works of this period, influenced his literary activity and made him a profounder and more serious writer. Anton himself admitted Melikhovo's influence.' In addition, Mikhail

Chekhov categorically states that Anton's direct dealings with peasants on the estate had a strong influence on both 'Peasants' and 'In the Gully'. As one would expect, Chekhov was a good master and life at Melikhovo was peaceful.

The story tells of a penniless, sick Moscow hotel waiter who returns to his native village to die, and it caused a furore. Tolstoy, greatly displeased at the mercilessly truthful description of peasant life, reacted angrily, stating: '"Peasants" is a sin. The author doesn't know the common people.' Chekhov's message is clear and uncompromising: life in villages could be far happier were it not for the overwhelming poverty and squalor, directly produced by the exploitation of the poor peasants by the rich. As matters stand, the only escape for the peasant from a life of grinding want, lies in drink and every church festival is made an excuse for a drunken spree:

> On Elijah's day they drank, on the Feast of the Assumption they drank, on the day of the Exaltation of the Cross they drank. The Feast of the Intercession was a parish holiday in Zhukovo, and the men celebrated it by going on a three-day binge. They drank their way through fifty roubles of communal funds and on top of this they had a whip-round from all the farms for some vodka. On the first day of the Feast, the Chikildeyevs slaughtered a sheep and ate it for breakfast, lunch and dinner, consuming vast quantities, and then the children got up during the night for another bite. During the entire three days Kiryak was terribly drunk – he drank everything away, even his cap and boots, and he gave Marya such a thrashing that they had to douse her with cold water. Afterwards everyone felt ashamed and sick.

Chekhov brilliantly describes the barbaric ignorance of the peasants, some of whom are like wild animals. Their grasp of Christianity is primitive, churchgoing being an empty ritual for them, and all they seem to know is when to fast and what food is forbidden on certain high holidays.

In this story we see how the poor peasants are ruthlessly exploited by the rich (or kulak) peasants, seeing in the *zemstvo* or rural council the cause of all their misfortune. Plagued by morbid superstition, they are terrified of all illness – even the most minor complaint; indeed, they live on the barest level of subsistence, easy prey for the strong and predatory. Consequently, Chekhov's picture of the peasants' sad lot contrasts sharply with Tolstoy's idealization of the peasant with his 'unsullied virtues', and in both 'Peasants' and 'In the Gully' he shows up the cardinal error of regarding these poor creatures as the living embodiment of God-like purity and true guardians of Christian morality.

Although the peasants had been officially emancipated in 1861, they were now no freer than they had been before. Their lot was even worse, and alcoholism, venereal disease and epidemics were far more prevalent in the 1890s than four decades previously. Old Osip takes a longing look in 'Peasants' at the 'golden past', before the emancipation: life then, although still hard, had a meaning, offered an excitement and variety that had now gone for ever.

Other writers, such as Grigorovich and, later, Bunin, painted even gloomier pictures of peasant life, and while Chekhov attacks the peasants for their lethargy, drunkenness and barbaric ways he yet finds some vindication for them:

> During the summer and winter months there were hours and days when these people appeared to live worse than cattle and life with them was really terrible. They were coarse, dishonest, filthy, drunk, always quarrelling and arguing among themselves, with no respect for one another and living in mutual fear and suspicion. Who maintains the pubs and makes the peasants drunk? The peasant. Who embezzles the village, school and parish funds and spends it all on drink? The peasant ... Yes, it was terrible living with these people; nevertheless, they were still human beings, suffering and weeping like other people and there was nothing in their lives which did not provide some excuse: killing work which made bodies ache all over at night, harsh winters, poor harvests, overcrowding, no help and nowhere to find it ...

After the death of Nikolay, Chekhov had intended continuing this story, describing Olga and Sasha's subsequent life in Moscow. But he never carried this out: perhaps he thought, and rightly so if this were the case, that the picture was complete, and that any continuation might weaken the overall effect.

'The Bishop' (1902) is one of the most deeply felt and affecting of all Chekhov's stories. Written at the time of his marriage to Olga Knipper, and in fact not long before the author's death, it portrays the last moments in the life of a bishop. A year before the story first appeared, Chekhov had written to Olga Knipper that the subject had been in his head for fifteen years. When the story was published it was highly acclaimed by contemporary critics and writers, especially by Ivan Bunin, a close friend, who wrote ecstatically: '"The Bishop" is an amazing piece of writing. Only someone whose sole preoccupation is with literature and has himself experienced these hellish torments can understand this work in all its beauty.' And the short story writer Kuprin stressed the astonishing accuracy of observation, stating that the characters in this story must have been based on real people – monks from the monastery near Melikhovo, Chekhov's estate. But Chekhov's brother Mikhail said that the prototype for the bishop was a Stepan Petrov, student of philology at Moscow University, who knew Chekhov when he was living in Moscow. This student later took holy orders and became Father Sergei; and when he went to Yalta, suffering from a nervous disorder, he often called on Chekhov. Chekhov's brother goes on to say that the subsequent frequent meetings Anton had with Father Sergei provided the basic material for the story. However, according to another source, Anton happened to see a photograph in a Yalta shop window of a certain Bishop Gribanovsky. He was intrigued, made inquiries into the bishop's life, and the present story was the result. Whatever the true source, this late work is a masterpiece and comes very close to being a prose-poem, so fine is the lyrical element, so subtle and telling the atmospheric details which run like leitmotivs throughout the story.

In the tortured mind of the bishop (and contemporary critics were quick to note the spiritual discord within him) and the final illumination in the face of death one can find a strong parallel in Tolstoy's *Death of Ivan Ilyich*: like Tolstoy's Ivan Ilyich, the closer he comes to death the happier he is.

The whole story has a dreamlike quality and the opening scene in the church takes on an almost hallucinatory nature as the bishop, who is conducting a service on the eve of Palm Sunday, surveys his congregation: 'lights had burned low, wicks needed snuffing and everything was obscured by a thick haze. The congregation rocked like the sea in the gloomy church and all those faces, old and young, male and female, looked exactly alike to Bishop Peter, who had not been feeling well for the past three days . . .'

When the service draws to a close, the church is filled with a 'gentle weeping' and the reader becomes aware that the bishop is doomed to die, very soon, that this is inevitable. All the signs at the opening of 'The Bishop' point towards this approaching death: the bishop feels unwell, with laboured breathing, dry throat and shaking legs – all characteristic symptoms of typhoid. After the bishop leaves the church, Chekhov finely contrasts the beauty of the moonlit night and the joyful ringing of Easter bells with the deep melancholy of the bishop.

Back in his monastery, the bishop's thoughts turn to his mother (whom he thought he had seen in that billowing sea of faces in the church) and to the golden age of his childhood – a time of innocent happiness and a recurring theme in Chekhov (cf. the beautiful evocation of childhood in another story in this selection, 'Gooseberries'). As he senses that death is drawing near, the bishop is filled with longing for 'dear, precious, unforgettable childhood!'. He feels that it has 'gone forever' and asks himself, 'Why does this time always seem brighter, gayer, richer than it is in reality?' In the bishop's conversations with the monks, especially with Father Sisoy (whose prototype was possibly a Father Anany who often visited Chekhov's parents), the author shows a mastery of colloquial ecclesiastical language.

As the illness worsens, the bishop asks Father Sisoy to massage him – a symbolic embalming, perhaps, and preparation for burial.

His mother and niece call on him. His mother is overawed in the presence of a bishop, although he is her own son, and is at a loss for words, so great is her embarrassment. Then the bishop's thoughts go flooding back to his student life, to the eight years he spent away from Russia, to happier times. All this had now gone forever and his routine duties become a burden and source of suffering for him and have the most enervating effect on his already weakened state. He is deeply worried and grieved by the fact that even his own parishioners and his mother are frightened of him, especially as he prides himself on his mild, gentle disposition.

As he goes to take another service, his mind once again fills with visions of the past, of a happy childhood, and the whole story is pervaded by contrast of past and present, of life and death. After Maundy Thursday all he desires, when he has returned to his room, is to climb into bed, and he requests the lay brother to close the shutters: the inner darkness of his consciousness is paralleled with the darkness in which he now wishes to repose and these states of gloom are vividly contrasted with a radiant, sunny nature, the joyful time of spring: 'the weather turned out sunny, warm and cheerful, and water bubbled along the ditches, while the never-ending, sweetly soothing song of the skylarks drifted in from the fields beyond the town. The trees, already in bud, smiled their welcome, while the fathomless, vast expanse of blue sky overhead floated away into the mysterious beyond.'

As he lies on his bed he grows highly irritable, weeps once more. His mother, realizing how serious his condition is, casts her shyness aside and talks naturally to him, calling him now by his childhood name, Paulie.

When he takes a further service, everything again assumes that same hallucinatory, visionary quality: all he can make out is a sea of blurred candle flames, indistinguishable faces among the congregation; yet again his mind turns to the past.

On the day before Easter Sunday he dies, while outside the whole of nature seems to be rejoicing, with birds singing and a brightly shining spring sun. As he lies on his deathbed he imagines himself as: 'just an ordinary, simple man walking swiftly and cheerfully across fields, beating his stick on the ground, under a broad, brilliant sky. Now he was as free as a bird and could go wherever he liked!'

The final delirium has brought peace of mind, resignation and spiritual illumination: now he feels like a natural, normal person. Soon after his death he is forgotten, as though he had never existed.

Throughout this story, Chekhov strikes a fine balance between the tortured, agonizing last moments of the bishop, conveyed by the repeated images of death, and the radiance of a seemingly indifferent nature. And a further contrast is made between the bishop's death and the time of rejoicing in the Resurrection of Christ: Christ's death is to be rejoiced in as he was to rise again, never to be forgotten; the bishop dies and is consigned to oblivion. The constant counterpoint of images of spring, resurrection and re-birth, and of death and disintegration gives the story great poetic beauty.

'The Bishop' is a perfect work of art. Chekhov attached such importance to it that he insisted it be printed without a single word being changed. Indeed, he gave instructions that he would prefer it not to be published at all if anything was altered by the censors, even the smallest detail – firm testimony to the essential unity and compression of the writing.

Like the world-weary professor in Chekhov's famous 'A Boring Story', the bishop desired to be loved for himself, not for his status as a bishop, a point sharply brought home by his ever-growing impatience with the trivia of church routine and the alienation his elevated position has caused between him and his subordinates. This impatience and dissatisfaction with the way he has had to spend his life is voiced in the splenetic outburst as he lies dying: 'Why am I a bishop? ... I should have been a village priest, a lay-reader or an ordinary monk. All of this crushes the life out of me...'

Only at death's door (like Ivan Ilyich) does he attain any peace of mind, approachable now and happy in the knowledge that he has become an ordinary human being again. Death is the true leveller.

The first chapter of 'The Russian Master' was originally published in 1889 as 'The Philistines', with a second chapter, 'The Russian Master', following in 1894. Both chapters were then published together under the story's present name.

Chekhov gives a gently satirical picture of middle-class life in a small provincial town, with all its vulgarity, bigotry and artificiality, which our hero finally rejects. At this period of his development, Chekhov was preoccupied with depictions of life in middle-class provincial society, particularly with the predatory, grasping female – described so well in a later story, included in this selection, 'Anna Round the Neck'. He had described his story as a 'light-hearted piece of nonsense from the lives of provincial guinea pigs' and the satire is conveyed with a light touch.

The story almost certainly takes place in a southern Russian town, possibly Chekhov's own birthplace, Taganrog. Nature here is exotic with the fragrance of flowering acacias and lilacs, melon plantations and olive groves. Its hero, Nikitin, is in love with Masha, a young woman from a rich family, who appears to be chiefly interested in horseriding. Nikitin achieves his aim, but in the end the blissful domestic idyll falls apart and the story closes with Nikitin, a schoolteacher, desperate to escape married life and the stifling atmosphere of the town with all its 'vulgarity, nothing but boring, insignificant people, pots of sour cream, jugs of milk, cockroaches, stupid women . . .'

The development of the narrative is typical of Chekhov: all appears serene and happy after the wedding, but then a change takes place – almost imperceptibly at first and very subtly interwoven – and disillusionment and nausea (as experienced by the hero) set in. This change of mood runs parallel with changes in nature: at the beginning of the story nature is radiant and sunny. However, when Nikitin comes to write his diary we find, 'as though they *were echoing my mood*,* the trees began to rustle, telling me that it was going to rain. The rooks are cawing and my Masha, who's just fallen asleep, has a peculiarly sad look.'

Soon after, the winter weather becomes irritatingly mild, the wind howls mournfully and it pours with rain when Nikitin returns from his club, where he has lost twelve roubles at cards. It is then he suddenly realizes the whole falsity of his position: a little earlier in the story he has tried to rationalize his position and convince himself that he has earned his happiness:

> But I don't look on my happiness as a chance happening, as though it suddenly dropped down from heaven. Our happiness is perfectly in the nature of things, in strict accord with the laws of logic. I believe that man is the creator of his own happiness and now I am enjoying the fruits of that creation. Yes, I can say without any false modesty that *I* created this happiness and I am its rightful possessor.

Now, returning from his club, he sees the whole falsity of his reasoning:

> Now he realized that he wasn't sorry about losing twelve roubles, because he got them for nothing in the first place. If he had been a

*My italics.

> workman, he would have treasured every kopek and wouldn't have been indifferent as to whether he won or lost. And he concluded that all this happiness had come to him without any effort on his part, that it had no point, and it was essentially just as much a luxury as medicine. If, like the overwhelming majority of people, he had been tormented with worrying where the next crust of bread was coming from or had been forced to struggle for his living, or if he had backache or a pain in the chest from *hard work*, then his supper, his warm comfortable flat and all that domestic happiness would have been an absolute necessity, a reward, something to enrich his life. But now all this had only some strange, vague significance for him.

The domestic idyll has become a nightmare and the only hope lies in escape from a way of life that is stifling him.

The following stories, 'Man in a Case', 'Gooseberries' and 'Concerning Love', can be termed a trilogy, each story being linked to the preceding one. The first, 'Man in a Case', was published in 1898 and Chekhov's brother Mikhail states that the prototype for the main character, Belikov, was Dyakonov, an inspector at the Taganrog gymnasium where Anton had studied, adding that his brother also drew on events at the school – the annual spring outing, for example. It is also possible that the prototype for the main character could have been the journalist Menshikov, editor of the journal *The Week*, as Chekhov refers to him in his diary for 1896: 'Menshikov goes around with galoshes in dry weather, carrying an umbrella so as not to perish from sunstroke, and is scared of washing in cold water . . .' In addition, Professor Serebryakov in *Uncle Vanya* never ventures out without umbrella and galoshes. Clearly, Chekhov was fascinated by this type of encapsulated, cocooned individual and 'Man in a Case' is his fullest portrayal of this strange manifestation of extreme eccentricity. Critics have justly pointed out the similarity of Chekhov's 'hero' to characters in Gogol and Goncharov, particularly in his automaton-like nature.

Belikov, whose only wish is to shield himself from any external influences within the protective cocoon he has built around himself, is the very incarnation of petty tyranny. Not only does he bully the students at the school where he teaches but hounds the adult community in the town, making their lives a veritable hell. He thrives on oppressing others with his ridiculously stringent rules and regulations, always keeping strictly to the letter of the law; as a result he has a deadening effect on his whole environment. Chekhov stresses the point that contemporary society as he saw it was a perfect breeding-ground for characters such as these. And, although Belikov dies, he warns that more will rise up.

While 'Man in a Case' is told by a schoolteacher, Burkin, the narrative in the second story of this trilogy, 'Gooseberries', is taken up by Burkin's friend Ivan Ivanovich, a vet, with whom he had been sheltering in a barn for the night, after returning late from a hunting expedition. The second story links the first and last and contemporary critics were quick to see the similarity of thematic material running through the three stories: lack of will, moral cowardice, pettiness and bigotry generated by a complacent society. Chekhov thought that all these defects could be pinned on his own generation.

In 'Gooseberries', Ivan Ivanovich, the vet, tells the story of his brother, who has the preposterous surname of Chimsha-Gimalaysky and, although only a minor government official, has aspirations to become one of the gentry, with his own country estate. In many ways he resembles the poor clerk in Gogol's famous story 'The Overcoat', obsessed with the acquisition of something that is really quite trivial and undergoing all kinds of deprivation to achieve his aim in life – in this case a country estate where he can grow gooseberries. There are many Gogolian echoes in this story, particularly in the comparisons of people to pigs: Chimsha-Gimalaysky grows as fat as a pig, seems about to grunt into his blanket; his dog is as fat as a pig and so is his cook. The moral connotations are quite clear in these recurring similes and they had been used to great effect by Chekhov's celebrated predecessor. 'Gooseberries' closes with a diatribe on happiness, seen as a state of hypnosis, affecting the supposedly educated classes and based on the misery of the masses:

> And I thought how many satisfied, happy people really do exist in this world! And what a powerful force they are! Just take a look at this life of ours and you will see the arrogance and idleness of the strong, the ignorance and bestiality of the weak. Everywhere there's unspeakable poverty, overcrowding, degeneracy, drunkenness,

> hypocrisy and stupid lies . . . And yet peace and quiet reign in every house and street . . . It's obvious that the happy man feels contented only because the unhappy ones bear their burden without saying a word . . . Someone ought to stand with a hammer at the door of every happy contented man, continually banging on it to remind him that there are unhappy people around and that however happy *he* may be at the time, sooner or later life will show him its claws and disaster will overtake him . . . But there isn't anyone holding a hammer, so our happy man goes his own sweet way and is only gently ruffled by life's trivial cares . . . All's well as far as *he's* concerned.

For Chekhov it was a matter of great concern that there was no one or nothing (at least in the closing decade of the last century) to administer this sharp shock in order to jolt people out of their complacency, narrow-mindedness and lack of positive ideals.

In turn, 'Gooseberries' is linked to 'Concerning Love', in which Alyokhin, who has been entertaining the vet and the teacher, tells in the first person of an experience in his own life. Here the narrator could have grasped happiness but in the end is shown to be too weak to win the lady with whom he has fallen in love: the situation is similar to Gurov's predicament in 'Lady with Lapdog', but in the latter story the hero takes positive steps to achieve his goal and does not give up like Alyokhin. As Belikov and Chimsha-Gimalaysky in the preceding stories have withdrawn from the real world and are content inside the artificial barriers they have erected around themselves, so Alyokhin is enclosed within his own little world and simply does not have the courage to break out of it. The message of these three stories is quite clear: man needs more than his own little patch of ground, he needs 'the whole wide world' and should try to make the best possible use of his abilities, instead of remaining content with what he has, lacking courage to take a positive step forwards. The human spirit is worthy of greater things than a few miserable gooseberry bushes and Chekhov saw the men of his generation as quite satisfied within the world of their own petty little domestic bliss and trivial amusements. Alyokhin could have won Anna had he acted more forcefully. But he merely sheds a few tears and weakly lets her go in the final parting on the train. His mistake was waiting for love and happiness to come to him of their own accord. Instead of breaking out of his own little world, he sublimates his energy slaving away on his farm, anaesthetizing himself as a result from the really pressing problems of life, shying away from a positive solution and living like a 'squirrel in a cage'.

'A Case History' (1898) concerns a doctor urgently summoned to attend an ostensibly sick girl, heiress to a cotton-printing factory not far from Moscow. The story is a strong indictment of the dehumanizing effects of industrialism. In his notebooks Chekhov had written: 'If you take a look at some factory in a backwater it strikes you as peaceful ... but look closer and you'll see the utter ignorance of its owners, blinded by their egoism, the terrible condition of the factory workers, rubbish, vodka and lice.' These remarks are repeated, almost word for word, in the story itself.

The doctor's first impressions of the factory and its surroundings are hardly favourable: 'They reached a wide open square, devoid of any grass. Here there were five enormous factory blocks with chimneys ... everything was covered with a rather strange grey deposit that could have been dust. Miserable little gardens and the managers' houses with their green or red roofs were scattered here and there, like oases in a desert.'

After examining the young girl, the doctor concludes that she is not really ill at all and clearly sees the cause of her nervous tension and nocturnal palpitations in severe frustration – possibly sexual and most certainly the result of the isolation brought about by her wealth and secure comfort. The whole irony of the situation, as the doctor sees it when he makes his carefully considered conclusion, lies in the fact that:

> Fifteen hundred or two thousand workers are slaving away, without a break, in unhealthy conditions, producing inferior cotton print, are half-starved and only now and then find relief from this nightmare in the pub. A hundred people supervise their work and the lives of these hundred supervisors are wasted entering fines in the record-book, swearing and being unfair to the workers ... But what exactly *are* these profits, how do they use them? ... As I see it, there's five factories turning out cheap cotton print ... just to keep Miss Christina [the governess] supplied with madeira and sturgeon.

Indeed, the only happy person in the house is the governess, both the girl and her mother being miserable creatures.

After his examination and searching questioning, the doctor sees hope for the girl in that she is aware of the spiritual aridity of her life, of the uselessness of her existence, as this very awareness produces sleepless nights and acute tension. In this insomnia there is something to be respected: 'now you can't sleep . . . Of course, this is better than being contented, sleeping soundly and thinking all's well with the world. Your insomnia is something *honourable*: whatever you may think, it's a good sign.'

The full horror of the industrial desert is conveyed by small, but significant, and carefully selected details: the strange metallic tapping made by the night watchman, which the doctor finds most unnerving, the red glow in windows which he compares to the eyes of an all-consuming devil, which has everyone in its grasp. The doctor takes a detached, clinical view of the so-called improvements in the factory workers' lives – the canteens, magic-lantern shows – and these measures strike him as mere palliatives, so that he compares the workers to an incurable patient who is given palliatives temporarily to sedate him. Chekhov's hostility to this industrial wasteland is everywhere apparent; only when the doctor takes his leave is there any ray of light and his talk to the girl appears to have had the right effect. In stark contrast to the barrenness of the factory complex, nature now becomes radiant and joyful, and the doctor drives away enjoying the warm sunshine: 'The larks were singing and the church bells rang out . . . along the road to the station Korolyov had forgotten all about factory workers, pile-dwellings, the devil and was thinking of the time – perhaps not far away – when life would be just as radiant and joyful as that calm Sunday morning.'

In that final speech to his patient, where he voices the hope that life (although he would never live to see it) would be better in fifty years' time, we find a direct parallel to Tuzenbakh's words in the third act of *The Three Sisters*.

The second peasant story in this selection, 'In the Gully', was published in 1900 and written at the request of Maxim Gorky and the editor of the radical journal *Life*. After 'Peasants', Chekhov was understandably apprehensive about the reception this new story might have at the hands of the censors, especially as it paints an even grimmer picture of peasant life, being surpassed in this respect by perhaps only Ivan Bunin's 'The Village' (1910) in unremitting gloom. In the year of its publication, Chekhov had written to Olga Knipper rather light-heartedly, saying that his story would be 'very strange, crowded with characters, with many landscape descriptions, a half-moon, a bittern making a booming noise in the far distance, sounding just like a cow locked in a shed'. A passage, almost identical to this, is incorporated in the story itself. Later, Chekhov's brother stated that Anton had taken various incidents from his visit to the penal settlement on Sakhalin and used them in the story. However, Chekhov stressed that the descriptions in 'Peasants' were based on life near his country estate of Melikhovo and wrote:

> I'm describing life as it really is in the central provinces, *that* I know best. The Khrymin merchants really do exist, only in actual fact they are far worse. From the age of eight their children take to vodka, lead a dissipated life in their adolescence and infect the whole neighbourhood with syphilis – I don't mention the latter in my story as it might spoil my artistic purpose. Lipa's child being scalded to death with boiling water is no unique event and is often encountered by country doctors.

The anecdote of the caviare, told at the beginning of the story, was apparently based on an actual occurrence recounted to Chekhov by Ivan Bunin. At all events, 'In the Gully' recalls life at Melikhovo some eighteen months earlier (the story was written in Yalta); Chekhov had always affirmed that he wrote solely by memory, never from immediate, direct experience: 'My memory has to sieve through my material so that only the important or typical remains, as on a filter.'

'In the Gully' was acclaimed by contemporary writers and critics, and its author was particularly praised for his deep sensitivity. In the year of publication, Gorky informed Chekhov that the story had made a great impression on Tolstoy. Gorky himself devoted a whole article to 'In the Gully', in which he wrote that the author, besides being a talented artist, was a 'creator of works of great social significance, with an acute understanding of the chaos, the stupidity of peasant life'. At the same time, he keenly saw that Chekhov was basically an optimist – for all the gloom conveyed by the story, which shows even more strongly than 'Peasants' the terrible lot of the peasant faced by ever-encroaching industrialization. If Chekhov wished us to take a moral from the story, it would be: wholesale industrialization, with its accompanying spoliation of the countryside, can have only a destructive effect on the peasant community. In fact, the rising tide of industrialism in the later nineteenth century led rapidly to the disintegration of village life, with subsequent mass movements of peasants to the towns to form the new urban industrial proletariat. Not only are the peasants ruthlessly exploited but nature itself is contaminated:

> Swamp fever was still rife here and even in summer there were slimy patches of mud – especially under fences – which lay in the broad shade of old, overhanging willows. There was always a smell of factory waste, of the acetic acid they used for processing the cotton. The factories – three cotton-printing works and one tannery – were not in the village itself, but a short distance away ... The waste from the tannery made the water in the small river stink horribly, the meadows were polluted by the effluent, the cattle in the village suffered from anthrax, and so it was ordered to close down.

The rich kulak peasants who profit from industrialization become deficient in all human values, commercial greed has a brutalizing effect on them all, and they treat the poor peasants like animals:

> On the eve of a Fast or on a saint's day festival (they usually took three days to celebrate them) when they used to fob the peasants off with rotten salt beef, which gave off such a revolting stench you could hardly go near the barrel; when they let the drunks pawn their scythes, caps, their wives' scarves; when the factory-hands, their heads reeling from cheap vodka, wallowed in the mud, so that the shamelessness of it all seemed to hang overhead in a thick haze ...

Chekhov had painted the same picture of the bestiality of peasant life in 'Peasants', where everyone seems to be immersed in a deep sink of depravity. The local government officials are equally corrupted, greedy and brutish:

> The chairman of the parish council and his clerk, who had been working together for as long as fourteen years now – during the whole course of which they had never signed a single document – and who never let anyone leave the office without first cheating and insulting him – had positioned their fat, well-fed selves next to each other. They had lived on lies for so long, it seemed that even the skin on their faces had taken on a peculiarly criminal complexion all of its own. The clerk's wife, a scraggy woman with a squint, had brought all her children along; just like a bird of prey she looked at the plates out of the corner of her eye and grabbed everything within reach, stuffing it away in her children's pockets and her own.

The weak are fleeced, counterfeit money is passed round and, in the end, the old Tsybukin, who had been one of the exploiters, now feeble and helpless, is thrown out of his house by his own daughter-in-law, a veritable snake in the grass.

But the grim picture is relieved: there *are* some good peasants and nature, away from the polluted land near the factories, is beautiful still: the descriptions of harvest-time and people coming to help are particularly fine and almost certainly based on Chekhov's own reminiscences of life at Melikhovo:

> On the slope on the far side they could see rye lying in stooks and sheaves, scattered all over the place as if blown around in a storm; some of the rye lay in freshly cut swathes. The oats were ready as well and shone like mother-of-pearl in the sun. It was the height of harvest-time, but that day was a rest day. The following morning, a Saturday, they would be gathering in the rye and hay and then they would rest again on the Sunday. Every day distant thunder rumbled; it was close and humid, and rain seemed to be in the air.

The following scene is almost Flemish in its picture of the peasants:

> Meanwhile more and more people kept pouring in from the fair at Kazansk. Peasant women, factory-hands wearing new caps,

> beggars, children ... A cart would rumble past in a cloud of dust, with an unsold horse (which seemed very pleased at the fact) trotting along behind it; then came an obstinate cow, which was being dragged along by the horns; then another cart rolled past, full of drunken peasants who let their legs dangle over the sides. One old woman came past with a boy who wore a large hat and big boots; he was exhausted by the heat and the weight of the boots, which didn't let him bend his knees, but in spite of this he kept blowing his toy trumpet for all he was worth.

Crutchy, the carpenter, and the brutally treated Lipa and her mother shed rays of light among the gloom and show there is hope yet. Chekhov, in a beautiful passage, describes Lipa and her mother resting at harvest-time:

> The sun had set and a thick, milk-white mist was rising over the river, the fences and the clearings near the factories. And now with darkness swiftly advancing and lights twinkling down below, when that mist seemed to be hiding a bottomless abyss, Lipa and her mother, who were born beggars and were resigned to stay beggars for the rest of their lives, surrendering everything except their own frightened souls to others – perhaps even *they* imagined, for one fleeting moment, that they mattered in that vast mysterious universe, where countless lives were being lived out, and that they had a certain strength and were better than someone else.

Chekhov's meaning is clear: those who suffer and endure pain are superior to their oppressors and will eventually have their just reward.

'Anna Round the Neck' was first published in 1895, but Chekhov made substantial revisions for the first collected edition of his works: these were chiefly in intensifying the satirical portraits in small-town society and in stressing the final and complete alienation of the heroine from her own family. In common with two other stories of this period ('The Wife' and 'Ariadne'), Chekhov depicts the metamorphosis of a newly married young woman from a poor family who, after marrying a rich but elderly pompous government official, takes full advantage of her newly discovered attractiveness to men and becomes a coquette and social climber, carried away in a world of charity balls, country outings and all the trivial social life of a small provincial town.

The first intimation of her newly discovered awareness of the power she can wield over men is given when she is spotted by a rich landowner, when the train carrying the honeymoon couple stops at a small country railway station; subsequently, in the final lines of the story, this gentleman 'befriends' her.

But it is at a charity ball where she causes a sensation, all the men there competing for her attention. Now, fully confident of her powers, she is able to flirt with everyone and completely neglect her tiresome husband. Indeed, her husband, who is a priggish bore, soon fades into the background, together with her pathetic, drunken, widowed father and her brothers, whom she cruelly disowns. The story shows very well how a seemingly innocent young woman can change into the type of predatory female so often found in Chekhov's work. All moral responsibility is abdicated by her and eventually, there is no doubt, she will become like one of the empty-headed society ladies she had met at her first charity ball.

What is most distinctive about Chekhov's work is the evocation of mood and atmosphere, the portrayal of elusive states of mind, fleeting sensations, and it is here that he is a true master, creating subtle effects by nuance, by carefully selected detail. Tolstoy clearly appreciated Chekhov's mastery of style, his ability to create that mood which typifies his works more than anything else, when he wrote: 'Chekhov is like an Impressionist painter and has a style all his own. At first glance it appears as if the painter has merely smeared his canvas with the first colour that came to hand, indiscriminately, so that the brush-strokes seem to bear no relationship to each other. But as soon as one steps back and surveys the work from a distance, one has the remarkable impression of a colourful, irresistible painting.' And Ivan Bunin, who like Chekhov was a supreme stylist and master of creating a uniquely individual atmosphere, lyrical and evocative, justly called him the 'singer of twilight moods'. But perhaps it was Maxim Gorky who paid the greatest possible tribute when he wrote: 'Chekhov is unapproachable as stylist . . . literary historians will in future say that the Russian language was created by Pushkin, Turgenev and Chekhov.' In his purity of style, in his elegiac mood, Chekhov is close to Turgenev, who undoubtedly influenced him strongly, especially in the writings of his middle years. Like Turgenev, Chekhov was acutely sensitive to the beauty of nature: in his depictions of subtle changes of light, cloud formations, the countryside flooded in moonlight, the elusive and mysterious sounds of forest creatures, Chekhov is close to the great novelist. In his character portraits, however – unlike Turgenev – Chekhov does not retard the narrative with lengthy, retrospective biographies. Carefully selecting significant detail he creates characters with a few telling brush-strokes.

For all his melancholy, for all the pictures of gloom, futility and sham ideals, Chekhov was basically an optimist, firmly believing that education and science would aid the development of the human personality and rouse it from its appalling lethargy and complacency. 'My holy of holies,' he wrote to Suvorin, 'is the human body, health, intelligence, talent, inspiration, love, and absolute freedom from coercion and falsehood, no matter how the last two manifest themselves.' Maxim Gorky, in his remarkable memoir of Chekhov, saw how positive a writer Chekhov was: 'No one understood so clearly as Anton Chekhov the tragic element in life's trivialities; before him no one was able to convey to people, with such ruthless truthfulness, the shamefulness and boredom of their life in all its monotony and dreariness.'

Chekhov does see hope for humanity in the unfettered development of the individual consciousness, as did Tolstoy (however much Chekhov disagreed with him on other matters), and this belief is conveyed to us by characters such as Sonya in *Uncle Vanya*, Sasha in 'Peasants', Tuzenbakh and Vershinin in *The Three Sisters*: all look forward to the time when life would eventually be worth living – however far away that might be.

R.W.

The Kiss

On 20 May, at eight o'clock in the evening, all six batteries of a reserve artillery brigade, on their way back to headquarters, stopped for the night at the village of Mestechki. At the height of all the confusion – some officers were busy with the guns, while others had assembled in the main square by the churchyard fence to receive their billetings – someone in civilian dress rode up from behind the church on a strange horse: it was small and dun-coloured with a fine neck and short tail, and seemed to move sideways instead of straight ahead, making small dancing movements with its legs as if they were being whipped. When the rider came up to the officers he doffed his hat and said, 'Our squire, His Excellency, Lieutenant-General von Rabbeck, invites you for tea and would like you to come now . . .'

The horse performed a bow and a little dance, and retreated with the same sideways motion. The rider raised his hat again and quickly disappeared behind the church on his peculiar horse.

'To hell with it!' some of the officers grumbled as they rode off to their quarters. 'We want to sleep and up pops this von Rabbeck with his tea! We know what *that* means all right!'

Every officer in the six batteries vividly remembered the previous year when they were on manoeuvres with officers from a Cossack regiment and had received a similar invitation from a landowning count, who was a retired officer. This hospitable and genial count had plied them with food and drink, would not hear of them returning to their billets and made them stay the night. That was all very well, of course, and they could not have hoped for better. But the trouble was that this retired officer was overjoyed beyond measure at having young men as his guests and he regaled them with stories from his glorious past until dawn, led them on a tour of the house, showed them his valuable paintings, old engravings and rare guns, and read out signed letters from eminent personages; and all this time the tired and weary officers listened, looked, pined for bed, and continuously yawned in their sleeves. When their host finally let them go, it was too late for bed.

Now, was this von Rabbeck one of the same breed? Whether he was or not, there was nothing they could do about it. The officers put clean uniforms on, smartened themselves up and went off en masse to look for the squire's house. On the square by the church they were told that they could either take the lower path leading down to the river behind the church, and then go along the bank to the garden, or they could ride direct from the church along the higher road which would bring them to the count's barns about a quarter of a mile from the village. The officers decided on the higher route.

'Who is this von Rabbeck?' they argued as they rode along. 'Is he the one who commanded a cavalry division at Plevna?'

'No, that wasn't von Rabbeck, just Rabbe, and without the "von".'

'It's marvellous weather, anyway!'

The road divided when they reached the first barn: one fork led straight on and disappeared in the darkness of the evening, while the other turned towards the squire's house on the right. The officers took the right fork and began to lower their voices ... Stone barns with red tiled roofs stood on both sides of the road and they had the heavy, forbidding look of some provincial barracks. Ahead of them were the lighted windows of the manor-house.

'That's a good sign, gentlemen!' one of the officers said. 'Our setter's going on in front. That means he scents game!'

Lieutenant Lobytko, a tall, strongly built officer, who was riding ahead of the others, who had no moustache (although he was over twenty-five there wasn't a trace of hair on his face), and who was renowned in the brigade for his keen senses and ability to sniff a woman out from miles away, turned round and said, 'Yes, there must be women here, my instinct tells me.'

The officers were met at the front door by von Rabbeck himself – a fine-looking man of about sixty, wearing civilian clothes. He said how very pleased and happy he was to see the officers as he shook hands, but begged them most sincerely, in the name of God, to excuse him for not inviting them to stay the night, as two sisters with their children, his brothers and some neighbours had turned up, and he didn't have one spare room.

The general shook everyone's hand, apologized and smiled, but they could tell from his face that he wasn't nearly as pleased to have guests as last year's count and he had only asked them as it was the done thing. And, as they climbed the softly carpeted stairs and listened, the officers sensed that they had been invited only because it would have caused embarrassment if they had *not* been invited. At the sight of footmen dashing around lighting the lamps in the hall and upstairs, they felt they had introduced a note of uneasiness and anxiety into the house. And how could any host be pleased at having nineteen strange officers descend on a house where two sisters, children, brothers and neighbours had already arrived, most probably to celebrate some family anniversary. They were met in the ballroom upstairs by a tall, stately old lady with black eyebrows and a long face – the living image of Empress Eugénie. She gave them a majestic, welcoming smile and said how glad and happy she was to have them as guests and apologized for the fact that she and her husband weren't able to invite the officers to stay overnight on this occasion. Her beautiful, majestic smile, which momentarily disappeared every time she turned away from her guests, revealed that in her day she had seen many officers, that she had no time for them now, and that she had invited them and was apologizing only because her upbringing and social position demanded it.

The officers entered the large dining-room where about ten gentlemen and ladies, old and young, were sitting along one side of the table having tea. Behind their chairs, enveloped in a thin haze of cigar smoke, was a group of men with a rather lean, young, red-whiskered man in the middle, rolling his 'r's as he spoke out loud in English. Behind them, through a door, was a bright room with light blue furniture.

'Gentlemen, there's so many of you, it's impossible to introduce *everyone*!' the general was saying in a loud voice, trying to sound cheerful. 'So don't stand on ceremony, introduce yourselves!'

Some officers wore very serious, even solemn expressions; others forced a smile, and all of them felt awkward as they bowed rather indifferently and sat down to tea.

Staff-Captain Ryabovich, a short, stooping officer, with spectacles and lynx-like side whiskers, was more embarrassed than anyone else.

While his fellow-officers were trying to look serious or force a smile, his face, lynx-like whiskers and spectacles seemed to be saying, 'I'm the shyest, most modest and most insignificant officer in the whole brigade!' When he first entered the dining-room and sat down to tea, he found it impossible to concentrate on any one face or object. All those faces, dresses, cut-glass decanters, steaming glasses, moulded cornices, merged into one composite sensation, making Ryabovich feel ill-at-ease, and he longed to bury his head somewhere. Like a lecturer at his first appearance in public, he could see everything in front of him well enough, but at the same time he could make little sense of it (physicians call this condition, when someone sees without understanding, 'psychic blindness'). But after a little while Ryabovich began to feel more at home, recovered his normal vision and began to take stock of his surroundings. Since he was a timid and unsociable person, he was struck above all by what he himself had never possessed – the extraordinary boldness of these unfamiliar people. Von Rabbeck, two elderly ladies, a young girl in a lilac dress, and the young man with red whiskers – Rabbeck's youngest son – had sat themselves very cunningly among the officers, as though it had all been rehearsed. Straight away they had launched into a heated argument, which the guests could not help joining. The girl in lilac very excitedly insisted that the artillery had a much easier time than either the cavalry or the infantry, while Rabbeck and the elderly ladies argued the contrary. A rapid conversational crossfire ensued. Ryabovich glanced at the lilac girl who was arguing so passionately about something that was so foreign to her, so utterly boring, and he could see artificial smiles flickering over her face.

Von Rabbeck and family skilfully drew the officers into the argument, at the same time watching their wine glasses with eagle eyes to check whether they were filled, that they had enough sugar, and one officer who wasn't eating biscuits or drinking any brandy worried them. The more Ryabovich looked and listened, the more he began to like this insincere but wonderfully disciplined family.

After tea the officers went into the ballroom. Lieutenant Lobytko's instinct had not failed him: the room was full of girls and young married women. Already this 'setter' lieutenant had positioned himself next to a young blonde in a black dress, bending over dashingly as though leaning on some invisible sabre, smiling and flirting with his shoulders. Most probably he was telling her some intriguing nonsense as the blonde glanced superciliously at his well-fed face and said, 'Really?'

If that 'setter' had had any brains, that cool 'Really?' should have told him that he would never be called 'to heel'.

The grand piano suddenly thundered out. The sounds of a sad waltz drifted through the wide-open windows and everyone remembered that outside it was spring, an evening in May, and they smelt the fragrance of the young leaves of the poplars, of roses and lilac. Ryabovich, feeling the effects of the brandy and the music, squinted at a window, smiled and watched the movements of the women. Now it seemed that the fragrance of the roses, the poplars and lilac wasn't coming from the garden but from the ladies' faces and dresses.

Rabbeck's son had invited a skinny girl to dance and waltzed twice round the room with her. Lobytko glided over the parquet floor as he flew up to the girl in lilac and whirled her round the room. They all began to dance . . . Ryabovich stood by the door with guests who were not dancing and watched. Not once in his life had he danced, not once had he put his arm round an attractive young woman's waist. He would usually be absolutely delighted when, with everyone looking on, a man took a young girl he hadn't met before by the waist and offered his shoulders for her to rest her hands on, but he could never imagine himself in that situation. There had been times when he envied his fellow-officers' daring and dashing ways and it made him very depressed. The realization that he was shy, round-shouldered, quite undistinguished, that he had a long waist, the lynx-like side whiskers, hurt him deeply. But over the years this realization had become something of a habit and as he watched his friends dance or talk out loud he no longer envied them but was filled with sadness.

When the quadrille began, young von Rabbeck went over to the officers who were not dancing and invited two of them to a game of billiards. They accepted and left the great hall with him. As he had nothing else to do, and feeling he would like to take at least some part in what was going on, Ryabovich trudged off after them. First they went into the drawing-room, then down a narrow corridor with a glass ceiling, then into a room where three sleepy footmen leapt up from a sofa the moment they entered. Finally, after passing through a whole series of rooms, young Rabbeck and company reached a small billiard-room and the game began.

Ryabovich, who never played any games except cards, stood by the table and indifferently watched the players, cue in hand, walking up and down in their unbuttoned tunics, making puns and shouting things he could not understand. The players ignored him, only turning round to say, 'I beg your pardon,' when one of them happened accidentally to nudge him with an elbow or prod him with a cue. Even before the first game was over, he was bored and began to feel he was not wanted, that he was in the way ... He felt drawn back to the ballroom and walked away.

As he walked back he had a little adventure. Halfway, he realized he was lost – he knew very well he had to go by those three sleepy footmen, but already he had passed through five or six rooms and those footmen seemed to have vanished into thin air. He realized his mistake, retraced his steps a little and turned to the right, only to find himself in a small, dimly lit room he had not seen on the way to the billiard-room. He stood still for a minute or so, opened the first door he came to with determination and entered a completely dark room. Ahead of him he could see light coming through a crack in the door and beyond was the muffled sound of a sad mazurka. The windows here had been left open as they had in the ballroom and he could smell poplars, lilac and roses ...

Ryabovich stopped, undecided what to do ... Just then he was astonished to hear hurried footsteps, the rustle of a dress and a female voice whispering breathlessly, 'At last!' Two soft, sweet-smelling arms (undoubtedly a woman's) encircled his neck, a burning cheek pressed against his and at the same time there was the sound of a kiss. But immediately after the kiss the woman gave a faint cry and shrank backwards in disgust – that was how it seemed to Ryabovich.

He was on the point of crying out too and he rushed towards the bright chink in the door.

His heart pounded away when he was back in the hall and his hands trembled so obviously that he hastily hid them behind his back. At first he was tormented by shame and he feared everyone there knew he had just been embraced and kissed, and this made him hesitate and look around anxiously. But when he had convinced himself that everyone was dancing and gossiping just as peacefully as before, he gave himself up to a totally new kind of sensation, one he had never experienced before in all his life. Something strange was happening to him ... his neck, which just a few moments ago had been embraced by sweet-smelling hands, seemed anointed with oil. And on his left cheek, just by his moustache, there was a faint, pleasant, cold, tingling sensation, the kind you get from peppermint drops and the more he rubbed the spot the stronger the tingling became. From head to heels he was overcome by a strange, new feeling which grew stronger every minute. He wanted to dance, speak to everyone, run out into the garden, laugh out loud. He completely forgot his stoop, his insignificant appearance, his lynx-like whiskers and 'vague appearance' (once he happened to hear some ladies saying this about him). When Rabbeck's wife went by he gave her such a broad, warm smile that she stopped and gave him a very searching look.

'I love this house so much!' he said, adjusting his spectacles.

The general's wife smiled and told him that the house still belonged to her father. Then she asked if his parents were still alive, how long he had been in the army, why he was so thin, and so on ... When Ryabovich had replied, she moved on, leaving him smiling even more warmly and he began to think he was surrounded by the most wonderful people ...

Mechanically, Ryabovich ate and drank everything he was offered at the dinner table, deaf to everything as he tried to find an explanation for what had just happened. It was a mysterious, romantic incident, but it wasn't difficult to explain. No doubt some girl or young married woman had a rendezvous with someone in that dark room, had waited for a long time, and then mistook Ryabovich for her hero in her nervous excitement. This was the most likely explanation, all the more so as Ryabovich had hesitated in the middle of the room, which made it look as though he were expecting someone ...

'But who *is* she?' he thought as he surveyed the ladies' faces. 'She must be young, as old ladies don't have rendezvous. And intelligent – I could tell from the rustle of her dress, her smell, her voice.'

He stared at the girl in lilac and found her very attractive. She had beautiful shoulders and arms, a clever face and a fine voice. As he gazed at her, Ryabovich wanted *her*, no one else, to be that mysterious stranger . . . But she gave a rather artificial laugh and wrinkled her long nose, which made her look old. Then he turned to the blonde in black. She was younger, simpler and less affected, with charming temples and she sipped daintily from her wine glass. Now Ryabovich wanted her to be the stranger. But he soon discovered that she had a featureless face and he turned to her neighbour . . . 'It's hard to say,' he wondered dreamily. 'If I could just take the lilac girl's shoulders and arms away, add the blonde's temples, then take those eyes away from the girl on Lobytko's left, *then*.' He merged them all into one, so that he had an image of the girl who had kissed him, the image he desired so much, but which he just could not find among the guests around the table.

After dinner the officers, well-fed and slightly tipsy by now, began to make their farewells and expressed their thanks. Once again the hosts apologized for not having them stay the night.

'Delighted, gentlemen, absolutely delighted,' the general was saying and this time he meant it – probably because people are usually more sincere and better-humoured saying good-bye to guests than welcoming them.

'Delighted! Glad to see you back any time, so don't stand on ceremony. Which way are you going? The higher road? No, go through the garden, it's quicker.'

The officers went into the garden, where it seemed very dark and quiet after the bright lights and the noise. They did not say a word all the way to the gate. They were half-drunk, cheerful and contented, but the darkness and the silence made them pause for thought. Probably they were thinking the same as Ryabovich: would they ever see the day when they would own a large house, have a family, a garden, when *they* too would be able to entertain people (however much of a pretence this might be), feed them well, make them drunk and happy?

As they went through the garden gate they all started talking at once and, for no apparent reason, laughed out loud. Now they were descending the path that led down to the river and then ran along the water's edge, weaving its way around the bushes, the little pools of water and the willows which overhung the river. The bank and the path were barely visible, and the far side was plunged in darkness. Here and there were reflections of the stars in the water, quivering and breaking up into little patches – the only sign that the river was flowing fast. All was quiet. Sleepy sandpipers called plaintively from the far bank and on the near side a nightingale in a bush poured out its song, ignoring the passing officers.

The men paused by the bush, touched it, but still the nightingale sang.

'That's a bird for you!' approving voices murmured. 'Here we are, right next to him and he doesn't take a blind bit of notice! What a rascal!'

The path finally turned upwards and came out on to the high road by the church fence. The officers were exhausted from walking up the hill and sat down for a smoke. On the far bank they could make out a dim red light and they tried to pass the time by guessing whether it was a camp fire, a light in a window, or something else . . . Ryabovich looked at it and imagined that the light was winking at him and smiling, as though it knew all about that kiss.

When he reached his quarters Ryabovich quickly undressed and lay on his bed. In the same hut were Lobytko and Lieutenant Merzlyakov, a gentle, rather quiet young man, who was considered well-educated in his own little circle. He was always reading the *European Herald* when he had the chance and took it with him everywhere. Lobytko undressed, paced up and down for a long time, with the expression of a dissatisfied man, and sent the batman for some beer.

Merzlyakov lay down, placed a candle near his pillow and immersed himself in the *European Herald*.

'Who *is* she?' Ryabovich wondered as he glanced at the grimy ceiling. His neck still felt as if it had been anointed with oil and he had that tingling sensation around his mouth – just like peppermint drops. He had fleeting visions of the lilac girl's shoulders and arms, the temples and truthful eyes of the blonde in black, waists, dresses, brooches. He tried to fix these visions firmly in his mind, but they kept dancing about, dissolving, flickering. When these visions vanished completely against that darkened background everyone has when he closes his eyes, he began to hear hurried steps, rustling dresses, the sound of a kiss and he was gripped by an inexplicable, overwhelming feeling of joy. Just as he was abandoning himself to it, he heard the batman come back and report that there wasn't any beer. Lobytko became terribly agitated and started pacing up and down again.

'Didn't I tell you he's an idiot?' he said, stopping first in front of Ryabovich, then Merzlyakov. 'A man must really be a blockhead and idiot to come back without any beer! The man's a rogue, eh?'

'Of course, you won't find any beer in this place,' Merzlyakov said without taking his eyes off the *European Herald*.

'Oh, do you really think so?' Lobytko persisted. 'Good God, put me on the moon and I'll find you beer and women right away! Yes, I'll go now and find some . . . Call me a scoundrel if I don't succeed!'

He slowly dressed and pulled on his high boots. Then he finished his cigarette in silence and left.

'Rabbeck, Grabbeck, Labbeck,' he muttered, pausing in the hall. 'I don't feel like going on my own, dammit! Fancy a little walk, Ryabovich?'

There was no reply, so he came back, slowly undressed and got into bed. Merzlyakov sighed, put the *European Herald* away and snuffed the candle.

'Hm,' Lobytko murmured as he puffed his cigarette in the dark.

Ryabovich pulled the blankets over his head, curled himself into a ball and tried to merge the visions fleeting through his mind into one fixed image. But he failed completely. Soon he fell asleep and his last waking thought was of someone caressing him and making him happy, of something absurd and unusual, but nonetheless exceptionally fine and joyful, that had entered his life. And his dreams centred around this one thought.

When he woke up, the sensation of oil on his cheek and the minty tingling near his lips had vanished, but the joy of yesterday still filled his heart. Delighted, he watched the window frames, gilded now by the rising sun, and listened intently to the street noises. Outside, just by the window, he could hear loud voices – Lebedetsky, Ryabovich's battery commander, who had just caught up with the brigade, was shouting at his sergeant – simply because he had lost the habit of talking softly.

'Is there anything else?' he roared.

'When they were shoeing yesterday, sir, someone drove a nail into Pigeon's hoof. The medical orderly put clay and vinegar on it and they're keeping the horse reined, away from the others. And artificer Artemyev got drunk yesterday and the lieutenant had him tied to the fore-carriage of an auxiliary field-gun.'

And the sergeant had more to report. Karpov had forgotten the new cords for the trumpets and the stakes for the tents, and the officers had spent the previous evening as guests of General von Rabbeck. During the conversation, Lebedetsky's head and red beard appeared at the window. He blinked his short-sighted eyes at the sleepy officers and bade them good morning.

'Everything all right?' he asked.

'One of the shaft-horses damaged its withers – it was the new collar,' Lobytko answered, yawning.

The commander sighed, pondered for a moment and said in a loud voice, 'I'm still wondering whether to pay Aleksandra a visit, I really ought to go and see how she is. Well, good-bye for now, I'll catch you up by evening.'

A quarter of an hour later the brigade moved off. As it passed the general's barns, Ryabovich looked to the right where the house was. The blinds were drawn in all the windows. Clearly, everyone was still asleep. And the girl who had kissed Ryabovich the day before was sleeping too. He tried to imagine her as she slept and he had a clear and distinct picture of the wide-open windows, the little green branches peeping into her bedroom, the morning freshness, the smell of poplars, lilac and roses, her bed and the chair with that dress which had rustled the day before lying over it, tiny slippers, a watch on the table. But the actual features of that face, that sweet, dreamy smile, exactly what was most characteristic of her, slipped through his imagination like mercury through the fingers. When he had ridden about a quarter of a mile, he looked back. The yellow church, the house, the river and garden were flooded in sunlight and the river, with its bright green banks and its waters reflecting the light blue sky and glinting silver here and there, looked very beautiful. Ryabovich took a last look at Mestechki and he felt so sad, as if he were saying farewell to what was very near and dear to him.

But there were only long-familiar, boring scenes ahead of him. On both sides of the road there were fields of young rye and buckwheat, where crows were hopping about. Ahead, all he could see was dust and the backs of soldiers' heads; and behind, the same dust, the same faces. The brigade was led by a vanguard of four soldiers bearing sabres and behind them rode the military choristers, followed by trumpeters.

Every now and then, like torchbearers in a funeral cortège, the vanguard and singers ignored the regulation distance and pushed on far ahead. Ryabovich rode alongside the first field-gun of the fifth battery and he could see the other four in front. These long, ponderous processions formed by brigades on the move can strike civilians as very peculiar, an unintelligible muddle, and non-military people just cannot fathom why a single field-gun has to be escorted by so many soldiers, why it has to be drawn by so many horses all tangled up in such strange harness, as if it really was such a terrible, heavy object. But Ryabovich understood everything perfectly well and for that reason he found it all extremely boring. He had long known why a hefty bombardier always rides with the officer at the head of every battery and why he is called an outrider. Immediately behind this bombardier came the riders on the first, then the middle-section trace-horses. Ryabovich knew that the horses to the left were saddle-horses, while those on the right were auxiliary – all this was very boring. The horsemen were followed by two shaft-horses, one ridden by a horseman with yesterday's dust still on his back and who had a clumsy-looking, very comical piece of wood fixed to his right leg. Ryabovich knew what it was for and did not find it funny. All the riders waved their whips mechanically and shouted now and again. As for the field-gun, it was an ugly thing. Sacks of oats covered with tarpaulin lay on the fore-carriage and the gun itself was hung with kettles, kitbags and little sacks: it resembled a small harmless animal which had been surrounded, for some reason, by men and horses. On the side sheltered from the wind a team of six strode along, swinging their arms. This gun was followed by more bombardiers, riders, shaft-horses and another field-gun – just as ugly and uninspiring as the first – lumbering along in the rear. After the second gun came a third, then a fourth with an officer riding alongside (there are six batteries to a brigade and four guns to a battery). The whole procession stretched about a quarter of a mile and ended with the baggage wagons, where a most likeable creature plodded thoughtfully along, his long-eared head drooping: this was Magar the donkey, brought from Turkey by a certain battery commander.

Ryabovich looked apathetically at all those necks and faces in front and behind. At any other time he would have dozed off, but now he was immersed in new, pleasant thoughts. When the brigade had first set off, he had tried to convince himself that the incident of the kiss was only some unimportant, mysterious adventure and that essentially it was trivial and too ridiculous for serious thought. But very quickly he waved logic aside and gave himself up to his dreams. First he pictured himself in von Rabbeck's drawing-room, sitting next to a girl who resembled both the girl in lilac and the blonde in black. Then he closed his eyes and imagined himself with another, completely strange girl, with very indeterminate features: in his thoughts he spoke to her, caressed her and leaned his head on her shoulder. Then he thought of war and separation, reunion, dinner with his wife and children . . .

'Brakes on!' rang out the command every time they went downhill. He shouted the command too, and feared that his own shouts would shatter his daydreams and bring him back to reality.

As they passed some estate, Ryabovich peeped over the fence into the garden. There he saw a long avenue, straight as a ruler, strewn with yellow sand and lined with young birches. With the eagerness of a man who has surrendered himself to daydreaming, he imagined tiny female feet walking over the yellow sand. And, quite unexpectedly, he had a clear mental picture of the girl who had kissed him, the girl he had visualized the previous evening during dinner. This image had planted itself in his mind and would not leave him.

At midday someone shouted from a wagon in the rear, 'Attention, eyes left! Officers!'

The brigadier drove up in an open carriage drawn by two white horses. He ordered it to stop near the second battery and shouted something no one understood. Several officers galloped over to him, Ryabovich among them.

'Well, what's the news?' asked the brigadier, blinking his red eyes. 'Anyone ill?'

When they had replied, the brigadier, a small skinny man, chewed for a moment, pondered and then turned to one of the officers: 'One of your drivers, on the third gun, has taken his knee-guard off and the devil's hung it on the fore-carriage. Reprimand him!'

He looked up at Ryabovich and continued: 'It strikes me your harness breeches are too long.'

After a few more tiresome comments, the brigadier glanced at Lobytko and grinned. 'You look down in the dumps today, Lieutenant

Lobytko. Pining for Madame Lopukhov, eh? Gentlemen, he's pining for Madame Lopukhov!'

Madame Lopukhov was a very plump, tall lady, well past forty. The brigadier, who had a passion for large women, no matter what age, suspected his officers nurtured similar passions. They smiled politely. Then the brigadier, delighted with himself for having made a very amusing, cutting remark, roared with laughter, tapped his driver on the back and saluted. The carriage drove off.

'All the things I'm dreaming about now and which seem impossible, out of this world, are in fact very ordinary,' Ryabovich thought as he watched the clouds of dust rising in the wake of the brigadier's carriage. 'It's all so very ordinary, everyone experiences it . . . The brigadier, for example. He was in love once, now he's married, with children. Captain Vachter is married and loved, despite having an extremely ugly red neck and no waistline. Salmanov is coarse and too much of a Tartar, but *he* had an affair that finished in marriage. I'm the same as everyone else . . . sooner or later I'll have to go through what they did . . .'

And he was delighted and encouraged by the thought that he was just an ordinary man, leading an ordinary life. Now he was bold enough to picture *her* and his happiness as much as he liked and he gave full rein to his imagination.

In the evening, when the brigade had reached its destination and the officers were resting in their tents, Ryabovich, Merzlyakov and Lobytko gathered round a trunk and had supper. Merzlyakov took his time, holding his *European Herald* on his knees and reading it as he slowly munched his food.

Lobytko could not stop talking and kept filling his glass with beer, while Ryabovich, whose head was rather hazy from dreaming all day long, said nothing as he drank. Three glasses made him tipsy and weak and he felt an irrepressible longing to share his new feelings with his friends.

'A strange thing happened to me at the Rabbecks,' he said, trying to sound cool and sarcastic. 'I went to the billiard-room, you know . . .'

He began to tell them, in great detail, all about the kiss, but after a minute fell silent. In that one minute he had told them everything and he was astonished when he considered how little time was needed to tell his story: he had imagined it would take until morning. After he heard the story, Lobytko – who was a great liar and therefore a great sceptic – looked at him in disbelief and grinned. Merzlyakov twitched his eyebrows and kept his eyes glued to the *European Herald* as he calmly remarked, 'Damned if I know what to make of it! Throwing herself round a stranger's neck without saying a word first . . . She must have been a mental case . . .'

'Yes, some kind of neurotic,' Ryabovich agreed.

'Something similar happened to me once,' Lobytko said, assuming a frightened look. 'Last year I was travelling to Kovno . . . second class. The compartment was chock-full and it was impossible to sleep. So I tipped the guard fifty kopeks . . . he took my luggage and got me a berth in a sleeper. I lay down and covered myself with a blanket. It was dark, you understand. Suddenly someone was touching my shoulder and breathing into my face. So I moved my arm and felt an elbow. I opened my eyes and – can you imagine! – it was a woman. Black eyes, lips as red as the best salmon, nostrils breathing passion, breasts like buffers! . . .'

'Just a minute,' Merzlyakov calmly interrupted. 'I don't dispute what you said about her breasts, but how could you see her lips if it was dark?'

Lobytko tried to wriggle out by poking fun at Merzlyakov's obtuseness and this jarred on Ryabovich. He went away from the trunk, lay down and vowed never again to tell his secrets.

Camp life fell back into its normal routine. The days flashed by, each exactly the same as the other. All this time Ryabovich felt, thought and behaved like someone in love. When his batman brought him cold water in the mornings, he poured it over his head and each time he remembered that there was something beautiful and loving in his life.

In the evenings, when his fellow-officers talked about love and women, he would listen very attentively, sitting very close to them and assuming the habitual expression of a soldier hearing stories about battles he himself fought in. On those evenings when senior officers, led by 'setter' Lobytko, carried out 'sorties' on the local village, in true Don Juan style, Ryabovich went along with them and invariably returned feeling sad, deeply guilty and imploring *her* forgiveness. In his spare time, or on nights when he couldn't sleep, when he wanted to recall his childhood days, his parents, everything that was near and dear to him, he would always find himself thinking of Mestechki instead, of that strange horse, of von Rabbeck and his wife, who looked like the Empress Eugénie, of that dark room with the bright chink in the door.

On 31 August he left camp – not with his own brigade, however, but with two batteries. All the way he daydreamed and became very excited, as though he were going home. He wanted passionately to see that strange horse again, the church, those artificial Rabbecks, the dark room. Some inner voice, which so often deceives those in love, whispered that he was *bound* to see her again. And he was tormented by such questions as: how could he arrange a meeting, what would she say, had she forgotten the kiss? If the worst came to the worst, he would at least have the pleasure of walking through that dark room and remembering . . .

Towards evening, that familiar church and the white barns appeared on the horizon. His heart began to pound. He did not listen to what the officer riding next to him was saying, he was oblivious of everything and looked eagerly at the river gleaming in the distance, at the loft above which pigeons were circling in the light of the setting sun.

As he rode up to the church and heard the quartermaster speaking, he expected a messenger on horseback to appear from behind the fence any minute and invite the officers to tea . . . but the quartermaster read the billeting list out, the officers dismounted and strolled off into the village – and no messenger came.

'The people in the village will tell Rabbeck we're here and he'll send for us,' Ryabovich thought as he went into his hut. He just could not understand why a fellow-officer was lighting a candle, why the batmen were hurriedly heating the samovars.

He was gripped by an acute feeling of anxiety. He lay down, then got up and looked out of the window to see if the messenger was coming. But there was no one. He lay down again but got up again after half an hour, unable to control his anxiety, went out into the street and strode off towards the church.

The square near the fence was dark and deserted. Some soldiers were standing in a row at the top of the slope, saying nothing. They jumped when they saw Ryabovich and saluted. He acknowledged the salute and went down the familiar path.

The entire sky over the far bank was flooded with crimson; the moon was rising. Two peasant women were talking loudly and picking cabbage leaves as they walked along the edge of a kitchen garden. Beyond the gardens were some dark huts. On the near bank everything was much the same as in May: the path, the bushes, the willows overhanging the river ... only there was no bold nightingale singing, no fragrant poplars or young grass. Ryabovich reached the garden and peered over the gate. It was dark and quiet and all he could see were the white trunks of the nearest birches and here and there little patches of avenue – everything else had merged into one black mass. Ryabovich looked hard, listened eagerly, and after standing and waiting for about quarter of an hour, without hearing a sound or seeing a single light, he trudged wearily away ...

He went down to the river, where he could see the general's bathing-hut and towels hanging over the rail on the little bridge. He went on to the bridge, stood for a moment and aimlessly fingered the towels. They felt cold and rough. He looked down at the water ... the current was swift and purled, barely audibly, against the piles of the hut. The red moon was reflected in the water near the left bank; tiny waves rippled through the reflection, pulling it apart and breaking it up into little patches, as if trying to bear it away.

'How stupid, how very stupid!' Ryabovich thought as he looked at the fast-flowing water. Now, when he hoped for nothing, that adventure of the kiss, his impatience, his vague longings and disillusionment appeared in a new light. He didn't think it at all strange that he hadn't waited for the general's messenger or that he would never see the girl who had kissed him by mistake. On the contrary, he would have thought it strange if he *had* seen her ...

The water raced past and he did not know where or why; it had flowed just as swiftly in May, when it grew from a little stream into a large river, flowed into the sea, evaporated and turned into rain. Perhaps this was the same water flowing past. To what purpose?

And the whole world, the whole of life, struck Ryabovich as a meaningless, futile joke. As he turned his eyes from the water to the sky, he remembered how fate had accidentally caressed him – in the guise of an unknown woman. He recalled the dreams and visions of that summer and his life seemed terribly empty, miserable, colourless . . . When he returned to his hut, none of the officers was there.

The batman reported that they had all gone to 'General Fontryabkin's' – he'd sent a messenger on horseback with the invitation. There was a brief flicker of joy in his heart, but he snuffed it out at once, lay on his bed and in defiance of fate – as though he wanted to bring its wrath down on his own head – he did not go to the general's.

Peasants

I

Nikolay Chikildeyev, a waiter at the Slav Fair in Moscow, was taken ill. His legs went numb and it affected his walk so much that one day he stumbled and fell down as he was carrying a tray of peas and ham along one of the passages. As a result, he had to give up his job. Any money he and his wife had managed to save went on medical expenses, so they now had nothing to live on. He got bored without a job, so he decided it was probably best to return to his native village. It's easier being ill at home – and it's cheaper; they don't say 'there's no place like home' for nothing.

It was late in the afternoon when he reached his village, Zhukovo. He had always remembered his old home from childhood as a cheerful, bright, cosy, comfortable place, but now, as he entered the hut, he was actually scared when he saw how dark, crowded and filthy it was in there. Olga, his wife, and his daughter, Sasha, who had travelled back with him, stared in utter bewilderment at the huge neglected stove (it took up nearly half the hut), black with soot and flies – so many flies! It was tilting to one side, the wall-beams were all askew, and the hut seemed about to collapse any minute. Instead of pictures, labels from bottles and newspaper-cuttings had been pasted over the wall next to the ikons. This was *real* poverty! All the adults were out reaping. A fair-haired, dirty-faced little girl of about eight was sitting on the stove, so bored she didn't even look up as they came in. Down below, a white cat was rubbing itself on the fire-irons. Sasha tried to tempt it over: 'Here Puss, here!'

'She can't hear you,' the little girl said, 'she's deaf.'

'How's that?'

'They beat her.'

From the moment they entered the hut, Nikolay and Olga could see the kind of life they led there. But they didn't make any comment, threw their bundles on to the floor and went out into the street without a word. Their hut was third from the end and seemed the poorest and oldest. The second hut was not much better, while the last one – the village inn – had an iron roof and curtains, was unfenced and stood apart from the others. The huts formed a single row and the whole peaceful, sleepy little village, with willows, elders and ash peeping out of the yards, had a pleasant look.

Beyond the gardens, the ground sloped steeply down to the river, like a cliff, with huge boulders sticking out of the clay. Paths threaded their way down the slope between the boulders and pits dug out by the potters, and bits of brown and red clay piled up in great heaps. Down below a bright green, broad and level meadow opened out – it had already been mown and the village cattle were grazing on it. The meandering river with its magnificent leafy banks was almost a mile from the village and beyond were more broad pastures, cattle, long strings of white geese, and then a similar steep slope on its far side. At the top stood a village, a church with five 'onion' domes, with the manor-house a little further on.

'What a lovely spot!' Olga said, crossing herself when she saw the church. 'Heavens, so much open space!'

Just then the bells rang for evensong (it was Saturday evening). Two little girls, who were carrying a bucket of water down the hill, looked back at the church to listen to them.

'It'll be dinner time at the Slav Fair now,' Nikolay said dreamily.

Nikolay and Olga sat on the edge of the cliff, watching the sun go down and the reflections of the gold and crimson sky in the river, in the church windows, in the air all around, which was gentle, tranquil, pure beyond description – such air you never get in Moscow.

But after the sun had set and the lowing cows and bleating sheep had gone past, the geese had flown back from the far side of the river and everything had grown quiet – that gentle light faded from the air and the shades of evening swiftly closed in.

Meanwhile the old couple – Nikolay's parents – had returned. They were skinny, hunchbacked, toothless and the same height. Marya and Fyokla, his sisters-in-law, who worked for a landowner on the other side of the river, had returned too. Marya – the wife of his brother Kiryak – had six children, while Fyokla (married to Denis, who was away on military service) had two. When Nikolay came into the hut and saw all the family there, all those bodies large and small sprawling around on their bunks, cradles, in every corner; when he saw how ravenously the old man and the woman ate their black bread, dipping it first in water, he realized that he had made a mistake coming here, ill as he was, without any money and with his family into the bargain – a real blunder!

'And where's my brother Kiryak?' he asked when they had greeted each other.

'He's living in the forest, working as a night watchman for some merchant. Not a bad sort, but he can't half knock it back!'

'He's no breadwinner!' the old woman murmured tearfully. 'Our men are a lousy lot of drunkards, they don't bring their money back home! Kiryak's a drinker. And the old man knows the way to the pub as well, there's no harm in saying it! The Blessed Virgin must have it in for us!'

They put the samovar on especially for the guests. The tea smelled of fish, the sugar was grey and had been nibbled at, and cockroaches ran all over the bread and crockery. The tea was revolting, just like the conversation, which was always about illness and how they had no money. But before they even managed to drink the first cup a loud, long drawn-out, drunken cry came from outside.

'Ma–arya!'

'Sounds like Kiryak's back,' the old man said. 'Talk of the devil.'

Everyone went quiet. And a few moments later they heard that cry again, coarse and drawling, as though it was coming from under the earth.

'Ma–arya!'

Marya, the elder sister, turned pale and huddled closer to the stove, and it was somehow strange to see fear written all over the face of that strong, broad-shouldered woman. Suddenly her daughter – the same little girl who had been sitting over the stove looking so apathetic – sobbed out loud.

'And what's the matter with you, you silly cow?' Fyokla shouted at her – she was strong and broad-shouldered as well. 'I don't suppose he's going to kill you.'

Nikolay learned from the old man that Marya didn't live in the forest, as she was scared of Kiryak, and that whenever he was drunk he would come after her, make a great racket and always beat her mercilessly.

'Ma–arya!' came the cry – this time right outside the door.

'Please, help me, for Christ's sake, my own dear ones . . .' Marya mumbled breathlessly, panting as though she had just been dropped into freezing water. 'Please protect me . . .'

Every single child in the hut burst out crying, and Sasha gave them one look and followed suit. There was a drunken coughing, and a tall man with a black beard and a fur cap came into the hut. As his face was not visible in the dim lamplight, he was quite terrifying. It was Kiryak. He went over to his wife, swung his arm and hit her across the face with his fist. She was too stunned to cry out and merely sank to the ground; the blood immediately gushed from her nose.

'Should be ashamed of yourself, bloody ashamed!' the old man muttered as he climbed up over the stove. 'And in front of guests. A damned disgrace!'

But the old woman sat there without saying a word, all hunched up, and seemed to be thinking; Fyokla went on rocking the cradle. Clearly pleased at the terrifying effect he had on everyone, Kiryak seized Marya's hand, dragged her to the door and howled like a wild animal, so that he seemed even more terrifying. But then he suddenly saw the guests and stopped short in his tracks.

'Oh, so you've arrived . . .' he muttered, letting go of his wife. 'My own brother, with family and all . . .'

He reeled from side to side as he said a prayer in front of the ikon, and his drunken red eyes were wide open. Then he continued, 'So my dear brother's come back home with his family . . . from Moscow. The great capital, that is, Moscow, mother of cities . . . Forgive me . . .'

He sank down on a bench by the samovar and started drinking tea, noisily gulping from a saucer, while no one else said a word. He drank about ten cups, then slumped down on the bench and started snoring.

They prepared for bed. As Nikolay was ill, they put him over the stove with the old man. Sasha lay down on the floor, while Olga went into the barn with the other women.

'Well, dear,' Olga said, lying down on the straw next to Marya. 'It's no good crying. You've got to grin and bear it. The Bible says:

"Whosoever shall smite thee on the right cheek, turn to him the other also . . ." Yes, dear!'

Then she told her about her life in Moscow, in a whispering, sing-song voice, about her job as a maid in some furnished flats.

'The houses are very big there and built of stone,' she said. 'There's ever so many churches – scores and scores of them, my dear, and them that live in the houses are all gentlefolk, so handsome and respectable!'

Marya replied that she had never been further than the county town, let alone Moscow. She was illiterate, did not know any prayers – even 'Our Father'. Both she and Fyokla, the other sister-in-law, who was sitting not very far away, listening, were extremely backward and understood nothing. Neither loved her husband. Marya was frightened of Kiryak and whenever he stayed with her she would tremble all over. And he stank so much of tobacco and vodka she nearly went out of her mind. If anyone asked Fyokla if she got bored when her husband was away, she would reply indignantly, 'to hell with him!' They kept talking a little longer and then fell silent . . .

It was cool and they could not sleep because of a cock crowing near the barn for all it was worth. When the hazy-blue light of morning was already filtering through every chink in the woodwork, Fyokla quietly got up and went outside. Then they heard her running off somewhere, her bare feet thudding over the ground.

II

Olga went to church, taking Marya with her. Both of them felt cheerful as they went down the path to the meadow. Olga liked the wide-open spaces, while Marya sensed that her sister-in-law was someone near and dear to her. The sun was rising and a sleepy hawk flew low over the meadows. The river looked gloomy, with patches of mist here and there. But a strip of sunlight already stretched along the hill on the far side of the river, the church shone brightly and crows cawed furiously in the manor-house garden.

'The old man's all right,' Marya was telling her, 'only Grannie's very strict and she's always on the warpath. Our own bread lasted until

Shrovetide, then we had to go and buy some flour at the inn. That put her in a right temper, said we were eating too much.'

'Oh, what of it, dear! You just have to grin and bear it. As it says in the Bible: "Come unto me, all ye that labour and are heavily laden." '

Olga had a measured, sing-song voice and she walked like a pilgrim, quick and bustling. Every day she read out loud from the Gospels, like a priest, and there was much she did not understand. However, the sacred words moved her to tears and she pronounced 'if whomsoever' and 'whither' with a sweet sinking feeling in her heart. She believed in God, the Holy Virgin and the saints. She believed that it was wrong to harm anyone in the wide world – whether they were simple people, Germans, gipsies or Jews – and woe betide those who were cruel to animals! She believed that all this was written down in the sacred books and this was why, when she repeated words from the Bible – even words she did not understand – her face became compassionate, radiant and full of tenderness.

'Where are you from?' Marya asked.

'Vladimir. But my parents took me with them to Moscow a long time ago, when I was only eight.'

They went down to the river. On the far side a woman stood at the water's edge, undressing herself.

'That's our Fyokla,' Marya said, recognizing her. 'She's been going across the river to the manor-house to lark around with the men. She's a real tart and you should hear her swear – something wicked!'

Fyokla, who had black eyebrows and who still had the youthfulness and strength of a young girl, leapt from the bank into the water, her hair undone, threshing the water with her legs and sending out ripples in all directions.

'A real tart!' Marya said again.

Over the river was a rickety wooden plank footbridge and right below it shoals of large-headed chub swam in the pure, clear water. Dew glistened on green bushes which seemed to be looking at themselves in the river. A warm breeze was blowing and everything became so pleasant. What a beautiful morning! And how beautiful life could be in this world, were it not for all its terrible, never-ending poverty, from which there is no escape! One brief glance at the village brought yesterday's memories vividly to life – and that enchanting happiness, which seemed to be all around, vanished in a second.

They reached the church. Marya stopped at the porch, not daring to go in, or even sit down, although the bells for evening service would not ring until after eight. So she just kept standing there.

During the reading from the Gospels, the congregation suddenly moved to one side to make way for the squire and his family. Two girls in white frocks and broad-brimmed hats and a plump, pink-faced boy in a sailor suit came down the church. Olga was very moved when she saw them and was immediately convinced that these were respectable, well-educated, fine people. But Marya gave them a suspicious, dejected look, as though they were not human beings but monsters who would trample all over her if she did not get out of the way. And whenever the priest's deep voice thundered out, she imagined she could hear that shout again – *Ma–arya!* – and she trembled all over.

III

The villagers heard about the newly arrived visitors and a large crowd was already waiting in the hut after the service. Among them were the Leonychevs, the Matveichevs and the Ilichovs, who wanted news of their relatives working in Moscow. All the boys from Zhukovo who could read or write were bundled off to Moscow to be waiters or bellboys (the lads from the village on the other side of the river just became bakers). This was a long-standing practice, going back to the days of serfdom when a certain peasant from Zhukovo called Luka (now a legend) had worked as a barman in a Moscow club and only took on people who came from his own village. Once these villagers had made good, they in turn sent for their families and fixed them up with jobs in pubs and restaurants. Ever since then, the village of Zhukovo had always been called 'Loutville' or 'Lackeyville' by the locals. Nikolay had been sent to Moscow when he was eleven and he got a job through Ivan (one of the Matveichevs), who was then working as an usher at the 'Hermitage' Gardens. Rather didactically Nikolay told the Matveichevs, 'Ivan was very good to me, so I must pray for him night and day. It was through him I became a good man.'

Ivan's sister, a tall old lady, said tearfully, 'Yes, my dear friend, we don't hear anything from them these days.'

'Last winter he was working at Aumont's,* but they say he's out of town now, working in some suburban pleasure gardens. He's aged terribly. Used to take home ten roubles a day in the summer season. But business is slack everywhere now, the old boy doesn't know what to do with himself.'

The woman looked at Nikolay's legs (he was wearing felt boots), at his pale face and sadly said, 'You're no breadwinner, Nikolay. How can you be, in your state!'

They all made a fuss of Sasha. She was already ten years old, but she was short for her age, very thin and no one would have thought she was more than seven, at the very most. This fair-haired girl with her big dark eyes and a red ribbon in her hair looked rather comical among the others, with their deeply tanned skin, crudely cut hair and their long faded smocks – she resembled a small animal that had been caught in a field and brought into the hut.

'And she knows how to read!' Olga said boastfully as she tenderly looked at her daughter. 'Read something, dear!' she said, taking a Bible from one corner. 'You read a little bit and these good Christians will listen.'

The Bible was old and heavy, bound in leather and with well-thumbed pages; it smelled as though some monks had come into the hut. Sasha raised her eyebrows and began reading in a loud, singing voice, 'And when they were departed, behold, the angel of the Lord . . . appeared to Joseph in a dream, saying, "Arise, and take the young child and his mother."'

'"The young child and his mother",' Olga repeated and became flushed with excitement.

'"And flee into Egypt . . . and be thou there until I bring thee word . . ."'

At the word 'until', Olga broke down and wept. Marya looked at her and started sobbing, and Ivan's sister followed suit. Then the old man had a fit of coughing and fussed around trying to find a present for his little granddaughter. But he could not find anything and finally

* Aumont's, a well-known amusement house.

gave it up as a bad job. After the reading, the neighbours went home, deeply touched and extremely pleased with Olga and Sasha.

When there was a holiday the family would stay at home all day. The old lady, called 'Grannie' by her husband, daughters-in-law and grandchildren, tried to do all the work herself. She would light the stove, put the samovar on, go to milk the cows and then complain she was worked to death. She kept worrying that someone might eat a little too much or that the old man and the daughters-in-law might have no work to do. One moment she would be thinking that she could hear the innkeeper's geese straying into her kitchen garden from around the back, and she would dash out of the hut with a long stick and stand screaming for half an hour on end by her cabbages that were as withered and stunted as herself; and then she imagined a crow was stalking her chickens and she would rush at it, swearing for all she was worth. She would rant and rave from morning to night and very often her shouting was so loud that people stopped in the street.

She did not treat the old man with much affection and called him 'lazy devil' or 'damned nuisance'. He was frivolous and unreliable and wouldn't have done any work at all (most likely he would have sat over the stove all day long, talking) if his wife hadn't continually prodded him. He would spend hours on end telling his son stories about his enemies and complaining about the daily insults he had apparently to suffer from his neighbours. It was very boring listening to him.

'Oh yes,' he would say, holding his sides. 'Yes, a week after Exaltation of the Cross, I sold some hay at thirty kopeks a third of a hundredweight, just what I wanted ... Yes, very good business. But one morning, as I was carting the hay, keeping to myself, not interfering with anyone ... it was my rotten luck that Antip Sedelnikov, the village elder, comes out of the pub and asks: "Where you taking that lot, you devil ... ?" and he gives me one on the ear.'

Kiryak had a terrible hangover and he felt very shamed in front of his brother.

'That's what you get from drinking vodka,' he muttered, shaking his splitting head. 'Oh God! My own brother and sister-in-law! Please forgive me, for Christ's sake. I'm so ashamed!'

For the holidays they bought some herring at the inn and made soup from the heads. At midday they sat down to tea and went on drinking until the sweat poured off them. They looked puffed out with all that liquid and after the tea they started on the soup, everyone drinking from the same pot. Grannie had what was left of the herring.

That evening a potter was firing clay on the side of the cliff. In the meadows down below, girls were singing and dancing in a ring. Someone was playing an accordion. Another kiln had been lit across the river and the girls there were singing as well and their songs were soft and melodious in the distance. At the inn and round about, some peasants were making a great noise with their discordant singing and they swore so much that Olga could only shudder and exclaim, 'Oh, good heavens!'

She was astonished that the swearing never stopped for one minute and that the old men with one foot in the grave were the ones who swore loudest and longest. But the children and the young girls were obviously used to it from the cradle and it did not worry them at all.

Now it was past midnight and the fires in the pottery kilns on both sides of the river had gone out. But the festivities continued in the meadow below and at the inn. The old man and Kiryak, both drunk; joined arms and kept bumping into each other as they went up to the barn where Olga and Marya were lying.

'Leave her alone,' the old man urged Kiryak. 'Let her be. She doesn't do any harm . . . it's *shameful* . . .'

'Ma–arya!' Kiryak shouted.

'Leave her alone . . . it's sinful . . . she's not a bad woman.'

They both paused for a moment near the barn, then they moved on.

'I lo–ove the flowers that bloom in the fields, oh!' the old man suddenly struck up in his shrill, piercing tenor voice. 'Oh, I do lo–ove to pick the flo–owers!'

Then he spat, swore obscenely and went into the hut.

IV

Grannie stationed Sasha near her kitchen garden and told her to watch out for stray geese. It was a hot August day. The geese could have got into the garden from round the back, but now they were busily pecking at some oats near the inn, peacefully cackling to each other. Only the gander craned his neck, as though he were looking out for the old woman with her stick. The other geese might have come up from the slope, but they stayed far beyond the other side of the river and resembled a long white garland of flowers laid out over the meadow.

Sasha stood there for a few moments, after which she felt bored. When she saw that the geese weren't coming, off she went down the steep slope. There she spotted Motka (Marya's eldest daughter), standing motionless on a boulder, looking at the church. Marya had borne thirteen children, but only six survived, all of them girls – not a single boy among them; and the eldest was eight. Motka stood barefooted in her long smock, in the full glare of the sun which burned down on her head. But she did not notice it and seemed petrified. Sasha stood next to her and said as she looked at the church, 'God lives in churches. People have ikon lamps and candles, but God has little red, green and blue lamps that are just like tiny eyes. At night-time God goes walking round the church with the Holy Virgin and Saint Nikolay . . . tap-tap-tap. And the watchman is scared stiff!' Then she added, mimicking her mother, 'Now, dear, when the Day of Judgement comes, every church will be whirled off to heaven!'

'Wha–at, with their be–ells too?' Motka asked in a deep voice, dragging each syllable.

'Yes, bells and all. On the Day of Judgement, all good people will go to paradise, while the wicked ones will be burnt in everlasting fire, for ever and ever. And God will tell my mother and Marya, "You never harmed anyone, so you can take the path on the right that leads to paradise." But he'll say to Kiryak and Grannie, "You go to the left, into the fire. And all those who ate meat during Lent must go as well." '

She gazed up at the sky with wide-open eyes and said, 'If you look at the sky without blinking you can see the angels.'

Motka looked upwards and neither of them said a word for a minute or so.

'Can you see them?' Sasha asked.

'Can't see nothing,' Motka said in her deep voice.

'Well, *I* can. There's tiny angels flying through the sky, flapping their wings and going buzz-buzz like mosquitoes.'

Motka pondered for a moment as she looked down at the ground and then she asked, 'Will Grannie burn in the fire?'

'Yes, she will, dear.'

From the rock down to the bottom, the slope was gentle and smooth. It was covered with soft green grass which made one feel like touching it or lying on it. Sasha lay down and rolled to the bottom. Motka took a deep breath and, looking very solemn and deadly serious, she lay down too and rolled to the bottom; on the way down her smock rode up to her shoulders.

'That was great fun,' Sasha said rapturously.

They both went up to the top again for another roll, but just then they heard that familiar, piercing voice again. It was really terrifying! That toothless, bony, hunchbacked old woman, with her short grey hair fluttering in the wind, was driving the geese out of her kitchen garden with a long stick, shouting, 'So you had to tread all over my cabbages, blast you! May you be damned three times and rot in hell, you buggers!'

When she saw the girls, she threw the stick down, seized a whip made of twigs, gripped Sasha's neck with fingers as hard and dry as stale rolls, and started beating her. Sasha cried out in pain and fear, but at that moment the gander, waddling along and craning its neck, went up to the old woman and hissed at her. When it returned to the flock all the females cackled approvingly. Then the old woman started beating Motka and her smock rode up again. With loud sobs and in utter desperation, Sasha went to the hut to complain about it. She was followed by Motka, who was crying as well, but much more throatily and without bothering to wipe the tears away. Her face was so wet it seemed she had just drenched it with water.

'Good God!' Olga said in astonishment when they entered the hut. 'Holy Virgin!'

Sasha was just about to tell her what had happened when Grannie started shrieking and cursing. Fyokla became furious and the hut was filled with noise. Olga was pale and looked very upset as she stroked Sasha's head and said consolingly, 'It's all right, it's nothing. It's sinful to get angry with your grandmother. It's all right, my child.'

Nikolay, who by this time was exhausted by the never-ending shouting, by hunger, by the fumes from the stove and the terrible stench, who hated and despised poverty, and whose wife and daughter made him feel ashamed in front of his parents, sat over the stove with his legs dangling and turned to his mother in an irritable, plaintive voice: 'You can't beat her, you've no right at all!'

'You feeble little man, rotting away up there over the stove,' Fyokla shouted spitefully. 'What the hell's brought you lot here, you parasites!'

Both Sasha and Motka and all the little girls, who had taken refuge in the corner, over the stove, behind Nikolay's back, were terrified and listened without saying a word, their little hearts pounding away.

When someone in a family has been terribly ill for a long time, when all hope has been given up, there are horrible moments when those near and dear to him harbour a timid, secret longing, deep down inside, for him to die. Only children fear the death of a loved one and the very thought of it fills them with terror. And now the little girls held their breath and looked at Nikolay with mournful expressions on their faces, thinking that he would soon be dead. They felt like crying and telling him something tender and comforting.

He clung to Olga, as though seeking protection, and he told her softly, tremulously, 'My dear Olga, I can't stand it any more here. All my strength has gone. For God's sake, for Christ's sake, write to your sister Claudia and tell her to sell or pawn all she has. Then she can send us the money to help us get out of this place.'

He went on in a voice that was full of yearning: 'Oh God, just one glimpse of Moscow is all I ask! If only I just could *dream* about my dear Moscow!'

When evening came and it was dark in the hut, they felt so depressed they could hardly speak. Angry Grannie sat dipping rye-crusts in a cup and sucking them for a whole hour. After Marya had milked the cow she brought a pail of milk and put it on a bench. Then Grannie poured it into some jugs, without hurrying, and she was visibly cheered by the thought that as it was the Feast of the Assumption (when milk was forbidden) no one would go near it. All she did was pour the tiniest little drop into a saucer for Fyokla's baby. As she was carrying the jugs with Marya down to the cellar, Motka suddenly started, slid down from the stove, went over to the bench where the wooden cup with the crusts was standing and splashed some milk from the saucer over them.

When Grannie came back and sat down to her crusts, Sasha and Motka sat watching her from the stove, and it gave them great pleasure to see that now she had eaten forbidden food during Lent and would surely go to hell for it. They took comfort in this thought and lay down to sleep. As Sasha dozed off she had visions of the Day of Judgement; she saw a blazing furnace, like a potter's kiln, and an evil spirit dressed all in black, with the horns of a cow, driving Grannie into the fire with a long stick, as *she* had driven the geese not so long ago.

V

After ten o'clock, on the eve of the Feast of the Assumption, the young men and girls who were strolling in the meadows down below suddenly started shouting and screaming and came running back to the village. People who were sitting up on the hill, on the edge of the cliff, could not understand at first what had happened.

'Fire! Fire!' came the desperate cry from below. 'We're on fire!'

The people up above looked round and were confronted by the most terrifying, extraordinary sight: on the thatched roof of one of the huts at the end of the village a pillar of fire swirled upwards, showering sparks everywhere like a fountain. The whole roof turned into a mass of bright flames and there was a loud crackling. The moonlight was dimmed by the glare and the whole village became enveloped in a red, flickering light. Black shadows stole over the ground and there was a smell of burning. The villagers had come running up the hill, were all out of breath and could not speak for trembling; they jostled each other and kept falling down, unable to see properly in that sudden blinding light and not recognizing one another. It was terrifying, particularly with pigeons flying around in the smoke above the fire, while down at the inn (they had not heard about the fire) the singing and accordion-playing continued as if nothing had happened.

'Uncle Semyon's hut's on fire!' someone shouted in a loud, rough voice.

Marya was dashing around near the hut, crying and wringing her hands and her teeth chattered – even though the fire was some distance away, at the far end of the village.

Nikolay emerged in his felt boots and the children came running out in their little smocks. Some of the villagers banged on an iron plate by the police constable's hut, filling the air with a loud clanging; this incessant, unremitting sound made your heart ache and made you go cold all over.

Old women stood holding ikons.

Sheep, calves and cows were driven out into the street from the yards; trunks, sheepskins and tubs were carried outside. A black stallion, normally kept apart from the herd – it had a tendency to kick and injure the others – was set loose and galloped once or twice through the village, whinnying and stamping, and then suddenly stopped near a cart and lashed out with its hind legs.

And the bells were ringing out in the church on the other side of the river. Near the blazing hut it was hot and so light that the tiniest blade of grass was visible.

Semyon, a red-haired peasant with a large nose, wearing a waistcoat and with his cap pulled down over his ears, was sitting on one of the trunks they had managed to drag out. His wife was lying face downwards moaning in despair. An old man of about eighty, shortish, with an enormous beard – rather like a gnome – and who was obviously in some way connected with the fire (although he came from another village), was pacing up and down without any hat, carrying a white bundle. A bald patch on his head glinted in the light of the fire. Antip Sedelnikov, the village elder – a swarthy man with the black hair of a gipsy – went up to the hut with an axe and, for some obscure reason, knocked out the windows, one after the other. Then he started hacking away at the front steps.

'Get some water, you women!' he shouted. 'Bring the fire-engine! And be quick about it!'

A fire-engine was hauled up by the same villagers who had just been drinking and singing at the inn. They were all dead-drunk and kept stumbling and falling over; all of them had a helpless look and they had tears in their eyes.

The village elder, who was drunk as well, shouted, 'Get some water, quick!'

The women and girls ran down to the bottom of the hill, where there was a spring, dragged up the full buckets and tubs, emptied them into the fire-engine and ran down again. Olga, Marya, Sasha and Motka all helped. The women and little boys helped to pump the water, making the hosepipe hiss, and the village elder began by directing a jet into the doorway, then through the windows, regulating the flow with his finger, which made the water hiss all the more.

'Well done, Antip!' the villagers said approvingly. 'Come on now!'

Antip climbed right into the burning hall from where he shouted, 'Keep on pouring. Try your best, you good Christians, on the *occasion of such an unhappy event.*'

The villagers crowded round and did nothing – they just gazed at the fire. No one had any idea what to do – no one was capable of doing anything – and close by there were stacks of wheat and hay, piles of dry brushwood, and barns. Kiryak and old Osip, his father, had joined in the crowd, and they were both drunk. The old man turned to the woman lying on the ground and said – as though trying to find some excuse for his idleness – 'Now don't get so worked up! The hut's insured, so don't worry!'

Semyon turned to one villager after the other, telling them how the fire had started.

'It was that old man with the bundle, him what worked for General Zhukov ... used to cook for him, God rest his soul. Along he comes this evening and says, "Let me stay the night, please." Well, we had a drink or two ... the old girl started messing around with the samovar to make the old man a cup of tea and she put it in the hall before the charcoal was out. The flames shot straight up out of the pipe and set the thatched roof alight, so there you are! *We* nearly went up as well. The old man's cap was burnt, a terrible shame.'

Meanwhile they banged away at the iron plate for all they were worth and the bells in the church across the river kept ringing. Olga ran breathlessly up and down the slope. As she looked in horror at the red sheep, at the pink doves fluttering around in the smoke, she was lit up by the fierce glow. The loud clanging had the effect of a sharp needle piercing her heart and it seemed that the fire would never go out, that Sasha was lost ... And when the ceiling in the hut collapsed with a loud crash, the thought that the whole village was bound to burn down now made her feel weak and she could not carry any more water. So she sat on the cliff, with the buckets at her side. Nearby, a little lower down, women were sitting and seemed to be wailing for the dead.

But just then some labourers and men from the manor across the river arrived in two carts, together with a fire-engine. A very young student came riding up in his unbuttoned white tunic. Axes started hacking away, a ladder was propped against the blazing framework and five men clambered up it at once, with the student leading the way. His face was red from the flames and he shouted in a hoarse, rasping voice, in such an authoritative way it seemed putting fires out was something he did every day. They tore the hut to pieces beam by beam, and they tore down the cowshed, a wattle fence and the nearest haystack.

Stern voices rang out from the crowd: 'Don't let them smash the place up. Stop them!'

Kiryak went off towards the hut with a determined look and as though intending stopping the newly arrived helpers from breaking the whole place up. But one of the workmen turned him round and hit him in the neck. There was laughter and the workman hit him again. Kiryak fell down and crawled back to the crowd on all fours.

Two pretty girls, wearing hats – they were probably the student's sisters – arrived from across the river. They stood a little way off, watching the fire. The beams that had been pulled down had stopped burning, but a great deal of smoke still came from them. As he manipulated the hose, the student directed the jet at the beams, then at the peasants and then at the women fetching the water.

'Georges!' the girls shouted, in anxious, reproachful voices. 'Georges!'

The fire was out now and only when they started going home did the villagers notice that it was already dawn and that everyone had that pale, slightly swarthy look which always seems to come in the early hours of the morning, when the last stars have faded from the sky. As they went their different ways, the villagers laughed and made fun of General Zhukov's cook and his burnt hat. Already they wanted to turn the fire into a joke – and they even seemed sorry that it was all over so quickly.

'You were a very good fireman,' Olga told the student. 'You should come to Moscow where we live, there's a fire every day.'

'You don't say, you're from *Moscow*?' one of the young ladies asked.

'Oh yes. My husband worked at the Slav Fair. And this is my daughter.'

She pointed to Sasha, who went cold all over and clung to her. 'She's from Moscow as well, Miss.'

The two girls said something in French to the student and he gave Sasha a twenty-kopek piece. When old Osip saw it, there was a sudden flicker of hope on his face.

'Thank God there wasn't any wind, sir,' he said, turning to the student, 'or everything would have gone up before you could say knife.' Then he lowered his voice and added timidly, 'Yes, sir, and you ladies, you're good people ... it's cold at dawn, could do with warming up ... Please give me a little something for a drink ...'

They gave him nothing and he sighed and slunk off home. Afterwards Olga stood at the top of the slope and watched the two carts fording the river and the two ladies and the gentleman riding across the meadow – a carriage was waiting for them on the other side.

When she went back into the hut she told her husband delightedly, 'Such fine people! And so good-looking. Those young ladies were like little cherubs!'

'They can damned well go to hell!' murmured sleepy Fyokla, in a voice full of hatred.

VI

Marya was unhappy and said that she longed to die. Fyokla, on the other hand, found this kind of life to her liking – for all its poverty, filth and never-ending bad language. She ate whatever she was given, without any fuss, and slept anywhere she could and on whatever she happened to find. She would empty the slops right outside the front door, splashing them out from the steps, and she would walk barefoot through the puddles into the bargain. From the very first day she had hated Olga and Nikolay, precisely because they did not like the life there.

'We'll see what you get to eat here, my posh Moscow friends,' she said viciously. 'We'll see!'

One morning, right at the beginning of September, the healthy, fine-looking Fyokla, her face flushed with the cold, brought two buckets of water up the hill. Marya and Olga were sitting at the table drinking tea.

'Tea *and* sugar!' Fyokla said derisively. 'Real ladies!' she added, putting the buckets down. 'Is it the latest fashion, then, drinking tea every day? Careful you don't burst with all that liquid inside you.' She gave Olga a hateful look and went on, 'Stuffed your fat mug all right in Moscow, didn't you, you fat cow!'

She swung the yoke and hit Olga on the shoulders; this startled the sisters-in-law so much all they could do was clasp their hands and say, 'Oh, good heavens!'

Then Fyokla went down to the river to do some washing and she swore so loudly the whole way there, they could hear her back in the hut.

The day drew to a close and the long autumn evening set in. In the hut they were winding silk – everyone, that is, except Fyokla, who had gone across the river.

The silk was collected from a nearby factory and the whole family earned itself a little pocket money – twenty kopeks a week.

'We were better off as serfs,' the old man said as he wound the silk. 'You worked, ate, slept – everything had its proper place. You had cabbage soup and kasha for your dinner and again for supper. You had as many cucumbers and as much cabbage as you liked and you could eat to your heart's content, if you felt like it. And they were stricter then, everyone knew his place.'

Only one lamp was alight, smoking and glowing dimly. Whenever anyone stood in front of it, a large shadow fell across the window and one could see the bright moonlight. Old Osip took his time as he told them all what life was like before the serfs were emancipated;* how, in those very same places where life was so dull and wretched now, they used to ride out with wolfhounds, borzois and skilled hunters. There would be plenty of vodka for the peasants during the battue. He told how whole cartloads of game were taken to Moscow for the young gentlemen, how badly behaved peasants were flogged or sent away to estates in Tver, while the good ones were rewarded. Grannie had stories

* The serfs were officially emancipated in 1861.

to tell as well. She remembered simply everything. She told of her mistress, whose husband was a drunkard and a rake and whose daughters all made absolutely disastrous marriages; one married a drunkard, another a small tradesman in the town, while the third eloped (with the help of Grannie, who was a girl herself at the time). In no time at all they all died of broken hearts (like their mother) and Grannie burst into tears when she recalled it all.

Suddenly there was a knock at the door and everyone trembled.

'Uncle Osip, put me up for tonight, please!'

In came General Zhukov's cook – a bald, little old man, the same cook whose hat had been burnt. He sat down, listened to the conversation and soon joined in, reminiscing and telling stories about the old days. Nikolay sat listening with his legs dangling from the stove and all he wanted to know was what kind of food they used to eat in the days of serfdom. They discussed various kinds of rissoles, cutlets, soups and sauces. The cook, who had a good memory as well, mentioned dishes that were not made any more. For example, there was some dish made from bulls' eyes called *morning awakening*.

'Did they make cutlets *à la maréchale* then?' Nikolay asked.

'No.'

Nikolay shook his head disdainfully and said, 'Oh, you little apology for a cook!'

The little girls who were sitting or lying on the stove looked down without blinking. There seemed to be so many of them, they were like cherubs in the clouds. They liked the stories, sighed, shuddered and turned pale with delight or fear. Breathlessly they listened to Grannie's stories, which were the most interesting, and they were too frightened to move a muscle. All of them lay down to sleep without saying a word. The old people, excited and disturbed by the stories, thought about the beauty of youth, now that it was past: no matter what it had *really* been like, they could only remember it as bright, joyful and moving. And now they thought of the terrible chill of death – and for them death was not far away. Better not to think about it! The lamp went out. The darkness, the two windows sharply outlined in the moonlight, the silence and the creaking cradle somehow reminded them that their lives were finished, nothing could bring them back. Sometimes one becomes drowsy and dozes off, and suddenly someone touches you on the shoulder, breathes on your cheek and you can sleep no longer, your whole body goes numb, and you can think of nothing but death. You turn over and death is forgotten; but then the same old depressing, tedious thoughts keep wandering around your head – thoughts of poverty, cattle fodder, about the higher price of flour and a little later you remember once again that your life has gone, that you can never re-live it.

'Oh God!' sighed the cook.

Someone was tapping ever so gently on the window – that must be Fyokla. Olga stood up, yawning and whispering a prayer as she opened the door and then drew the bolt back in the hall. But no one came in and there was just a breath of chill air from the street and the sudden bright light of the moon. Through the open door she could see the quiet, deserted street and the moon itself sailing across the heavens.

Olga called out, 'Who is it?'

'It's me,' came the answer, 'it's me.'

Fyokla was standing near the door, pressing close to the wall, and she was stark naked. She was trembling with the cold and her teeth chattered. In the bright moonlight she looked very pale, beautiful and strange. The shadow and the brilliant light playing over her skin struck Olga particularly vividly and those dark eyebrows and firm young breasts were very sharply outlined.

'It was them beasts on the other side of the river, they stripped me naked and sent me away like this . . .' she muttered. 'I've come all the way home without nothing on . . . stark naked . . . Give me some clothes.'

'Come into the hut!' Olga said softly and she too started shivering.

'I don't want the old people to see me!'

But in actual fact Grannie had already become alarmed and was grumbling away, while the old man asked, 'Who's there?'

Olga fetched her own smock and skirt and dressed Fyokla in them. Then they both tiptoed into the hut, trying not to bang the doors.

'Is that you, my beauty?' Grannie growled angrily when she realized who it was. 'You little nightbird, want a nice flogging, do you?'

'It's all right, it's all right, dear,' Olga whispered as she wrapped Fyokla up.

Everything became quiet again. They always slept badly in the hut, every one of them would be kept awake by obsessive, nagging thoughts – the old man by his backache, Grannie by her worrying and evil mind, Marya by her fear and the children by itching and hunger.

And now their sleep was as disturbed as ever and they kept tossing and turning, and saying wild things; time after time they got up for a drink of water.

Suddenly Fyokla started bawling in her loud, coarse voice, but immediately tried to pull herself together and broke into an intermittent sobbing which gradually became fainter and fainter until it died away completely. Now and again the church on the other side of the river could be heard striking the hour, but in the most peculiar way: first it struck five and then three.

'Oh, my God!' sighed the cook.

It was hard to tell, just by looking at the windows, whether the moon was still shining or if dawn had already come. Marya got up and went outside. They could hear her milking the cow in the yard and telling it, 'Ooh, keep still!' Grannie went out as well. Although it was still dark in the hut, by now every object was visible.

Nikolay, who had not slept the whole night, climbed down from the stove. He took his tail-coat out of a green trunk, put it on, smoothed the sleeves as he went over to the window, held the tails for a moment and smiled. Then he carefully took it off, put it back in the trunk and lay down again.

Marya returned and started lighting the stove. Quite clearly she was not really awake yet and she was still coming to as she moved around. Most probably she had had a dream or suddenly remembered the stories of the evening before, since she said, 'No, *freedom** is best,' as she sensuously stretched herself in front of the stove.

VII

The 'gentleman' arrived – this was how the local police inspector was called in the village. Everyone knew a week beforehand exactly when and why he was coming. In Zhukovo there were only forty households, but they were so much in arrears with their taxes and rates that over two thousand roubles were overdue.

* Marya means freedom from serfdom.

The inspector stopped at the inn. There he 'imbibed' two glasses of tea and then set off on foot for the village elder's hut, where a crowd of defaulters was waiting for him. Antip Sedelnikov, the village elder, despite his lack of years (he had only just turned thirty) was a very strict man and always sided with the authorities, although he was poor himself and was always behind with his payments. Being the village elder obviously amused him and he enjoyed the feeling of power and the only way he knew to exercise this was by enforcing strict discipline. At village meetings everyone was scared of him and did what he said. If he came across a drunk in the street or near the inn he would swoop down on him, tie his arms behind his back and put him in the village lock-up. Once he had even put Grannie there for swearing when she was deputizing for Osip at a meeting and he kept her locked up for twenty-four hours. Although he had never lived in a town or read any books, somehow he had managed to accumulate a store of various clever-sounding words and he loved using them in conversation, which made him respected, if not always understood.

When Osip entered the elder's hut with his rent-book, the inspector – a lean old man with long grey whiskers, in a grey double-breasted jacket – was sitting at a table in the corner near the stove, writing something down. The hut was clean and all the walls were gay and colourful with pictures cut out of magazines. In the most conspicuous place, near the ikons, hung a portrait of Battenberg, once Prince of Bulgaria. Antip Sedelnikov stood by the table with his arms crossed.

'This one 'ere owes a hundred and nineteen roubles, your honour,' he said when it was Osip's turn. ' 'E paid a rouble before Easter, but not one kopek since.'

The inspector looked up at Osip and asked, 'How come, my dear friend?'

'Don't be too hard on me, your honour,' Osip said, getting very worked up, 'just please let me explain, sir. Last summer the squire from Lyutoretsk says to me, "Sell me your hay, Osip, sell it to me . . ." Why not? I had about a ton and a half of it, what the women mowed in the meadows . . . well, we agreed the price . . . It was all very nice and proper.'

He complained about the elder and kept turning towards the other peasants as though summoning them as witnesses. His face became red and sweaty and his eyes sharp and evil-looking.

'I don't see why you're telling me all this,' the inspector said. 'I'm asking *you* why you're so behind with your rates. It's *you* I'm asking. None of you pays up, so do you think *I'm* going to be responsible!'

'But I just can't!'

'These words have no *consequences*, your honour,' the elder said. 'In actual fact those Chikildeyevs belong to the *impecunious* class. But if it please your honour to ask the others, the whole reason for it is vodka. And they're real troublemakers. They've no *comprehension*.'

The inspector jotted something down and told Osip in a calm, even voice, as though asking for some water, 'Clear off!'

Shortly afterwards he drove away and he was coughing as he climbed into his carriage. From the way he stretched his long, thin back one could tell that Osip, the elder and the arrears at Zhukovo were no more than dim memories, and that he was now thinking about something that concerned him alone. Even before he was half a mile away, Antip Sedelnikov was carrying the samovar out of the Chikildeyevs' hut, pursued by Grannie, who was shrieking for all she was worth, 'I won't let you have it, *I won't*, blast you!'

Antip strode along quickly, while Grannie puffed and panted after him, nearly falling over and looking quite ferocious with her hunched back. Her shawl had slipped down over her shoulders and her grey hair, tinged with green, streamed in the wind. Suddenly she stopped and began beating her breast like a real rebel and shouted in an even louder sing-song voice, just as though she were sobbing, 'Good Christians, you who believe in God! Heavens, we've been trampled on! Dear ones, we've been persecuted. Oh, please help us!'

'Come on, Grannie,' the elder said sternly, 'time you got some sense into that head of yours!'

Life became completely and utterly depressing without a samovar in the Chikildeyevs' hut. There was something humiliating, degrading in this deprivation, as though the hut itself were in disgrace. It wouldn't have been so bad if the elder had only taken the table, all the benches and pots instead – then the place wouldn't have looked so bare as it did now. Grannie yelled, Marya wept and the little girls looked at her and wept too. The old man felt guilty and sat in one corner, his head downcast and not saying a word. Nikolay did not say a word either: Grannie was very fond of him and felt sorry for him, but now all compassion was forgotten as she suddenly attacked him with a stream of reproaches and insults, shaking her fists right under his nose. He was to blame for everything, she screamed. And in actual fact, why had he sent them so little, when in his letters he had boasted that he was earning fifty roubles a month at the Slav Fair? And why did he have to come with his family? How would they pay for the funeral if he died here . . . ? Nikolay, Olga and Sasha made a pathetic sight.

The old man wheezed, picked his cap up and went off to see the elder. Already it was getting dark. Antip Sedelnikov was soldering something near the stove, puffing his cheeks out. The air was heavy with fumes. His skinny, unwashed children – they were no better than the Chikildeyev children – were playing noisily on the floor, while his ugly, freckled, pot-bellied wife was winding silk. It was a wretched, miserable family – with the exception of Antip, who was handsome and dashing. Five samovars stood in a row on a bench. The old man offered a prayer to Battenberg and said, 'Antip, have pity on us, give us the samovar back, for Christ's sake!'

'Bring me three roubles – then you can have it back.'

'I haven't got them!'

Antip puffed his cheeks out, the fire hummed and hissed and its light gleamed on the samovars. The old man rumpled his cap, pondered for a moment and said, 'Give it back!'

The dark-faced elder looked jet-black, just like a sorcerer. He turned to Osip and said in a rapid, stern voice, 'It all depends on the magistrate. At the administrative meeting on the 26th inst. you can announce your grounds for dissatisfaction, orally or in writing.'

Osip did not understand one word of this, but he seemed satisfied and went home.

About ten days later the inspector turned up again, stayed for an hour and then left. About this time the weather was windy and cold. The river had frozen over long ago, but there still hadn't been any snow and everyone was miserable, as the roads were impassable. On one holiday, just before evening, some neighbours dropped in at Osip's for a chat. The conversation took place in the dark – it was considered sinful to work, so the fire had not been lit. There was a little news –

most of it unpleasant: some hens had been confiscated from two or three households that were in arrears and taken to the council offices where they died, since no one bothered to feed them. Sheep were confiscated as well – they were taken away with their legs tied up and dumped into a different cart at every village; one died. And now they were trying to decide who was to blame.

'The local council, who else?' Osip said.

'Yes, of course, it's the council.'

The council was blamed for everything – tax arrears, victimization, harassment, crop failures, although not one of them had any idea what the function of the council was. And all this went back to the times when rich peasants who owned factories, shops and inns had served as councillors, became dissatisfied, and cursed the council when they were back in their factories and inns. They discussed the fact that God hadn't sent them any snow: firewood had to be moved, but it was impossible to drive or walk because of all the bumps in the road. Fifteen or twenty years ago – or even earlier – the local gossip in Zhukovo was much more interesting. In those times every old man looked as though he was hiding some secret, knew something, and was waiting for something. They discussed deeds with golden seals, allotments and partition of land, hidden treasure and they were always hinting at something or other. But now the people of Zhukovo had no secrets at all: their entire lives were like an open book, which anyone could read and all they could talk about was poverty, cattle feed, lack of snow . . .

They fell silent for a while: then they remembered the hens and the sheep and tried to decide whose fault it was.

'The council's!' Osip exclaimed gloomily. 'Who else!'

VIII

The parish church was about four miles away, at Kosogorovo, and the people only went there when they really had to – for christenings, weddings or funerals. For ordinary prayers they went to the church across the river. On saints' days (when the weather was fine) the young girls put on their Sunday best and crowded along to Mass, making a very cheerful picture as they walked across the meadows in their yellow and green dresses. But when the weather was bad everyone stayed at home. Pre-communion services were held in the parish church. The priest fined anyone who had not prepared for Communion during Lent fifteen kopeks as he went round the huts at Easter with his cross.

The old man didn't believe in God, for the simple reason that he rarely gave him a moment's thought. He admitted the existence of the supernatural, but thought that it could only affect women. Whenever anyone discussed religion or the supernatural with him, or questioned him, he would reluctantly reply as he scratched himself, 'Who the hell knows!'

The old woman believed in God, but only in some vague way. Everything in her mind had become mixed up and no sooner did she start meditating on sin, death and salvation, than poverty and everyday worries took charge and immediately she forgot what she had originally been thinking about. She could not remember her prayers and it was usually in the evenings, before she went to bed, that she stood in front of the ikons and whispered, 'to the Virgin of Kazan, to the Virgin of Smolensk, to the Virgin of the Three Arms . . .'

Marya and Fyokla would cross themselves and prepare to take the sacrament once a year, but they had no idea what it meant. They hadn't taught their children to pray, had told them nothing about God and never taught them moral principles: all they did was tell them not to eat forbidden food during fast days. In the other families it was almost the same story: hardly anyone believed in God or understood anything about religion. All the same, they loved the Bible dearly, with deep reverence; but they had no books, nor was there anyone to read or explain anything to them. They respected Olga for occasionally reading to them from the Gospels, and spoke to her and Sasha very politely.

Olga often went to festivals and services in the neighbouring villages and the county town, where there were two monasteries and twenty-seven churches. Since she was rather scatterbrained, she tended to forget all about her family when she went on these pilgrimages. Only on the journey home did she suddenly realize, to her great delight, that she had a husband and daughter, and then she would smile radiantly and say, 'God's been good to me!'

Everything that happened in the village disgusted and tormented her. On Elijah's day they drank, on the Feast of the Assumption they drank, on the day of the Exaltation of the Cross they drank. The Feast of the Intercession was a parish holiday in Zhukovo, and the men celebrated it by going on a three-day binge. They drank their way through fifty roubles of communal funds and on top of this they had a whip-round from all the farms for some vodka. On the first day of the Feast, the Chikildeyevs slaughtered a sheep and ate it for breakfast, lunch and dinner, consuming vast quantities, and then the children got up during the night for another bite. During the entire three days Kiryak was terribly drunk – he drank everything away, even his cap and boots, and he gave Marya such a thrashing that they had to douse her with cold water. Afterwards everyone felt ashamed and sick.

However, even in Zhukovo or 'Lackeyville', a truly religious ceremony was once celebrated. This was in August, when the ikon of the Life-giving Virgin was carried round the whole district, from one village to another. The day on which the villagers at Zhukovo expected it was calm and overcast. Right from the morning the girls, in their Sunday best, had left their homes to welcome the ikon and towards evening it was carried in procession into the village with the church choir singing and the bells in the church across the river ringing out loud. A vast crowd of villagers and visitors filled the street; there was noise, dust, and a terrible crush . . . The old man, Grannie, and Kiryak all held their hands out to the ikon, looked at it hungrily and cried out tearfully, 'Our Protector, holy Mother!'

It was as though everyone suddenly realized that there wasn't just a void between heaven and earth, that the rich and the strong had not grabbed everything yet, that there was still someone to protect them from slavery, crushing, unbearable poverty – and that infernal vodka.

'Our Protector, holy Mother!' Marya sobbed. 'Holy Mother!'

But the service was over now, the ikon was taken away and everything returned to normal. Once again those coarse drunken voices could be heard in the pub.

Only the rich peasants feared death, and the richer they became, the less they believed in God and salvation – if they happened to donate candles or celebrate Mass, it was only for fear of their departure from this world – and just to be on the safe side. The peasants who weren't so well off had no fear of death.

Grannie and the old man had been told to their faces that their lives were over, that it was time they were gone, and they did not care. They had no qualms in telling Fyokla, right in front of Nikolay, that when he died her husband Denis would be discharged from the army and sent home. Far from having any fear of death, Marya was only sorry that it was such a long time coming, and she was glad when any of her children died.

Death held no terrors for them, but they had an excessive fear of all kinds of illness. It only needed some trifle – a stomach upset or a slight chill – for the old woman to lie over the stove, wrap herself up and groan out loud, without stopping, 'I'm dy–ing!' Then the old man would dash off to fetch the priest and Grannie would receive the last sacrament and extreme unction. Colds, worms and tumours that began in the stomach and worked their way up to the heart were everyday topics. They were more afraid of catching cold than anything else, so that even in summer they wrapped themselves in thick clothes and stood by the stove warming themselves. Grannie loved medical treatment and frequently went to the hospital, telling them there that she was fifty-eight, and not seventy: she reasoned if the doctor knew her real age he would refuse to have her as a patient and would tell her it was time she died, rather than have hospital treatment. She usually left early in the morning for the hospital, taking two of the little girls with her, and she would return in the evening, cross and hungry, with drops for herself and ointment for the little girls. Once she took Nikolay with her; he took the drops for about two weeks afterwards and said they made him feel better.

Grannie knew all the doctors, nurses and quacks for twenty miles around and she did not like any of them. During the Feast of the Intercession, when the parish priest went round the huts with his cross, the lay-reader told her about an old man living near the town prison, who had once been a medical orderly in the army and who knew some very good cures. He advised her to go and consult him, which Grannie did. When the first snows came she drove off to town and brought a little old man back with her: he was a bearded, Jewish convert to Christianity who wore a long coat and whose face was completely covered with blue veins. Just at that time some jobbing tradesmen happened to be working in the hut – an old tailor with terrifying spectacles was cutting a waistcoat from some old rags and two young men were making felt boots from wool. Kiryak, who had been given the sack for drinking and lived at home now, was sitting next to the tailor mending a horse-collar. It was cramped, stuffy and evil-smelling in the hut. The convert examined Nikolay and said that he should be bled, without fail.

He applied the cupping glasses, while the old tailor, Kiryak and the little girls stood watching – they imagined that they could actually see the illness being drawn out of Nikolay. And Nikolay also watched the cup attached to his chest slowly filling with dark blood and he smiled with pleasure at the thought that something was really coming out.

'That's fine,' the tailor said. 'Let's hope it does the trick, with God's help.'

The convert applied twelve cups, then another twelve, drank some tea and left. Nikolay started shivering. His face took on a pinched look, like a clenched fist, as the women put it; his fingers turned blue. He wrapped himself tightly in a blanket and a sheepskin, but he only felt colder. By the time evening came he was very low. He asked to be laid on the floor and told the tailor to stop smoking. Then he fell silent under his sheepskin and passed away towards morning.

IX

What a harsh winter it was and what a long one!

By Christmas their own grain had run out, so they had to buy flour. Kiryak, who was living at home now, made a dreadful racket in the evening, terrifying everyone, and in the mornings he was tormented by self-disgust and hangovers; he made a pathetic sight. Day and night a hungry cow filled the barn with its lowing, and this broke Grannie and Marya's hearts. And, as though on purpose, the frosts never relented in their severity and snowdrifts piled up high. The winter dragged on: a real blizzard raged at Annunciation and snow fell at Easter.

However, winter finally drew to an end. At the beginning of April it was warm during the day and frosty at night – and still winter hadn't surrendered. But one warm day did come along at last and it gained the upper hand. The streams flowed once more and the birds began to sing again. The entire meadow and the bushes near the river were submerged by the spring floods and between Zhukovo and the far side there was just one vast sheet of water with flocks of wild duck flying here and there. Every evening the fiery spring sunset and rich luxuriant clouds made an extraordinary, novel, incredible sight – such clouds and colours that you would hardly think possible seeing them later in a painting.

Cranes flashed past overhead calling plaintively, as though inviting someone to fly along with them. Olga stayed for a long while at the edge of the cliff watching the flood waters, the sun, the bright church which seemed to have taken on a new life, and tears poured down her face; a passionate longing to go somewhere far, far away, as far as the eyes could see, even to the very ends of the earth, made her gasp for breath. But they had already decided to send her back to Moscow as a chambermaid and Kiryak was going with her to work as a hall porter or at some job or other. Oh, if only they could go soon!

When everything had dried out and it was warm, they prepared for the journey. Olga and Sasha left at dawn, with rucksacks on their backs, and both of them wore bast shoes. Marya came out of the hut to see them off. Kiryak wasn't well and had to stay on in the hut for another week. Olga gazed at the church for the last time and thought about her husband. She did not cry, but her face broke out in wrinkles and became ugly, like an old woman's. During that winter she had grown thin, lost her good looks and gone a little grey. Already that pleasant appearance and agreeable smile had been replaced by a sad, submissive expression that betrayed the sorrow she had suffered and there was something blank and lifeless in her, as though she were deaf. She was sorry to leave the village and the people there. She remembered them carrying Nikolay's body and asking for prayers to be said at each hut, and how everyone wept and felt for her in her sorrow. During the summer and winter months there were hours and days when these people appeared to live worse than cattle, and life with them was really terrible. They were coarse, dishonest, filthy, drunk, always quarrelling and arguing amongst themselves, with no respect for one another and living in mutual fear and suspicion. Who maintains the pubs and makes the peasants drunk? The peasant. Who embezzles the village, school and parish funds and spends it all on drink? The peasant. Who robs his neighbour, sets fire to his house and perjures himself in court for a bottle of vodka? Who is the first to revile the peasant at district council and similar meetings? The peasant. Yes, it was terrible living with these people; nevertheless, they were still human beings, suffering and weeping like other people and there was nothing in their lives which did not provide some excuse: killing work which made bodies ache all over at night, harsh winters, poor harvests, overcrowding, without any help and nowhere to find it. The richer and stronger cannot help, since they themselves are coarse, dishonest and drunk, using the same foul language. The most insignificant little clerk or official treats peasants like tramps, even talking down to elders and churchwardens, as though this is their right. And after all, could one expect help or a good example from the mercenary, greedy, dissolute, lazy people who come to the village now and then just to insult, fleece and intimidate the peasants? Olga recalled how pathetic and down-trodden the old people had looked when Kiryak was taken away for a flogging that winter . . . and now she felt sorry for all these people and kept glancing back at the huts as she walked away.

Marya went with them for about two miles and then she made her farewell, prostrating herself and wailing out loud, 'Oh, I'm all alone again, a poor miserable wretch . . .'

For a long time she kept wailing, and for a long time afterwards Olga and Sasha could see her still kneeling there, bowing as though someone were next to her and clutching her head, while the rooks circled above.

The sun was high now and it was warm. Zhukovo lay far behind. It was very pleasant walking on a day like this. Olga and Sasha soon forgot both the village and Marya. They were in a gay mood and everything around was a source of interest. Perhaps it was an old burial mound, or a row of telegraph poles trailing away heaven knows where and disappearing over the horizon, with their wires humming mysteriously. Or they would catch a glimpse of a distant farm-house, deep in foliage, with the smell of dampness and hemp wafting towards them and it seemed that happy people must live there. Or they would see a horse's skeleton lying solitary and bleached in a field. Larks poured their song out untiringly, quails called to each other and the corncrake's cry was just as though someone was tugging at an old iron latch.

By noon Olga and Sasha reached a large village. In its broad street they met that little old man who had been General Zhukov's cook. He was feeling the heat and his sweaty red skull glinted in the sun. Olga and the cook did not recognize one another at first, but then they both turned round at once, realized who the other was and went their respective ways without a word. Olga stopped by the open windows of a hut which seemed newer and richer than the others, bowed and said in a loud, shrill sing-song voice, 'You good Christians, give us charity, for the sake of Christ, so that your kindness will bring the kingdom of heaven and lasting peace to your parents . . .'

'Good Christians,' Sasha chanted, 'give us charity for Christ's sake, so that your kindness, the kingdom of heaven . . .'

The Bishop

I

It was the eve of Palm Sunday and night service had begun at the old convent of St Peter. By the time they had started giving out the willow branches, it was nearly ten, lights had burned low, wicks needed snuffing and everything was obscured by a thick haze. The congregation rocked like the sea in the gloomy church and all those faces, old and young, male and female, looked exactly alike to Bishop Peter, who had not been feeling well for the past three days; to him they all appeared to have exactly the same look in their eyes as they came forward for palms. The doors couldn't be seen through the haze and the congregation kept moving forward in a seemingly never-ending procession. A woman's choir was singing and a nun was reading the lessons.

How hot and stuffy it was – and the service was so long! Bishop Peter felt tired. He was breathing heavily and panting, his throat was dry, his shoulders ached from weariness and his legs were shaking. Now and then he was unpleasantly disturbed by some 'God's fool' shrieking up in the gallery. Then, all of a sudden, just as though he were dreaming or delirious, the bishop thought that he could see his mother, Marya Timofeevna (whom he had not seen for nine years) – or an old woman who looked like her – make her way towards him in the congregation, take her branch and gaze at him with a cheerful, kindly, joyful smile as she walked away and was lost in the crowd. For some reason tears trickled down his cheeks. He felt calm enough and all was well, but he stood there quite still, staring at the choir on his left, where the lessons were being read, unable to make out a single face in the dusk – and he wept. Tears glistened on his face and beard. Then someone else, close by, burst out crying, then another a little further away, then another and another, until the entire church was gradually filled with a gentle weeping. But about five minutes later the nuns were singing, the weeping had stopped and everything was normal again.

Soon the service was over. As the bishop climbed into his carriage, homeward bound, the whole moonlit garden was overflowing with the joyful, harmonious ringing of heavy bells. White walls, white crosses on graves, white birches, dark shadows, the moon high above the convent – everything seemed to be living a life of its own, beyond the understanding of man, but close to him nonetheless. It was early April, and after that mild day it had turned chilly, with a slight frost, and there was a breath of spring in that soft, cold air. The road from the convent to the town was sandy and they had to travel at walking pace. In the bright, tranquil moonlight churchgoers were trudging through the sand, on both sides of the carriage. They were all silent and deep in thought; and everything around was so welcoming, young, so near at hand – the trees, the sky, even the moon – that one wished it would always be like this.

The carriage finally reached the town and rumbled down the main street. The shops were already closed, except Yerakin's (a merchant millionaire), where electric lighting was being tested, violently flashing on and off while a crowd of people looked on. Dark, wide, deserted streets followed, then the high road (built by the council) on the far side of town, then the open fields, where the fragrance of pines filled the air. Suddenly a white, crenellated wall loomed up before the bishop, with a lofty belfry beyond, flooded by the moonlight, and with five, large gleaming golden 'onion' cupolas next to it – this was Pankratiev Monastery, where Bishop Peter lived. And here again, far above, was that same tranquil, pensive moon. The carriage drove through the gates, crunching over the sand, and here and there he caught fleeting glimpses of dark figures of monks in the moonlight; footsteps echoed on flagstones.

'Your mother called while you were out, your grace,' the lay brother announced as the bishop went into his room.

'My mother? When did she come?'

'Before evening service. First she asked where you were, then she drove off to the convent.'

'So I *did* see her in the church then – goodness gracious!' The bishop laughed joyfully.

'She asked me to inform your grace that she'll be coming tomorrow,' the lay brother went on. 'There's a little girl with her, her granddaughter, I suppose. They're staying at Ovsyannikov's inn.'

'What's the time now?'

'Just past eleven.'

'Oh, that's a shame.'

The bishop sat meditating in his drawing-room for a little while, hardly believing that it was so late. His arms and legs were aching all over, and he had a pain in the back of his neck; he felt hot and uncomfortable. After he had rested, he went to his bedroom and sat down again, still thinking about his mother. He could hear the lay brother going out and Father Sisoy coughing in the next room. The monastery clock struck the quarter. The bishop changed into his nightclothes and began to say his prayers. As he carefully read those old, long-familiar words he thought of his mother. She had nine children and about forty grandchildren. Once she had lived with her husband, a deacon, in a poor village. This was for a long, long time, from her seventeenth to her sixtieth year. The bishop remembered her from his early childhood, almost from the age of three, and how he had loved her! Dear, precious, unforgettable childhood! It had gone forever and was irrevocable. Why does this time always seem brighter, gayer, richer than it is in reality? How tender and caring his mother had been when he was ill as a child and a young man! And now prayers mingled with his memories, which flared up even brighter now, like flames – and these prayers did not disturb his thoughts about his mother.

When he had finished his prayers, he undressed and lay down. The moment darkness closed in all around him he had visions of his late father, his mother, his native village of Lesopolye . . . Creaking wheels, bleating sheep, church bells ringing out on bright summer mornings, gipsies at the window – how delightful it was thinking about these things! He recalled the priest at Lesopolye – that gentle, humble, good-hearted Father Simeon who was very short and thin, but who had a terribly tall son (a theological student) with a furious-sounding bass voice. Once his son had lost his temper with the cook and called her 'Ass of Jehudiel', which made Father Simeon go very quiet, for he was only too ashamed of not being able to remember where this particular ass was mentioned in the Bible. He was succeeded at Lesopolye by Father Demyan, who drank until he saw green serpents and even earned the nickname Demyan Snake-eye. Matvey Nikolayevich, the village schoolmaster, a former theological student, had been a kind, intelligent man, but a heavy drinker as well. He never beat his pupils, but for some reason always had a bundle of birch twigs hanging on the wall with the motto in dog Latin underneath: *Betula kinderbalsamica secuta*.* He had a shaggy black dog called Syntax.

The bishop laughed. About five miles from Lesopolye was the village of Obnino with its miracle-working ikon, carried in procession round the neighbouring villages every summer, when bells would ring out all day long – first in one village, then in another. On these occasions the bishop (who was called 'Little Paulie') thought that the very air was quivering with joy and he would follow the ikon bareheaded, barefoot, smiling innocently, immeasurably happy in his simple faith. Now he remembered that the congregations at Obnino were always quite large, and that the priest there, Father Alexei, had managed to shorten the services by making his deaf nephew Ilarion read out the little notices and inscriptions pinned to the communion bread – prayers 'for the health of' and 'for the departed soul of'. Ilarion read these out, occasionally getting five or ten kopeks for his trouble, and only when he had gone grey and bald, when life had passed him by, did he suddenly notice a piece of paper with 'Ilarion is a fool' written on it. Little Paulie had been a backward child, at least until he was fifteen years old, and he was such a poor pupil at the church school that they even considered sending him to work in a shop. Once when he was collecting the mail from Obnino post office, he had stared at the clerks there for a long time, after which he asked, 'May I inquire how you're paid, monthly or daily?'

The bishop crossed himself and turned over in an effort to stop thinking about such things and go to sleep.

'Mother's here,' he remembered – and he laughed.

The moon peered in at the window, casting its light on the floor, where shadows lay.

A cricket chirped. In the next room Father Sisoy was snoring away, and there was a solitary note in his senile snoring, making one think of an orphan or a homeless wanderer. At one time Sisoy had been a diocesan bishop's servant and he was called 'Father ex-housekeeper'. He

* A linguistic hotchpotch, ostensibly meaning 'a curative birch for beating children'.

was seventy, and now lived in a monastery about ten miles from the town. But he stayed in town whenever he had to. Three days before, he had gone to the Pankratiev Monastery, and the bishop had taken him into his own rooms, so that they could have a leisurely chat about church affairs and local business.

At half past one the bell rang for matins. The bishop could hear Father Sisoy coughing and mumbling ill-humouredly, after which he got up and started pacing up and down in his bare feet.

The bishop called out, 'Father Sisoy!', upon which Sisoy went back to his room, reappearing a little later in his boots, with a candle in his hand. Over his underclothes he was wearing a cassock and an old, faded skull-cap.

'I can't get to sleep,' the bishop said as he sat down. 'I must be ill, I just don't know what's wrong! It's so hot!'

'Your grace must have caught a cold. You need a rub-down with candle grease.'

Sisoy stood there for a few minutes and said to himself with a yawn, 'Lord forgive me, miserable sinner that I am.'

Then he said out loud, 'Those Yerakins have got electric lights now, I don't like it!'

Father Sisoy was old, skinny, and hunchbacked and he was always complaining. His eyes were angry and bulging, like a crab's.

'Don't like it,' he repeated as he went out, 'don't want nothing to do with it!'

II

Next day, Palm Sunday, the bishop celebrated mass in the cathedral, after which he visited the diocesan bishop, called on a very old general's wife, who was extremely ill, and finally went home. After one o'clock he had some rather special guests to lunch – his aged mother and his eight-year-old niece, Katya.

Throughout the meal the spring sun shone through the windows overlooking the yard, glinting cheerfully on the white tablecloth and in Katya's red hair. Through the double windows they could hear the rooks cawing in the garden and the starlings singing.

'It's nine years since we last saw each other,' the old lady was saying. 'But when I saw you yesterday in the convent – heavens, I thought, you haven't changed one bit, only you're thinner now and you've let your beard grow. Blessed Virgin! Everyone cried at the service, they just couldn't help it. When I looked at you I cried too, quite suddenly, just don't know why. It's God's will!'

Although she said this with affection, she was clearly quite embarrassed, wondering whether she should address him formally or as a close relative, whether she could laugh or not. And she seemed to think she was more a deacon's widow than a bishop's mother. All this time Katya looked at her right reverend uncle without blinking an eyelid, apparently trying to guess what kind of man he was. Her hair welled up like a halo from her comb and velvet ribbon; she had a snub nose and cunning eyes. Before lunch she had broken a glass and her grandmother kept moving tumblers and wine glasses out of her reach during the conversation. As he listened to his mother, the bishop recalled the time, many, many years ago when she took him and his brothers and sisters to see some relatives, who were supposed to be rich. Then she had her hands full with the children. Now she had grandchildren, and here she was with Katya.

'Your sister Barbara has four children,' she told him. 'Katya's the eldest. Father Ivan – your brother-in-law – was taken ill, God knows with what, and he passed away three days before Assumption. Now my poor Barbara has to go round begging.'

The bishop inquired about Nikanor, his eldest brother.

'He's all right, thank God. He doesn't have much, but he makes ends meet, thank God. But there's just one thing: his son Nicholas, my little grandson, didn't want to go into the Church and he's at university, studying to be a doctor. He thinks that's better, but who knows? It's the will of God.'

'Nicholas cuts up dead people,' Katya said, spilling water over her lap.

'Sit still, child,' her grandmother said calmly, taking a tumbler out of her hands. 'You must pray before you eat.'

'It's been such a long time since we met,' the bishop observed, tenderly stroking his mother's arm and shoulder. 'When I was abroad I missed you, mother, I really missed you!'

'That's very kind of you!'

'I used to sit during the evenings by an open window, all on my own, when suddenly I'd hear a band playing and then I'd long for Russia. I felt I would have given *anything* just to go home, to see you . . .'

His mother beamed all over but immediately pulled a serious face and repeated, 'That's very kind of you!'

Then he had a sharp change of mood. As he looked at his mother, he was puzzled by this obsequious, timid expression and tone of voice. What was the reason? – it wasn't at all like her.

He felt sad and irritated. And now he had the same headache as yesterday, and a killing pain in the legs. Moreover, the fish was unappetizing, had no flavour at all and it made him continually thirsty.

After lunch two rich landowning ladies arrived and they sat for over an hour and a half without saying a word, making long faces. The Father Superior, a taciturn man, who was rather hard of hearing, came on some business. Then the bells rang for evensong, the sun sank behind the forest and the day was over. As soon as he came back from the church, the bishop hurriedly said his prayers, went to bed and tucked himself up more warmly than usual.

The thought of the fish at lunch lingered very unpleasantly in his mind. First the moonlight disturbed him, then he could hear people talking. Father Sisoy was most likely talking politics in the next room, or the drawing-room, perhaps.

'The Japanese are at war now and fighting. Like the Montenegrins they are, ma'am, the same tribe, both were under the Turkish yoke.'

Then the bishop's mother was heard to say, 'Well then, after we said our prayers, hum – and had a cup of tea, we went to see Father Yegor at Novokhatnoye, hum . . .'

From those continual 'had a cup of tea's or 'drank a drop's, one would have thought that all she ever did in her life was drink tea. Slowly and phlegmatically the bishop recalled the theological college and academy. For three years he had taught Greek in the college, and then he could no longer read without spectacles; afterwards he became a monk and then inspector of schools. Then he took his doctorate. At the age of thirty-two he was appointed rector of the college and made Father Superior. Life was so pleasant and easy then, that it seemed it would continue like that forever. But then he was taken ill, lost a lot of weight and nearly went blind. As a result he was obliged, on his doctors' advice, to drop everything and go abroad.

'And then what?' Sisoy asked in the next room.

'Then we had tea,' the bishop's mother replied.

'Father, you've got a green beard!' Katya suddenly exclaimed with a surprised laugh. The bishop laughed too, remembering that grey-haired Father Sisoy's beard actually did have a greenish tinge.

'Heavens, that girl's a real terror,' Sisoy said in a loud, angry voice. 'Such a spoilt child! Sit still!'

The bishop recalled the newly built white church, where he had officiated when he was abroad. And he remembered the roar of that warm sea. He had a five-roomed flat there with high ceilings, a new desk in the study and a library. He had read and written a lot. He remembered feeling homesick for his native Russia and how that blind beggar woman who sang of love and played the guitar every day under his window had always reminded him of the past. But eight years had gone by, and he was recalled to Russia. By now he was a suffragan bishop, and his entire past seemed to have disappeared into the misty beyond, as though it had all been a dream. Father Sisoy came into the bedroom carrying a candle.

'Oho, asleep already, your grace?'

'What's the matter?'

'Well, it's still quite early, ten o'clock – even earlier perhaps. I've brought a candle so I can give you a good greasing.'

'I've a temperature,' the bishop said and sat down. 'But I really must take something, my head's terrible . . .'

Sisoy took the bishop's shirt off and started rubbing his chest and back with candle grease.

'Yes, that's it, there, that's it. Oh Christ in heaven! There . . . I went into town today and called on Father – what's his name? – Sidonsky and I had tea with him. Don't care for him much. Lord save us! No, I don't care for him . . .'

III

The diocesan bishop, old, very stout, and afflicted with rheumatism or gout, had been bedridden for over a month. Bishop Peter called on him almost every day and himself saw to the villagers who came for his advice and help. But now *he* was ill he was struck by the futility and triviality of their tearful petitions. Their ignorance and timidity infuriated him and the sheer weight of all those petty, trifling matters they came to see him about depressed him. He felt that he understood the diocesan bishop who, in his younger days, had written *Studies in Free Will*, but who seemed now to be completely obsessed by these trifles, having forgotten everything else, never giving any thought to God. While he was abroad, the bishop must have lost touch completely with Russia and things were not easy for him now. The peasants seemed so coarse, the ladies who came for help so boring and stupid, the theological students and their teachers so ignorant and sometimes so uncivilized, like savages. And all those incoming and outgoing documents – they could be counted by the thousand – what documents! The senior clergy, all over the diocese, were in the habit of awarding good conduct marks to junior priests, young or old, even to wives and children, and all this had to be discussed, scrutinized and solemnly recorded in official reports. There was never any let-up, not even for a minute, and Bishop Peter found this played on his nerves the whole day long: only when he was in church could he relax.

He found it quite impossible to harden himself against the fear he aroused in people (through no desire of his own) despite his gentle, modest nature. Everyone in the province struck him as small, terrified and guilty when he looked at them. Everyone – even the senior clergy – quailed when he was around, all of them threw themselves at his feet. Not so long before, an old country priest's wife, who had come begging some favour, was struck dumb with fear and left without saying one word, her mission unaccomplished. As the bishop could never bring himself to say a bad word about anyone in his sermons, and felt too much compassion to criticize, he found himself flying into tempers, getting mad with his petitioners and throwing their applications on the floor. Never had anyone spoken openly and naturally to him, as man to man, during the whole time he was there. Even his old mother seemed to have been transformed – now she was *quite* a different person! And he asked himself how she could chatter away to Sisoy and laugh so much, while with *him*, her own son, she was so withdrawn and embarrassed – which wasn't like her at all. The only one to feel free and easy and who would speak his mind in his presence was old Sisoy, who had spent his whole life attending bishops and who had outlived eleven of them. This was why the bishop felt at ease with him, although he was, without question, a difficult, cantankerous old man.

After Tuesday morning service the bishop received parish petitioners at the episcopal palace, which upset and angered him no end: afterwards he went home. Once again he felt ill and longed for his bed. But hardly had he reached his room than he was told that a young merchant called Yerakin, a most charitable man, had come on a most urgent matter. He just could not turn him away. Yerakin stayed for about an hour, and spoke so loud he nearly shouted, making it almost impossible to understand a word he said.

'God grant – well, you know,' he said as he left. 'Oh, most *certainly*! Depending on the circumstances, your grace. I wish you – well, you know!'

Then the Mother Superior from a distant convent arrived. But by the time she had left, the bells were ringing for evensong and he had to go to church.

That evening the monks' singing was harmonious and inspired; a young, black-bearded priest was officiating. When he heard the 'bridegroom who cometh at midnight' and 'the mansion richly adorned', he felt neither penitent nor sorrowful, but a spiritual peace and calm as his thoughts wandered off into the distant past, to his childhood and youth, when they had sung of that same bridegroom and mansion. Now that past seemed alive, beautiful, joyful, such as it most probably had never been. Perhaps, in the next world, in the life to come, we will remember that distant past and our life on earth below with just the same feelings. Who knows? The bishop took his seat in the dark chancel, and the tears flowed. He reflected that he had attained everything a man of his position could hope for; and his faith was still strong. All the same, there were things he did not understand, something was lacking. He did not want to die. And still it seemed that an integral part of his life, which he had vaguely dreamed of at some time, had vanished; and precisely the same hopes for the future which he had nurtured in his childhood, at the college and abroad, still haunted him.

'Just listen to them sing today!' he thought, listening intently. 'How wonderful!'

IV

On Maundy Thursday he celebrated mass and ritual washing of feet in the cathedral. When the service was over and the congregation had gone home, the weather turned out sunny, warm and cheerful, and water bubbled along the ditches, while the never-ending, sweetly soothing song of the skylarks drifted in from the fields beyond the town. The trees, already in bud, smiled their welcome, while the fathomless, vast expanse of blue sky overhead floated away into the mysterious beyond.

When he arrived home the bishop had his tea, changed, climbed into bed and ordered the lay brother to close the shutters. It was dark in the bedroom. How tired he felt, though, how his legs and back ached with that cold numbing pain – and what a ringing in his ears! He felt that it was ages since he last got some sleep, absolutely ages, and every time he closed his eyes there seemed to be some little trifling thought that flickered into life in his brain and kept him awake. And, just like yesterday, he could hear voices and the clink of glasses and teaspoons through the walls of the adjoining rooms. His mother, Marya, was cheerfully telling Father Sisoy some funny story while the priest kept commenting in a crusty, disgruntled voice, 'Damn them! Not on your life! What for!' Once more the bishop felt annoyed, then offended, when he saw that old lady behaving so naturally and normally with strangers, while with him, her own son, she was so timid and inarticulate, always saying the wrong thing and even trying to find an excuse to stand up, as she was too shy to sit down. And what about his father? Had he been alive, he would probably have been unable to say one word with his son there.

In the next room something fell on the floor and broke. Katya must have dropped a cup or saucer, because Father Sisoy suddenly spat and said angrily, 'That girl's a real terror, Lord forgive me, miserable sinner! She won't be satisfied until she's broken everything!'

Then it grew quiet except for some sounds from outside. When the bishop opened his eyes, Katya was in his room, standing quite still and looking at him. As usual, her red hair rose up above her comb like a halo.

'Is that you, Katya?' he asked. 'Who keeps opening and shutting that door downstairs?'

'I can't hear anything,' she replied, listening hard.

'Listen – someone's just gone through.'

'That was your stomach rumbling, Uncle!'

He laughed and stroked her head.

'So cousin Nicholas cuts dead bodies up, does he?' he asked after a short silence.

'Yes, he's studying to be a doctor.'

'Is he nice?'

'Yes, he's all right, but he's a real devil with the vodka!'

'What did your father die of?'

'Daddy was always weak and terribly thin, then suddenly he had a bad throat. I became ill as well, and my brother Fedya too – all of us had bad throats. Daddy died, but we got better, Uncle.'

Her chin trembled and tears welled up in her eyes and trickled down her cheeks. 'Your grace,' she said in a thin little voice, weeping bitterly now, 'Mummy and I were left with nothing . . . please give us a little money, please Uncle, dear!'

He burst out crying too and for a while was so upset he couldn't say a word. Then he stroked her hair, touched her shoulder and said, 'Never mind, little girl, it's all right. Soon it will be Easter Sunday and we'll have a little talk then . . . Of course I'll help you . . .'

Then his mother came in, quietly and timidly, and turned and prayed to the ikon. Seeing that he was awake she asked, 'Would you like a little soup?'

'No thanks, I'm not hungry.'

'Looking at you now, I can see you're not well. And I'm not surprised. On your feet all day long. Good God, it really hurts me to see you like this. Well, Easter's not far away and you can have a rest then, God willing. But I won't bother you any more with my nonsense. Come on, Katya, let the bishop sleep.'

He could recall her talking to some rural dean in that mock-respectful way a long, long time ago, when he was still a small boy. Only from her unusually loving eyes and the anxious, nervous look she darted at him as she left the room could one tell that she was actually his mother. He closed his eyes and appeared to have fallen asleep, but twice he heard the clock striking, then Father Sisoy coughing in the next room. His mother came into the room again and watched him anxiously for a minute. He heard some coach or carriage drive up to the front steps. Suddenly there was a knock and the door banged: in came the lay brother, shouting, 'Your grace.'

'What's the matter?'

'The carriage is ready, it's time for evening service.'

'What's the time?'

'Quarter past seven.'

He got dressed and went to the cathedral. Throughout the entire twelve lessons from the Gospels he had to stand motionless in the centre; he read the first, the longest and most beautiful, himself. A lighthearted mood came over him. He knew that first lesson ('Now is the Son of Man glorified') by heart. Now and again he raised his eyes as he read and he saw a sea of lights on both sides of him, heard the candles sputtering. But he could not make any faces out as he used to do in years gone by, and he felt that this was the very same congregation he had seen when he was a boy and a young man, and he felt that it would be the same year after year – for how long God alone knew. His father had been a deacon, his grandfather a priest, and his great-grandfather a deacon. In all likelihood his entire family, from the time of the coming of Christianity to Russia, had belonged to the clergy and his love of ritual, of the priesthood, of ringing bells was deep, innate and ineradicable. He always felt active, cheerful and happy when he was in church, especially when he was officiating, and this was how he felt now. Only after the eighth lesson had been read did he feel that his voice was weakening, he could not even hear himself cough and he had a splitting headache; he began to fear he might fall down any moment. In actual fact his legs had gone quite numb, there was no longer any feeling in them. He just could not make out how he was managing to keep on his feet at all and didn't fall over.

It was a quarter to twelve when the service finished. The moment he arrived home, the bishop undressed and went to bed without even saying his prayers. He was unable to speak and thought his legs were about to give way. As he pulled the blanket over him he had a sudden urge, an intolerable longing to go abroad. He felt that he could even sacrifice his life, so long as he didn't have to look at those miserable cheap shutters any more, those low ceilings, and he yearned to escape from that nasty monastery smell.

For a long time he heard someone's footsteps in the next room, but he just could not recollect whose they could be.

Finally the door opened and in came Sisoy with candle and tea cup.

'In bed already, your grace?' he asked. 'I've come to give you a good rub-down with vodka and vinegar. It'll do you the world of good if it's well rubbed in. Lord above! There, that's it . . . I've just been to the monastery. Don't like it there! I'm leaving tomorrow, master, I've had enough. Oh, Jesus Christ!'

Sisoy was incapable of staying very long in one place and he felt as though he had already spent a whole year at the Pankratiev Monastery. But the hardest thing was making any sense out of what he said, discovering where his home really was, whether he loved anyone or anything, whether he believed in God. He did not really know himself why he had become a monk – he never gave the matter any thought – and he had long forgotten the time when he had taken his vows. It was as if he had come into this world as a monk.

'Tomorrow I'm off, damn it all!'

'I'd like to have a talk with you, but I never seem to get round to it,' the bishop said softly and with great effort. 'But I don't know anyone or anything here.'

'I'll stay until Sunday if you like, but after that I'm off, damn it!'

'Why am I a bishop?' the bishop continued in his soft voice. 'I should have been a village priest, a lay-reader or an ordinary monk. All of this crushes the life out of me . . .'

'What? Heavens above! Now . . . there! You can have a good sleep now, your grace. Whatever next! Good night!'

The bishop did not sleep the whole night. At about eight o'clock in the morning he had an intestinal haemorrhage. The lay brother panicked and rushed off, first to the Father Superior, then he went to the monastery doctor, Ivan Andreyevich, who lived in town. This doctor, a plump old man with a long grey beard, gave the bishop a thorough examination, kept shaking his head and frowning, after which he said, 'Did you know it's typhoid, your grace?'

Within an hour of the haemorrhage, the bishop had turned thin, pale, and he had a pinched look. His face became wrinkled, his eyes dilated and he seemed suddenly to have aged and shrunk. He felt thinner and weaker and more insignificant than anyone else, and it seemed the entire past had vanished somewhere far, far away and would never be repeated or continued.

'How wonderful!' he thought. 'How wonderful!'

His old mother arrived. She was frightened when she saw his wrinkled face and dilated eyes, and she fell on her knees by the bed and started kissing his face, shoulders and hands. And somehow she too thought that he had become thinner, weaker and more insignificant than anyone else; she forgot that he was a bishop and kissed him like a much-loved child.

'Darling Paulie,' she said. 'My own flesh and blood . . . my little son . . . What's happened to you? Paul, answer me.'

Katya stood there, pale and solemn, unable to understand what had happened to her uncle and why her grandmother had such a pained expression, why she spoke so sadly and emotionally. But the bishop just could not articulate a simple word, understood nothing that was going on and he felt that he was just an ordinary, simple man walking swiftly and cheerfully across fields, beating his stick on the ground, under a broad, brilliant sky. Now he was as free as a bird and could go wherever he liked!

'Paul, my angel, my son!' the old lady said. 'What's the matter, dear, *please* answer!'

'Leave him alone,' Sisoy said angrily as he crossed the room. 'Let him sleep, there's nothing you can do . . . nothing . . .'

Three doctors arrived, consulted together and left. That day seemed never-ending, unbelievably long, and then came a seemingly endless night. Just before dawn on the Saturday, the lay brother went up to the old lady, who was lying on a couch in the drawing-room, and asked her to come to the bedroom as the bishop had just departed this world.

Next day was Easter Sunday. There were forty-two churches in the town and six monasteries and the sonorous, joyful, incessant pealing of bells lay over it, from morn till night, rippling the spring air. Birds sang and the sun shone brightly. The big market square was noisy, swings rocked back and forwards, barrel organs played, an accordion squealed and drunken shouts rang out.

In the afternoon there was pony-trotting down the main street. In brief, it was all so cheerful, gay and happy, just as it had been the year before and as it probably would be in the years to come.

A month later a new suffragan bishop was appointed. No one remembered Bishop Peter any more and soon they forgot all about him. Only the old lady (the late bishop's mother) who was now living with her brother-in-law, a deacon in an obscure provincial town, talked about her son to the women she met when she went out in the evening to fetch her cow from pasture; then she would tell them about her children, her grandchildren, about her son who had been a bishop. And she spoke hesitantly, afraid they would not believe her. Nor did they all believe her, as it happened.

The Russian Master

I

There was a sound of horses' hooves clattering over wooden floors and the black Count Nulin was first led out of the stables, then the white Giant, and then Mayka, his sister. All three of them were fine, valuable horses. Old Shelestov turned to his daughter Masha as he saddled Giant and said, 'Come on, Marie Godefroi,* get up! Off you go!'

Masha Shelestov was the youngest in the family. Although she was already eighteen, the others still treated her as a little girl, calling her Manya or Manyusya. But ever since a circus visited the town – and she had been a most enthusiastic spectator – everyone started calling her Marie Godefroi. 'Let's go!' she cried as she mounted Giant.

Her sister Varya mounted Mayka, Nikitin Count Nulin, the officers mounted their horses and the long, handsome cavalcade made a colourful picture with the officers' white tunics and the ladies' black riding-habits as it slowly moved out of the yard.

When everyone was on horseback and had ridden out into the street, Nikitin noticed that for some reason Masha was looking at no one else except him. She watched him and Count Nulin anxiously and then she said, 'Sergei, mind you hold him tight on the bit. Don't let him shy, he's only pretending.'

Whether it was because her Giant was great pals with Count Nulin or just pure coincidence, she rode beside Nikitin the whole time, as she had yesterday and the day before. And he looked tenderly, joyfully and delightedly at her small shapely body astride that proud white animal, at her fine profile, at her top hat which did not suit her at all and only made her look older; and as he listened, without understanding very much, he thought: 'I swear by God I won't be afraid any more and I'll make my feelings plain *today* ...'

It was six in the evening, a time when the white acacias and lilac

* A celebrated equestrienne of the time.

smell so strongly that the very air and trees seem numbed by their own fragrance. A band was already playing in the town gardens. Horses' hooves rang out along the road; everywhere there was laughter, talking and the sound of gates banging. Soldiers whom they passed saluted the officers and boys from the high school bowed to Nikitin. Clearly, everyone taking a stroll or hurrying to the park to hear the band found the cavalcade very pleasant to look at. And how warm it was! And how soft the clouds looked as they lay scattered here and there across the sky, how gentle and inviting the shadows of poplars and acacias seemed – shadows that spread right across that wide street to darken the houses on the other side up to their balconies and first floors!

They left the town and trotted along the high road. Here there was no longer acacia or lilac perfume and the music had died away – there were only sweet-smelling fields, the young green rye and wheat, squeaking marmots and cawing crows. Wherever one looked, there was greenery all around, broken only by black patches of melon plantations here and there and the white row of apple trees that had finished blossoming in the cemetery to the far left. They rode past the slaughterhouses, the brewery, and they overtook a military band hurrying to the country gardens.

'I don't deny it. Polyansky has a very fine horse,' Masha told Nikitin, nodding at the officer at Varya's side. 'But it has its faults. Now, that white spot on the left leg is just *not* right, and just look how it jibs. It's too late to train it now, it will go on jibbing till the day it dies.'

Like her father, Masha was terribly keen on horses. It really hurt her to see someone else with a fine horse and she liked finding faults with other people's horses. Nikitin did not have a clue about horses, and holding the reins in, curbing, trotting or galloping meant nothing to him. The only thing that worried him was looking clumsy and ill-at-ease on horseback – Masha must be more attracted to the officers who were all so used to the saddle. This was the reason why he was jealous of them.

When they were passing the country gardens, someone suggested stopping for a drink of soda-water, and so they rode in. There were only oaks in these gardens and they had just come into bud, so they could see the whole park – with its bandstand, little tables and swings, and crows' nests like huge fur hats – quite clearly through the young foliage. The riders and their ladies dismounted by one of the tables and ordered soda-water. Some of their friends who were already strolling round the gardens came up to greet them – among them an army doctor in jackboots and the bandmaster, who was waiting for his men to arrive. The doctor must have taken Nikitin for a student as he asked him, 'Are you here on holiday?'

'No, I *live* here,' Nikitin replied. 'I'm a teacher at the high school.'

'Really?' the doctor said, surprised. 'So young and a teacher already?'

'Young, am I? I'm *twenty-six* . . . for heaven's sake!'

'Yes, you've a beard and moustache. But you certainly don't look more than twenty-two or three. Really, you look so young!'

'What a bloody cheek!' Nikitin thought. 'He thinks I'm a whipper-snapper!' He became very angry when anyone said how young he looked – especially when there were women or schoolboys around. Ever since he had taken a teacher's job in that town, he had come to detest his own youthful looks. The schoolboys weren't afraid of him, old men called him 'young man' and the young ladies were more eager to dance with him than listen to his long speeches. He would have given a great deal now to be ten years older.

They left the gardens and rode up to the Shelestovs' farm. They halted by the gate and sent for Praskovya, the estate manager's wife, to bring them some fresh milk. No one drank any – they just stared at one another, laughed and galloped off home. The band was already playing in the country gardens as they rode back, the sun had set behind the cemetery and half the sky had turned crimson in the evening glow.

Masha rode beside Nikitin again. He wanted to tell her how passionately he loved her, but he was afraid the officers and Varya might hear and he said nothing. Masha remained silent as well, and he felt that he knew the reason for her silence and why she was riding with him. He was so happy that the whole earth and sky, the town lights, the black silhouette of the brewery – all of this, in his eyes, blended into something beautiful and welcoming, and it seemed Count Nulin was walking on air and wanted to climb that crimson sky.

They reached the house. A samovar was already boiling away on a garden table and old Shelestov was sitting on one side of it with his friends – officials from the circuit court. As usual, he was finding fault with something: 'That's the behaviour of a lout, sir,' he was saying. 'An utter lout, sir. Yes, a lout, I say!'

Ever since he had fallen in love with Masha, Nikitin found everything at the Shelestovs' highly agreeable – the house, the gardens, afternoon tea, the wickerwork chairs and the old nanny – even that word 'lout' which the old man loved so much. Only he could not stand the swarms of dogs and cats and the Egyptian doves that cooed so mournfully in the large cage on the terrace.

There were so many watch-dogs and house-dogs that, since his first meeting with the Shelestovs, he could recognize only two of them – Midge and Haddock.

Midge was a small, mangy, hairy-muzzled, nasty little cur and it was both vicious and spoilt. It hated Nikitin. Whenever it saw him, it cocked its head, bared its teeth and snarled away at him, 'Grrr grrr-rrr . . .' Then it would sit under his chair; but whenever he tried to drive it out, it would let fly with a series of ear-splitting yelps. His hosts would merely say, 'Don't be afraid, she doesn't bite. She's a good dog.'

Haddock was an enormous, black, long-legged hound with a tail as stiff as a poker. During dinner and tea it usually shuffled around silently under the table, slapping its tail on shoes and table-legs. It was a good-natured, stupid dog, but Nikitin just could not endure it, since it rested its nose on his lap at mealtimes and dribbled all over his trousers. More than once he had tried to rap its wide forehead with his knife handle, flipped it on the nose, cursed and complained, but nothing saved his trousers from being soiled.

After the ride, tea, jam, biscuits and butter tasted good. They all drank their first glass in silence, with great relish, but were already arguing when they were on their second. It was invariably Varya who started these arguments during meals. She was already twenty-three, very pretty – prettier even than Masha – and the family regarded her as the cleverest and most highly cultivated person in that house. As one might expect from an elder daughter who had taken her late mother's place, she behaved responsibly and sternly. As lady of the house she wore a blouse when they had company and she called the officers by their surnames. She treated Masha like a child and spoke to her like a schoolmistress, and she called herself an old maid – in other words, she was convinced that she was going to get married.

She never failed to turn any conversation, even about the weather, into an argument. She was particularly fond of taking everyone literally, catching them out with self-contradictions and quibbling about everything. You only had to start a conversation and she would immediately stare you in the face and interrupt you with, 'Please, please, Petrov, you said exactly the *opposite* the day before yesterday!' Or she would say, sneering, 'However, I see that you advocate the principles of the Third Department.* Congratulations!' If you made a joke or a pun, you would immediately hear a voice saying, 'That's as old as the hills,' or 'That's feeble!' If an officer tried to be witty she would leer contemptuously and exclaim, 'That's barrack-room humour!' She rolled her 'r's so impressively that Midge always echoed her from under a chair, 'Gr-rrr . . .'

And now a row started over tea because Nikitin made some remarks about school exams.

'Come, come, Mr Nikitin,' Varya interrupted, 'you say it's hard for the boys. May I ask, whom shall we blame? For example, you set form eight an essay on "Pushkin as psychologist". In the first place, you should *never* set them such difficult subjects. Secondly, how can you call Pushkin a psychologist? Now, Shchedrin, or Dostoyevsky – that's quite a different matter. But Pushkin's a great poet and nothing else.'

'Shchedrin is Shchedrin† and Pushkin is Pushkin,' Nikitin gloomily replied.

'I know you don't do any Shchedrin at the high school, but that's not the point. Just tell me why you think Pushkin was a psychologist?'

'Surely you can't mean he *wasn't*? I can give plenty of examples if you like.' And Nikitin recited a few passages from *Eugene Onegin* and *Boris Godunov*.

'I don't see any psychology there,' Varya sighed. 'A psychologist is someone who describes the nuances of the human soul, but you only quoted pretty poetry, nothing more.'

Nikitin took umbrage and said, 'I know what sort of psychology you want – someone to work on my fingers with a blunt saw so that I scream like hell – that's your idea of psychology.'

* The Third Department was a section of the secret police, particularly responsible for censorship.

† M. Saltykov-Shchedrin was a satirical novelist (1826–89).

'A feeble reply! However, you still haven't proved why Pushkin is a psychologist.'

Whenever Nikitin was forced into arguments that for him were all too stereotyped, bigoted and so on, he usually leapt from his seat, clutching his head with both hands and ran groaning from one corner of the room to the other. And he did just that. He jumped up, clutched his head, walked round the table groaning and then sat down a little distance away.

The officers came to his defence. Staff-Captain Polyansky tried to persuade Varya that Pushkin really was a psychologist and quoted two lines from Lermontov to prove it. Lieutenant Gernet said that if Pushkin hadn't been a psychologist they would never have erected a monument to him in Moscow.

'That's the work of a lout,' came a voice from the end of the table. 'And that's what I told the governor. I said, "That's sheer loutishness, sir!"'

'I don't intend arguing with you any more,' Nikitin shouted. 'He will reign for ever! Enough!' Then he screamed at Haddock, which had rested its head and paws on his lap, 'Get off, you filthy hound!'

The dog snarled back from under the table, 'Grr-rrr ...'

'Now admit you're in the wrong!' Varya shrieked. 'Admit it!'

But just then some young ladies arrived and the argument died a natural death. Everyone went into the ballroom. Varya sat down at the piano and played some dance-music. First they did a waltz, then a polka, then a quadrille *en grand rond*, with Staff-Captain Polyansky leading the way through all the rooms. Then they danced a waltz again.

The old people sat there smoking and watching the young ones dance. Among them was Shebaldin, director of the local savings bank and highly respected for his love of literature and the theatre. He had founded the local 'musico-dramatic circle', and acted in the productions himself, invariably playing the part of a comical footman, or reciting 'The Sinful Woman'* in a sing-song voice. The townspeople called him a mummy, since he was tall, very skinny and wiry with a perpetually solemn expression and dim lifeless eyes. So deep was his love of the theatre, he shaved his moustache and beard, which made him look even more like a mummy.

* 'The Sinful Woman', a poem by A. K. Tolstoy (1817–75).

After the *grand rond*, he coughed rather hesitantly, sidled up to Nikitin and said, 'I had the pleasure of being present at that argument over tea. I fully concur with your opinion. We are men of the same mind, and I would very much like to have a good talk with you. Have you read Lessing's *Hamburgische Dramaturgie*?'

'No, can't say I have.'

Shebaldin was horrified, waved his hands about as though he had burned his fingers and retreated without saying anything more. Shebaldin's whole look, his question and subsequent surprise struck Nikitin as funny; however, he reflected, 'It really is embarrassing. Here I am, a teacher of literature and I haven't read Lessing yet. That I *must* do.'

Before supper everyone, young and old, sat down to play forfeits. There were two packs of cards; one was dealt out and the other laid face downwards on the table.

'Whoever has this,' old Shelestov said solemnly, holding up the top card of the second pack, 'has to go straight to the nursery and kiss nanny.'

The pleasure of kissing nanny fell to Shebaldin. Everyone crowded round him and led him to the nursery, laughing and clapping their hands as they made him kiss her. It was all very noisy, with everyone shouting . . .

'Not so passionately!' Shelestov shouted, laughing so much that he cried. 'Not so passionately!'

Nikitin's forfeit was to hear everyone confess. He sat at a table in the middle of the room and they draped his head with a shawl. The first to come to confession was Varya.

'I know the sins you have committed,' Nikitin began as he peered through the darkness at her severe profile. 'Tell me, young lady, why do you go for a walk with Polyansky every day? *Oh, not for nothing, not for nothing is she with a hussar!*'*

'That's feeble,' Varya said, walking away.

Then two large shining motionless eyes appeared below the shawl. Nikitin could distinguish that beloved profile and that very familiar, precious smell reminding him of Masha's room.

'Marie Godefroi,' he said in a voice so tender and soft he did not

* Inaccurate quotation from an epigram by Lermontov.

recognize it as his own, 'what sin have you come to confess?'

Masha screwed her eyes up and stuck the tip of her tongue out at him. Then she laughed and walked away. A minute later she was already in the middle of the room clapping her hands and calling out, 'Supper, supper, supper!' And everyone piled into the dining-room.

During supper Varya started arguing again – this time with her father. Polyansky ate heartily, drank red wine and told Nikitin how once, during a winter campaign, he had stood in a swamp all night long up to his knees in water; the enemy was near, so they couldn't speak or smoke. It was a cold night, very dark, and there was a biting wind. Nikitin listened and glanced at Masha out of the corner of his eye. She looked at him without moving or blinking an eyelid, as if she were deep in thought or daydreaming ... He found this pleasant and agonizing at the same time.

'Why does she look at me like that?' he thought miserably. 'It's embarrassing, people might notice. Oh, she's so young, so naïve!'

The guests began to depart around midnight. As Nikitin passed through the gates, a window banged open on the first floor and Masha appeared.

'Sergei!' she called.

'What can I do for you?'

'Just this ...' Masha murmured, evidently trying to think up some excuse. 'Just this ... Polyansky promised to bring his camera round one of these days and photograph all of us. We must get together.'

'Good.'

Masha disappeared, the window slammed and immediately afterwards he could hear someone playing the piano.

'Oh, what a house!' Nikitin thought as he crossed the street. 'A house where the only sighing comes from Egyptian doves – and that's only because they can't express their joy any other way!'

But the Shelestovs were not the only family who led a gay life. Nikitin wasn't more than about two hundred steps away when he heard a piano again, this time from another house. He walked on a little further and saw a peasant playing the balalaika at the front gate. In the garden an orchestra struck up a medley of folk songs.

Nikitin lived in an eight-roomed flat (which he rented for 300 roubles a year), about a quarter of a mile from the Shelestovs, with his friend Ippolit, who taught geography and history at the school. This Ippolit, who was still fairly young, snub-nosed, with a reddish beard and a coarse stupid-looking face – like a factory worker's, but friendly all the same – was sitting at the table marking his students' maps. In his opinion map-making was the most important and essential part of geography – in history it was dates. He would stay up all night marking maps with a blue pencil or compiling tables of dates.

'What a magnificent day!' Nikitin said as he came in. 'I'm amazed that you can stay cooped up in here.'

Ippolit wasn't very talkative: either he said nothing at all or he just spoke in platitudes. This was how he replied then: 'Yes, beautiful weather. It's May now and soon it will *really* be summer. But summer's different from winter. In winter we have to light stoves, but in summer it's warm without them. In summer you can open the window at night and it's still warm, but in winter it's cold, even with double frames.'

Nikitin hadn't sat there for more than a minute when he became bored: 'Good night!' he said, yawning as he got up. 'I wanted to tell you some romantic little story concerning me – but all you can think about is geography! The moment I mention love all you can do is reply: "When was the battle of Kalka?" To hell with your battles and Cape Chukotskys!'

'Why are you getting so angry?'

'It's so annoying!'

Deeply irritated that he hadn't yet declared his love to Masha and that he didn't have anyone to discuss it with now, he went to his study and lay on the couch. It was dark and quiet, and as he lay there he began to imagine that in two or three years' time he would have to go to St Petersburg for some reason and that Masha would go to the station with him and start crying as she saw him off. In St Petersburg he'd get a long pleading letter from her, asking him to return at once. And he would write back, starting his letter with 'My dear little mousie'.

'Yes, that's just right, "my dear little mousie",' he said laughing.

He felt uncomfortable lying there, so he put his hands behind his head and let his legs dangle over the back of the couch. Now he felt more comfortable. Meanwhile the light at the window had become distinctly brighter, and the sleepy cocks outside started crowing. Nikitin kept thinking about his return from St Petersburg, with Masha at the station to meet him, shrieking with joy and flinging her arms round his neck. Even better, he might play a trick on her and come back at night without anyone knowing; the cook would let him in, and then he would tiptoe into her bedroom, quietly take his clothes off and – plop into bed! She would wake up and then, oh, what joy!

Now there was broad daylight, the study and windows vanished. Masha was sitting saying something on the steps of the same brewery they had passed when they had gone riding. She took Nikitin by the arm and went off with him to that park where the crows' nests in the oaks looked like hats. One nest started rocking, out popped Shebaldin's head and he shouted very loudly, 'You haven't read Lessing!'

Nikitin shook all over and opened his eyes. Ippolit was standing by the couch, throwing his head back as he put his tie on.

'Get up, it's time for school . . .' he was saying. 'You shouldn't sleep in your clothes. That spoils them. You should sleep in a bed, without any clothes.' And as usual he started rambling on and on about things that were common knowledge.

Nikitin's first class was Russian language with the second form. When he entered the classroom, at exactly nine o'clock, he looked at the blackboard and saw that someone had written M.S. in large letters – there was no doubt that they stood for Masha Shelestova.

'Those little devils have managed to sniff it out . . .' Nikitin thought. 'How do they know?'

The second literature class was with the fifth form, and there someone had written M.S. on the blackboard too. When the lesson was over and he had turned towards the door, the boys started shouting, 'Hurray for Shelestova!' – just as though they were sitting in a theatre.

Sleeping in his clothes had given him a headache, and the general inactivity left him feeling limp: the boys who were expecting a short break before the exams weren't doing any work, and as a result felt listless and kept getting up to mischief out of sheer boredom. Nikitin felt listless as well, was blind to the boys' pranks, and every now and then walked over to the window. He saw the street shining brightly in the sun. Above the houses was the light blue translucent sky and some birds, and far, far away, beyond the green gardens and houses, was a vast boundless expanse with hazy blue groves and a puff of smoke from a passing train . . .

Just then two officers in white tunics walked down the street in the shade of the acacias, swishing their riding-crops.

Then a crowd of grey-bearded Jews with peaked caps rode past in a brake. A governess was strolling along with the headmaster's granddaughter. Haddock had scampered off somewhere with two other mongrels. And then along came Varya, wearing a simple grey dress and red stockings, with a *European Herald* in her hand – evidently she had just been to the library . . .

But he had to survive more classes, right up to three o'clock! And after that he couldn't go home or to the Shelestovs', as he had to do some private coaching at the Woolfs'. Mr Woolf, a rich Jew who had converted to Lutheranism, did not send his children to the high school, but had them taught privately at home by some of the teachers, paying them five roubles a lesson . . .

'I'm so bored, bored, bored,' he thought.

At three o'clock he went to the Woolfs' and he felt he had been there for ages and ages. He left at five and at seven he was due back at the school for a staff meeting which involved drawing up the time-table for the fourth and sixth forms' oral exams.

It was late when he left school for the Shelestovs'; his heart thumped and his face was burning. For the past few weeks he always had a whole speech prepared, complete with prologue and conclusion; now he didn't have a single word ready. He felt terribly confused and all he could be sure of was that he would declare his love today *without fail* and that delaying any more was simply out of the question.

'I'll ask her to come out into the garden,' he thought, 'and I'll tell her after we've had a little walk.'

The entrance-lobby was deserted. He went into the hall, then the drawing-room. There was no one there either. He could hear Varya arguing upstairs with someone and the dressmaker's scissors snipping away in the nursery.

There was a little room in the house that had three different names: the small room, the intercommunicating room and the dark room. A large old cupboard, in which they kept medicine, gunpowder and hunting-gear stood there. A narrow wooden staircase, where the cats slept, led up to the first floor. There were two doors, one leading into the nursery, the other into the drawing-room. Just as Nikitin entered this room, meaning to go upstairs, the nursery door opened with such a bang that the staircase and cupboard shook. In ran Masha, wearing a dark dress, with a piece of blue material in her hands. Without seeing Nikitin, she dashed towards the stairs.

'Stop,' Nikitin said. 'Good evening, Marie Godefroi, would you care to . . .' He puffed and panted and was at a loss for words. With one hand he caught hold of her arm and grasped the piece of cloth with the other. She was half-scared, half-startled, and she looked at him with her big eyes.

'Please . . .' Nikitin went on, fearing that she might go on her way, 'there's something I *must* tell you . . . Only it's not very convenient in here. I just *can't* . . . I'm in no position . . . Do you understand, Marie Godefroi, I just can't, that's all . . .'

The dark cloth fell to the floor and Nikitin took Masha by the other arm. She turned pale and moved her lips; then she backed away from Nikitin until she was in the corner between the wall and the cupboard.

'On my word of honour, I assure you,' he said softly. 'On my word of honour, Masha.'

She tossed her head back, but he managed to kiss her on the lips, pressing her cheeks with his fingers to make the kiss last as long as possible, with the result that he ended up with her in the corner between cupboard and wall. She twined her arms around his neck and snuggled her head against his chin.

The Shelestovs' garden was large, about ten acres in all. There were about twenty old maples and limes, the rest were fruit trees: cherry, apple, pear, wild chestnut, silvery olive . . . Everywhere there were flowers.

Nikitin and Masha ran along the paths without saying a word, laughing and now and again suddenly firing questions at each other which neither bothered to answer. A half-moon shone over the garden and sleepy tulips and irises rose up from the dim grass which was faintly illuminated in its pale light and they too seemed to be begging for declarations of love.

When Nikitin and Masha were back in the house, the officers and ladies had already assembled and were dancing a mazurka. Once more Polyansky led everyone through the room *en grand rond*, once more they played forfeits after the dance.

Before supper, when the guests had left the hall for the dining-room, Masha, who was alone now with Nikitin, pressed close to him and said, '*You* speak to Papa and Varya. I feel ashamed . . .'

After supper he had a word with the old man. Shelestov listened, pondered for a moment and then told him, 'I'm deeply obliged to you for the honour you accord my daughter and myself. However, please allow me to talk to you as a friend. I shall say what I have to, not as a father, but as one gentleman to another. Will you please tell me why you wish to get married so young? Only peasants marry young, but of course, they're only louts. But why should *you* want to? For a man to put himself in chains at such a young age, what pleasure can there be in that?'

'I'm not young at all,' Nikitin said, very offended. 'I'm twenty-six.'

'Papa, the vet's come to see the horse!' Varya cried out from the other room.

And the conversation came to an end. Varya, Masha and Polyansky saw Nikitin back home. When they reached the gate, Varya said, 'Why does your mysterious Mitropolit* keep hiding himself away? He could at least pay us a visit.'

The enigmatic Ippolit was sitting on his bed taking his trousers off when Nikitin came in.

'Don't go to bed, my dear chap!' Nikitin panted, 'don't go to bed!'

Ippolit quickly put his trousers on again and anxiously asked, 'What's the matter?'

Nikitin sat next to his friend and gave him a startled look, as if surprised at himself, and continued, 'Just imagine, I'm getting married! To Masha Shelestova. I proposed today.'

'What of it? She seems a nice enough girl. But she's very young, though.'

'Yes, she's young,' Nikitin sighed, uneasily shrugging his shoulders. 'Very, very young.'

'I used to teach her once at the high school, I know her well. She wasn't bad at geography but terrible at history. And she didn't pay attention in class.'

* Pun on Ippolit, *Mitropolit* meaning metropolitan in the Greek Orthodox Church.

Nikitin suddenly felt sorry for his friend and wanted to cheer him up with a few kind words.

'My dear chap, why don't *you* get married?' he asked. 'Come on, Ippolit, why don't you marry *Varya*, for example? She's a wonderful, excellent girl. It's true she's fond of arguing, but on the other hand what a heart she has! She was only just asking about you. Marry her, dear chap! What do you say?'

He knew very well that Varya would never marry that boring man, with his snub nose; all the same, he still tried to persuade him. But *why*?

'Marriage is a serious step,' Ippolit said after a moment's reflection. 'One has to think carefully, weigh up all the pros and cons, otherwise it's no good. It never hurts to be sensible, especially when it comes to marriage, when a man, having ceased to be a bachelor, begins a new life.'

And he rambled on about things that were long familiar to everyone. Nikitin didn't stop to listen, but said good night and went back to his room. He rapidly undressed and got into bed, so that he could turn his thoughts all the more quickly to his good fortune, to Masha, to the future. He smiled as he suddenly remembered that he still hadn't read Lessing. 'I *must* read him . . .' he thought. 'On the other hand, why should I? To hell with him!'

Exhausted by all his happiness, he fell asleep immediately, the smile staying on his face until morning came. He dreamed about horses' hooves clattering over wooden floors, about black Count Nulin, the first horse to be brought out of the stables, followed by white Giant, then his sister Mayka . . .

II

'It was very crowded and noisy in the church and once someone even shouted out loud, so that the priest who was marrying Masha and me peered over his spectacles at the congregation and said sternly, "Don't wander round the church, don't make any noise, keep still and pray. You should fear God."

'Two of my friends were my best men, while Masha's were Staff-Captain Polyansky and Lieutenant Gernet. The choir sang magnificently. The sputtering candles, the glitter, the ladies' dresses, the officers, the sea of cheerful, contented faces, Masha's strange, ethereal expression – the whole setting and the words of the marriage vows moved me to tears and filled me with exultation. I considered how my life had suddenly blossomed, how it had now acquired a truly poetic beauty! Two years ago I was still a student living in cheap rooms in the Neglinny, without money or relatives and – as it seemed to me then – without any future. But now I was a high school teacher in one of the best provincial towns, well provided for, loved and spoilt. And I thought that all the crowd had congregated just for *me*, that the three chandeliers were burning for *me*, that the priest was bellowing away, that the choir was doing its best for *me* and that that young creature who was shortly to be my wife was looking so young, so elegant and so full of joy just for *me*. I recalled our first meeting, the trips to the country, the proposal and the weather, which seemed to have stayed fine the whole summer just for my sake. And now I was actually experiencing and had grasped hold of that happiness which had seemed possible only in novels and stories when I was living in the Neglinny.

'After the ceremony all the guests crowded and jostled around Masha and myself to express their sincere pleasure, to congratulate us and wish us happiness. A brigadier-general, an old man of about seventy, congratulated only Masha and told her in his senile, rasping voice – it was so loud, everyone in the church could hear – "I hope, my dear, that you will be the same lovely rose as you were *before* the wedding."

'The officers, headmaster and all the teachers smiled out of good manners and I too realized that I was smiling pleasantly – and artificially. That dear Ippolit, who taught history and geography and who always kept repeating what was long familiar to everyone, shook my hand firmly and said with feeling, "Up to now you weren't married and you lived on your own. But now you're married, you'll be living together with someone else."

'From the church we went to a two-storeyed house that hadn't been whitewashed and which is now my dowry. Besides the house, Masha was given a plot of waste ground, called Melitonov, complete with a lodge. And there were a great deal of hens and ducks, so people said, which would run wild without anyone there to look after them. When we reached the house I began to unwind, sprawled out on the couch in my new study and lit my pipe. It was all so snug and cosy – something I had never known before – but just then the guests shouted "hurray" and a terrible band out in the hall played all kinds of rubbish – with flourishes. Varya, Masha's sister, ran into my study with a glass in her hand, looking strangely tense, as though she had a mouth full of water: clearly she wanted to run off somewhere, but suddenly she gave a very loud laugh and burst out sobbing. Her glass tinkled as it rolled over the floor. We caught hold of her under the arms and led her away.

'"No one is capable of understanding!" she murmured later when she was lying down on the nurse's bed in the most remote room in the house. "*No one*, no one at all! Good God, no one understands!"

'But everyone realized only too well that she was the elder sister, that she was still not married and that she was crying not from jealousy, but from the sad realization that time was running out for her and that perhaps even now it was too late. When the quadrille started she was already in the hall, her tear-stained face smothered with powder. And I saw Captain Polyansky holding a dish of ice-cream in front of her while she ate from it with a spoon . . .'

'It's already past five in the morning. I started this diary just to describe my overwhelming happiness, in all its many aspects, and I thought of writing about six pages and reading them to Masha later that morning. But strange to say, my thoughts got so muddled up, everything became vague, as if I had dreamed it all and the only distinct recollection I have is that incident with Varya and I feel like writing *poor Varya*! I could go on all day just sitting here and writing *poor Varya*! And, as though they were echoing my mood, the trees began to rustle, telling me that it was going to rain. The rooks are cawing and my Masha, who's just fallen asleep, has a peculiarly sad look.'

For a long time afterwards Nikitin did not touch his diary. At the beginning of August there were examinations that had to be taken again, and the entrance exams as well; after Assumption there were the usual classes. He normally left for school after eight and by nine he was already pining for Masha and his new house and kept looking at his watch. He made a boy from a lower form read a passage for dictation to the class and, while they were writing, he sat by the window-sill daydreaming, his eyes closed. Whether he was dreaming of the future or musing over the past, everything, without exception, appeared beautiful, just like a fairy-tale. In the senior forms they were reading Gogol's or Pushkin's prose out loud, which made him feel sleepy. People, trees, fields, horses loomed up in his imagination and he sighed and exclaimed – as though enraptured by the author – 'How wonderful!'

For the lunch-break Masha would send him his lunch wrapped up in a serviette as white as snow and he would eat it slowly, pausing frequently to prolong the enjoyment, while Ippolit, who usually made do with a solitary roll, would watch him respectfully and enviously, and utter some platitude, such as: 'People can't exist without food.'

After school Nikitin went off to do some private coaching and when he finally arrived home, after five o'clock, he would feel both glad and apprehensive, as though he had been away for a whole year. He would run up the stairs, puffing away, and when he found Masha he would embrace and kiss her and solemnly swear that he loved her and could not exist without her. He would assure her that he had missed her terribly and asked her, with great trepidation, if she was well and why she looked so miserable. Then the two of them would have dinner. Afterwards he would lie down on the couch in the study and smoke, while she sat next to him whispering all the news.

For him the happiest days now were Sundays and school holidays, when he could be home all day long. At these times he would enjoy a life that was innocent, but particularly pleasant, putting him in mind of a pastoral idyll. He would spend every moment watching his sensible and capable Masha organizing their little home; and to prove that *he* was needed in the house, he would do something quite useless, such as rolling the carriage out of the shed and giving it a thorough inspection. With their three cows, Masha managed to run a real dairy and she kept lots of jugs of milk and pots of sour cream in the cellar and larder, which she stored for making butter. Sometimes, just for a joke, Nikitin would ask for a glass of milk. This would frighten her, as it was a breach of routine, but he would laugh and embrace her, and tell her, 'Come on, I was only joking, my treasure, only joking!' Or he would make fun of her fussiness – when, for example, she found useless, stone-hard scraps of sausage or cheese in the larder and solemnly announced, 'The servants can finish those in the kitchen.' He would point out that these scraps were only fit for mousetraps, but she would hotly retort that men knew nothing about housekeeping, that servants would not be at all surprised if you sent a whole load of savouries down to the kitchen, and in the end he would agree and embrace her rapturously. He found the truth of what she said most unusual, quite amazing; but anything that happened to clash with his own convictions he found naïve and touching.

Sometimes, when the philosophical mood took him, he would talk about all manner of abstract topics, while she listened and stared at him inquisitively. 'I'm so extremely happy with you, my dearest,' he said, playing with her fingers, undoing a plait of her hair and then tying it up again. 'But I don't look on my happiness as a chance happening, as though it suddenly dropped down from heaven. Our happiness is perfectly in the nature of things, in strict accord with the laws of logic. I believe that man is the creator of his own happiness and now I am enjoying the fruits of that creation. Yes, I can say without any false modesty that *I* created this happiness and I am its rightful possessor. You know all about my past. I was an orphan and I was brought up in poverty, had an unhappy childhood, was miserable when I was in my teens and it was all a struggle. It was the path that I paved towards happiness . . .'

In October the school suffered a terrible loss: Ippolit was taken ill with erysipelas of the head and died. Two days before his death he became delirious, but even then he could only repeat all those old familiar truths: 'The Volga flows into the Caspian . . . Horses eat oats and hay . . .'

The school was closed for the funeral. Fellow-teachers and pupils carried the coffin and the school choir sang 'God Is Holy' all the way to the cemetery. Three priests, two deacons, everyone from the high school for boys, the church choir in full ceremonial tunics, made up the procession. People in the street crossed themselves as the solemn cortège passed by and said, 'God grant us all a death like that.'

When he arrived home from the cemetery Nikitin, who was feeling deeply moved, found his diary on the table and wrote: 'Today Ippolit Ryzhytsky was buried. May your mortal remains rest in peace, humble toiler! Masha, Varya and all the women at the funeral shed genuine tears, perhaps because they knew that this boring, downtrodden man had never known the love of a woman. I had wanted to say a few warm words at my friend's grave, but I was warned that the headmaster wouldn't be too pleased if I did, since he'd never liked him. It strikes me that this is the first day since I was married that I feel down in the dumps . . .'

Nothing else particularly interesting happened for the rest of the term. The winter was mild, without any frost, and there was sleet; towards Epiphany the wind howled mournfully, as though it was still autumn and thawed ice flowed down from the roofs. On the morning of the day of the Blessing of the Water the police couldn't let anyone go near the river, as the ice was breaking up and looked black. But for all the miserable weather, Nikitin's life was just as happy as it had been during the summer. And he even found time for yet another useless diversion – he learned to play whist. Only one thing worried and annoyed him at times, however, and stood in the way of complete happiness – the dogs and cats which were part of the dowry. Every room, especially in the mornings, smelled like a menagerie and it was absolutely impossible to get rid of the stench. The cats often fought with the dogs. The spiteful Midge was fed ten times a day, still wouldn't accept Nikitin and kept growling at him.

One day, during Lent, he was returning home at midnight from a game of cards at his club. It was raining and all around it was dark and muddy. Nikitin felt an unpleasant aftertaste in his mouth and he just could not guess the reason for it: was it because he had lost twelve roubles at the club, or because one of the partners had remarked, when he was settling up, that he had pots of money – obviously referring to the dowry? The twelve roubles did not worry him and the partner hadn't really said anything insulting. But it was unpleasant all the same. He did not even feel like going home.

'Ugh, how nasty!' he said, stopping by a lamp-post.

Now he realized that he wasn't sorry about losing twelve roubles, because he got them for nothing in the first place. If he had been a workman, he would have treasured every kopek and wouldn't have been indifferent as to whether he won or lost. And he concluded that all this happiness had come to him without any effort on his part, that it had no point, and it was essentially just as much a luxury as medicine. If, like the overwhelming majority of people, he had been tormented with worrying where the next crust of bread was coming from or had been forced to struggle for his living, or if he had backache or a pain in the chest from *hard work*, then his supper, his warm, comfortable flat and all that domestic happiness would have been an absolute necessity, a reward, something to enrich his life. But now all this had only some strange, vague significance for him.

'Ugh, how *nasty*!' he said, realizing only too well that these thoughts were in themselves a bad sign.

When he arrived home, Masha was in bed. She was breathing evenly and there was a smile on her face – evidently she was having a very enjoyable sleep. The white cat lay next to her, rolled up in a ball, miaowing. When Nikitin lit a candle and a cigarette, Masha woke up and thirstily drank a glass of water.

'I must have eaten too much fruit jelly,' she said, laughing.

'Have you been to see my family?'

'No, I didn't go.'

Nikitin already knew that Captain Polyansky (Varya had been entertaining high hopes of him over the past few weeks) had been transferred to one of the western provinces and was already making his farewell calls in the town – and as a result it was depressing in his father-in-law's house.

'Varya called earlier this evening,' Masha said as she sat down. 'She didn't say anything, but I could see from her face how hard it was for the poor thing. I can't stand Polyansky myself. He's fat, flabby and his cheeks wobble when he walks or dances. Not my idea of a great passion. All the same, I think he was a respectable sort of man.'

'But I still think he's respectable.'

'But why did he treat Varya so badly?'

'Badly?' Nikitin asked, beginning to feel irritated by the white cat which was stretching itself and arching its back. 'As far as I know he didn't propose and he made no promises either.'

'But why did he call so often? He should have kept away if he had no intention of marrying her.'

Nikitin snuffed the candle and got into bed. But he didn't feel like sleeping or lying down. It seemed his head had become huge and empty, like a barn, and that several quite new and peculiar thoughts were wandering around it in the form of long shadows. He thought that besides that soft lamp-light which smiled on his domestic happiness, besides that little world, where life was so peaceful and sweet – for him as well as that cat – some other world *must* exist . . . And he conceived a passionate, burning desire to become part of it, to get a job in a factory or a large workshop somewhere, to give lectures, to write, to publish, to make a noise, to exhaust himself with work, to suffer . . . He yearned for something that would take such a firm hold on him that he would be oblivious of his own existence, become indifferent to his personal happiness with all its limited range of sensations. And suddenly he visualized that close-shaven Shebaldin so clearly, that he seemed to be right next to him, muttering in a horrified voice, 'Haven't read Lessing? You're a long way behind! Oh God, you've really let yourself go to seed!'

Masha drank some more water. He looked at her neck, her full shoulders and bosom, and remembered the word that the brigadier had used at the church: a *rose*. He murmured 'rose' and burst out laughing.

He was answered by a growl from the sleepy Midge, from underneath the bed. He felt a sharp twinge of spite, like a blow with a cold hammer, and he felt like saying something rude to Masha – even like jumping up and hitting her. His heart started pounding away.

'So, you are implying,' he asked, trying to control himself, 'that simply because I kept calling at the house, I would have *had* to marry you, come what may?'

'Of course. You know that only too well.'

'That's charming.'

A minute later he said 'charming' again.

To calm himself – and to avoid saying something he might regret – Nikitin went to his study and lay down on the couch, without any pillow; then he lay down on the carpet.

'What nonsense!' he said, still trying to calm himself. 'You're a teacher, you belong to one of the noblest of professions . . . Why do you need another kind of world? What rubbish!'

But immediately he reassured himself that he had no right to call himself a teacher at all, only a clerk, just as deficient in talent and personality as that Czech teacher of Greek. He had never felt any vocation for the profession, knew nothing about the theory of teaching and had never been interested in it; he had no idea how to handle children. He did not know if what he taught had any importance and perhaps he even taught things that were unnecessary. The late Ippolit didn't try to conceal his stupidity and his colleagues and the students knew all about him and what they could expect from him. But as for Nikitin, *he* knew how to hide his dim-wittedness like the Czech and was clever enough to fool anyone, artfully misleading everyone into believing that all was going nice and smoothly, thank God. These fresh thoughts frightened Nikitin and he immediately rejected them as idiotic, thinking it was all to do with his nerves, and that soon he would be laughing at himself for being so silly.

And in actual fact, towards morning, he was already laughing at his own irritability and calling himself an old woman. All the same, he clearly realized that he would probably never have peace of mind again, that he would never be happy in that two-storeyed house that hadn't been whitewashed. He suspected that all his illusions had faded away and that a new kind of life had already begun, a life which made him feel restless, fully alert and which clashed with peace of mind and personal happiness.

On the next day (which was a Sunday) he went to the school chapel, where he saw the Head and the other teachers. It struck him that they were only concerned with carefully concealing their ignorance and dissatisfaction with life, and he gave them agreeable smiles and talked about trivial matters, so as not to betray his own restlessness. Then he went to the station, watched the mail train come and go, and he felt very pleased being on his own, without having to talk to anyone.

Back home he found his father-in-law and Varya, who had been invited to dinner. Varya's eyes were tear-stained and she complained of a headache, but Mr Shelestov ate a great deal and talked about the unreliability of young men of today and about how they lacked gentlemanly qualities.

'Sheer loutishness!' he said. 'And I'll tell them straight: sheer loutishness, my dear sir!'

Nikitin smiled pleasantly and helped Masha entertain the guests. But after dinner he went to his study and locked himself in.

The March sun shone brightly and its warm rays came through the windows and fell on the table. Although it was only the twentieth of the month, it was dry enough to drive around on wheels and starlings chattered noisily in the garden. He felt that Masha would come into the room any minute, put her arm round his neck and tell him that the saddle-horses or the carriage were waiting at the front door; she would ask him what she should wear in case it was cold. Spring had begun, just as wonderful as last year, and it promised similar days of joy ... But Nikitin was thinking how nice it would be to take his holidays now, to travel to Moscow and stay in the Neglinny in his old rooms. In the next room they were having coffee and talking about Captain Polyansky; but he tried to not listen and wrote in his diary: 'Where *am* I, for heaven's sake? I'm surrounded by nothing but vulgarity, nothing but boring, insignificant people, pots of sour cream, jugs of milk, cockroaches, stupid women ... There's nothing more terrible, more damaging to one's pride, more depressing than vulgarity. I must run away from here, escape *today*, or I'll go mad.'

Man in a Case

Two men who had come back very late from a hunting expedition had to spend the night in a barn belonging to Prokofy, the village elder, at the edge of Mironositskoye. They were Ivan Ivanovich, the vet, and Burkin, the schoolteacher. The vet had a rather strange double-barrelled surname – Chimsha-Gimalaysky – that did not suit him at all, and everyone simply called him Ivan Ivanovich. He lived on a studfarm near the town and had come on the expedition just to get some fresh air, while Burkin, the teacher, regularly stayed every summer with a local count and his family, and knew the area very well.

They were still awake. Ivan Ivanovich, who was tall and thin, with a long moustache, was sitting outside the door, smoking his pipe in the full light of the moon. Burkin was lying on the hay inside, invisible in the dark.

They were telling each other different stories and happened to remark on the fact that Mavra, the village elder's wife, a healthy, intelligent woman, had never left her native village in her life, had never seen a town or a railway, had been sitting over her stove for the past ten years and would only venture out into the street at night.

'And what's so strange about that!' Burkin said. 'There's so many of these solitary types around, like hermit crabs or snails, they are, always seeking safety in their shells. Perhaps it's an example of atavism, a return to the times when our ancestors weren't social animals and lived alone in their dens. Or perhaps it's simply one of the many oddities of human nature – who knows? I'm not a scientist and that kind of thing's not really my province. I only want to say that people like Mavra are not unusual. And you don't have to look far for them – take Mr Belikov for example, who died two months ago in my home town. He taught Greek at the same high school. Of course, you must have heard of him. His great claim to fame was going around in galoshes, carrying an umbrella even when it was terribly warm, and he invariably wore a thick, padded overcoat. He kept this umbrella in a holder and his watch in a grey chamois leather pouch. And the penknife he used for sharpening pencils had its own little case. His face seemed to have its own cover as well, as he always kept it hidden inside his upturned collar. He wore dark glasses, a jersey, stuffed his ears with cotton wool and always had the top up when he rode in a cab. Briefly, this man had a compulsive, persistent longing for self-encapsulation, to create a protective cocoon to isolate himself from all external influences. The real world irritated and frightened him and kept him in a constant state of nerves. Perhaps, by forever praising the past and what never even happened, he was trying to justify this timidity and horror of reality. The ancient languages he taught were essentially those galoshes and umbrella in another guise, a refuge from everyday existence.

' "Oh, Greek is so melodious, so beautiful," he would say, savouring his words. And as if to prove his point he would screw his eyes up, raise one finger and pronounce the word: *Anthropos*.

'Belikov tried to bury his thoughts inside a rigid case. Only official regulations and newspaper articles, in which something or other was prohibited, had any meaning for him. For him, only rules forbidding students to be out in the streets after nine in the evening or an article outlawing sexual intercourse were unambiguous and authoritative: the thing was prohibited – and that was that! But whenever anything was allowed and authorized, there was something dubious, vague and equivocal lurking in it. When a dramatic society or a reading-room, or a tea-shop in town, was granted a licence, he would shake his head and softly say, "That's all very well, of course, but there *could* be trouble!"

'The least infringement, deviation, violation of the rules reduced him to despair, although you may well ask what business was it of his *anyway*? If a fellow-teacher was late for prayers, or if news of some schoolboy mischief reached his ears, or if he spotted a schoolmistress out late at night with an officer, he would get very heated and say over and over again, "There *could* be trouble." At staff meetings he really got us down with his extreme caution, his suspiciousness and his positively encapsulated notions about current wretched standards of behaviour in boys' and girls' schools, about the terrible racket students made in class and once again he would say, "Oh dear, what if the authorities got to hear? Oh, there *could* be trouble! Now, what if we expelled that Petrov in the second form and Yegorov in the fourth?" Well then, what with all his moaning and whining, what with those dark glasses and that pale little face (you know, it was just like a ferret's), he terrorized us so much that we had to give in. Petrov and Yegorov were given bad conduct marks, put in detention and finally were both expelled. He had the strange habit of visiting us in our digs. He would call in on some teacher and sit down without saying a word, as though he were trying to spy something out. After an hour or two he would get up and go. He called it "maintaining good relations with my colleagues". These silent sessions were clearly very painful for him and he made them only because he felt it was his duty to his fellow-teachers. All of us were scared of him, even the Head. It was quite incredible really, since we teachers were an intelligent, highly respectable lot, brought up on Turgenev and Shchedrin. And yet that miserable specimen, with that eternal umbrella and galoshes, kept the whole school under his thumb for fifteen whole years! And not only the school, but the whole town! Our ladies gave up their Saturday amateur theatricals in case he found out about them. And the clergy were too frightened to eat meat or play cards when he was around. Thanks to people like Belikov, the people in this town have lived in fear of *everything* for the last ten or fifteen years. They are frightened of talking out loud, sending letters, making friends, reading books, helping the poor or teaching anyone to read and write . . .'

Ivan Ivanovich wanted to say something and coughed, but first he lit his pipe, peered up at the moon and said in a slow deliberate voice, 'Yes, those intelligent, decent people had read their Shchedrin and Turgenev, their Henry Buckles and so on . . . , but still they gave in and put up with it. That's exactly my point.'

Burkin continued, 'Belikov and I lived in the same house and on the same floor. His room was right opposite mine and we saw a lot of each other. I knew his private life intimately. At home it was the same story: dressing-gown, night-cap, shutters, bolts, and a whole series of various prohibitions and restrictions – and all those "There *could* be trouble"s.

Fasting was bad for you and as he couldn't touch meat on days forbidden by the Church – or people might say Belikov didn't observe fasts – he would eat perch cooked in animal fat, food that couldn't be faulted, being neither one thing nor the other. He didn't have any female servants for fear people might "think the wrong thing", but he had a male cook, Afanasy, an old, drunken sixty-year-old half-wit, who had once been a batman in the army and who could knock up a meal of sorts. This Afanasy was in the habit of standing at the door with arms folded, always muttering the same old thing with a profound sigh, "There's been an awful lot of *that* about lately!"

'Belikov's bedroom was small, like a box in fact, and the bed was a four-poster. He would pull the blankets right up over his head when he got into it. The room was hot and stuffy, the wind would rattle the bolted doors and make the stove hum. Menacing sighs would drift in from the kitchen. He was terrified under those blankets, afraid of the trouble there *could* be, afraid that Afanasy might cut his throat, afraid of burglars. Then all night long he would have nightmares and, when we left for school together in the morning, he would look pale and depressed. Obviously the thought of that crowded school for which he was heading terrified him, deeply repelled his whole being – even walking next to me was an ordeal for this lone wolf. "The students are terribly noisy in class," he would tell me, as if seeking an excuse for his low spirits. "It's simply *shocking*."

'And this teacher of Greek, this man in his case, nearly got married once, believe it or not.'

Ivan Ivanovich took a quick look into the barn and said, 'You must be joking!'

'Oh, yes, he nearly got married, strange as it may seem. A new history and geography master was appointed, a Ukrainian called Mikhail Kovalenko. He came here with his sister Barbara. He was young, tall, dark-skinned and had enormous hands. From his face you could tell he had a deep bass voice, the kind that really seems to come booming straight out of a barrel. The sister wasn't what you might call young, though – about thirty, I'd say – and like her brother she was tall, with the same figure, dark eyebrows and red cheeks – in short, not the spinsterish type and a real beauty, always bright and jolly, singing Ukrainian songs and roaring with laughter. The least thing sent her into fits of loud laughter. I remember now, the first time we really got to know the Kovalenkos was at the Head's name-day party. Among all those stiff, intensely boring pedagogues (they only went to parties because they had to) we suddenly saw this new Aphrodite rising from the foam. She walked hands on hips, laughing, singing, dancing. She sang "Breezes of the South Are Softly Blowing" with great feeling and followed one song with another, enchanting all of us – even Belikov. "Ukrainian is like classical Greek in its softness and agreeable sonority," he said with a sugary smile as he sat down next to her.

'She was flattered and she gave him a stirring lecture about life on her farm down in Gadyach where Mummy lived, where they grew such marvellous pears and melons and *pubkins*: Ukrainians like calling pumpkins "pubkins", that's the way they talk there. And they made borshch with sweet little red beets, "Oh, *so* delicious – *frightfully* tasty!"

'We listened, and listened, and suddenly the same thought dawned on all present. "They'd make a very nice couple," the Head's wife told me quietly.

'For some reason this reminded us that our Belikov wasn't married and we wondered why we hadn't thought of it before, why we had completely overlooked this most important part of his life. What did he think of women, how would he answer this vital question? We hadn't been at all interested before – perhaps we couldn't bring ourselves to believe that this man who could wear galoshes in all kinds of weather, who slept in a four-poster, could be capable of loving.

' "He's well over forty and she's thirty," the Head's wife went on. "I think she'd accept him."

'Oh, the stupid, trivial things boredom makes us provincials do! And all because we can never get anything right. For example, why this sudden impulse to marry off our dear Belikov – surely not the ideal husband! The Head's wife, the inspector's wife and all the mistresses who taught at the high school suddenly brightened up, looked prettier even, as if they had discovered a purpose in life. The Head's wife took a box at the theatre and who do we see sitting next to her but a radiant, happy Barbara, holding some kind of fan, with Belikov at her side, so small and hunched up you'd have thought he'd been dragged from his house with a pair of tongs. If I gave a party, the ladies would absolutely insist on my inviting both Belikov and Barbara. Briefly, the wheels had been set in motion. It turned out that Barbara wasn't against marriage. Living with her brother wasn't very cheerful and apparently they'd argue and squabble for days on end. Just picture the scene for yourself: Kovalenko, that lanky, healthy boor walking down the street in his embroidered shirt, a tuft of hair falling on to his forehead from under his cap. In one hand a bundle of books, in the other a thick knobbly stick. Then his sister following close behind, loaded with books as well.

'"But Michael, you haven't read it!" she says in a loud, argumentative voice. "I'm telling you, I swear it's the truth, you've *never* read it!"

'"And I'm telling you that I *have*!" Kovalenko thunders back, banging his stick on the pavement.

'"Goodness gracious, Michael, don't lose your temper. It's only a matter of *principle* we're arguing about!"

'"But I'm telling you I *have* read it!" Kovalenko shouts, even louder.

'And when they had visitors they'd be at each other's throats again. She must have been fed-up with that kind of life and wanted her own little place – and then of course there was her age. She couldn't pick or choose any more, so anyone would do, even a Greek teacher. In fact most of the young ladies here aren't too choosy, as long as they find a husband. Anyway, Barbara began to show a decided liking for Belikov.

'And what about Belikov? He'd behave just the same at Kovalenko's as he did with us. He would go and sit down and say nothing, while Barbara would sing "Breezes of the South" for him or gaze at him thoughtfully with her dark eyes, or suddenly break into loud peals of laughter.

'In love affairs and above all in marriage a little persuasion plays a large part. Everyone, his colleagues and their wives, tried to persuade Belikov to get married – there was nothing else for him to live for. We all congratulated him and tried to look serious, and came out with such banal remarks as "marriage is a serious step". Barbara was good-looking and interesting. What's more, the daughter of a privy councillor, with a farm in the Ukraine. But most important, she was the first woman ever to treat Belikov with any warmth or affection. This turned his head and he made up his mind that he really should get married.'

'Now *that* would have been the best time to relieve him of his galoshes and umbrella,' Ivan Ivanovich muttered.

'But can you imagine, that proved impossible,' Burkin said. 'He put Barbara's portrait on his desk and kept coming to see me and chatting about her, about family life, about marriage being a serious step. He often visited the Kovalenkos, but he did not change his way of life one jot. In fact, it was the reverse, and his decision to get married had a rather morbid effect on him. He grew thin and pale and seemed to withdraw even further into his shell.

' "I like Barbara," he told me, with a weak, wry little smile, "and I know that everyone should get married ... but hm ... it's all been so *sudden* ... I must think about it ..."

' "Why?" I asked. "Just go ahead, that's all there is to it."

' "No, marriage is a serious step, one has to carefully consider the impending duties and responsibilities – you never know – in case there's trouble. I'm so worried I can't sleep at all. And to be honest, I'm scared. She and her brother have peculiar ideas, they have a strange way of talking, you know, and they're a bit too smart. You can get married and before long find yourself mixed up in something – you never know."

'So he didn't propose, but kept putting it off, much to the annoyance of the Head's wife and all the ladies. He continually weighed up the "impending duties and responsibilities" and at the same time went for a walk with Barbara nearly every day, perhaps because he thought he should do that in his position, and kept calling on me to discuss family life. Most likely he would have proposed in the long run and we would have had another of those unnecessary, stupid marriages – thousands of them are made every day, the fruit of boredom and having nothing to do – if a *kolossalische Skandal* hadn't suddenly erupted. Here I must say that Barbara's brother had taken a violent dislike to Belikov from the start, he just couldn't stand him.

' "I just don't understand," he told us, shrugging his shoulders, "how you can stomach that ugly little sneak. Really, gentlemen, how *can* you live in this place! The air is foul, stifling. Call yourselves pedagogues, teachers? You're lousy bureaucrats and this isn't a temple of learning, it's more like a police station and it has the sour stink of a sentry-box. No, my friends, I'm hanging on just a bit longer, then it's off to the farm to catch crayfish and teach the peasants. Yes, I'll be gone while you'll be here with your Judas, blast his guts!"

'Or he'd laugh out loud until the tears flowed – first in that deep bass, then in a thin squeaky tone. "Why does he hang around my room, what's he after? He just sits and gapes," he'd say, helplessly spreading his hands out.

'He even thought up a nickname for Belikov – Mr Creepy-Crawly. Naturally we didn't tell him his sister intended marrying this Mr Creepy-Crawly. Once, when the Head's wife hinted how nice it would be if his sister settled down with such a reliable, universally respected person as Belikov, he frowned and growled, "That's nothing to do with me. She can marry a viper if she wants. I don't go poking my nose into other people's business."

'Now listen to what happened next. Some practical joker drew a caricature of Belikov walking in his galoshes, his umbrella open, the bottoms of his trousers rolled up, and Barbara on his arm. Underneath was the caption *The Lovesick Anthropos*. It caught him to a tee, amazing. The artist must have worked many a long night, as all the teachers at the boys' and girls' high schools, as well as lecturers at the theological college *and* local civil servants – they all got a copy. So did Belikov, and it had the most depressing effect on him.

'Next Sunday, the first of May, we left the house together. All the teachers and their pupils had arranged to meet first at the school and then go out of town for a walk in the woods. Off we went, with Belikov looking green and gloomier than a storm cloud.

' "What wicked, evil people there are!" he said, his lips trembling. I really felt sorry for him. Then, as we were on our way, Kovalenko suddenly came bowling along on a bicycle, followed by his sister, also on one – she was flushed and looked worn-out, but still cheerful and happy.

' "We're going on ahead!" she shouted. "What wonderful weather, oh, *frightfully* wonderful!"

'And they both disappeared from view. Belikov changed colour from green to white and he looked stunned. He stopped, looked at me and asked, "Would you mind telling me what's going on? Are my eyes deceiving me? Do you think it's proper for high school teachers, for *ladies*, to ride bicycles?"

'"What's improper?" I said. "Let them cycle to their heart's content!"

'"What are you saying!" he shouted, amazed at my indifference. "What *do* you mean?" He was so shocked he wouldn't go any further and turned back home.

'All next day he kept nervously rubbing his hands together and quivering, and from his face we could see he wasn't well. He stayed away from school – for the first time in his life. And he didn't eat any lunch. Towards evening he put some warmer clothes on, although it was a perfect summer's day, and he plodded off to the Kovalenkos. Barbara had gone out, only her brother was home.

'"Please take a seat," Kovalenko muttered coldly. He was scowling and looked sleepy – he'd just been taking a nap after his meal and was in a terrible mood.

'After sitting for ten minutes without a word, Belikov began: "I've come to get something off my chest. I'm deeply upset. Some comedian has produced a cartoon in which myself and another person – close to both of us – are made to look silly. I consider it my duty to assure you that in no way am I involved, that I have never given grounds for such ridicule. On the contrary I have invariably conducted myself as a person of the highest integrity."

'Kovalenko boiled up inside, and said nothing. Belikov waited and then continued in a soft, sad voice, "And there's something else. I've been teaching for a long time, you're only just beginning, and I consider it my duty, as a senior colleague, to give you some words of warning. You ride a bicycle: that's a pastime which is utterly improper for a tutor of young people."

'"How so?" Kovalenko asked in his deep voice.

'"Do I need to make it any clearer, Mr Kovalenko, don't you get my meaning? If teachers start riding bicycles, what are we to expect from the pupils? That they'll take to walking on their heads, I dare say! There's nothing in the school rules that states it's allowed, so that means you *can't*. I was horrified yesterday! When I saw your sister, my eyes went dim. A woman or young girl on a *bicycle* – that's shocking!"

'"What exactly do you want?"

'"Only one thing, Mr Kovalenko. To warn you. You're a young man, with your future before you and you should watch your behaviour *very* carefully. You don't obey the rules, oh, no! You wear an embroidered shirt, you're always carrying books in the street, and now there's the bicycle. The Head will get to hear all about your sister and yourself cycling, then the governors ... That's not very nice, is it?"

'"If my sister and I go cycling that's no one else's business," Kovalenko said, turning purple. "And if anyone starts poking his nose into my private and personal affairs I'll tell him to go to hell!"

'Belikov turned white and got up. "If you take that tone with me I must conclude this conversation. And I beg you never to use such expressions about the authorities in my presence. You should have some respect for authority."

'"Did I say anything nasty about them?" Kovalenko said, looking at him angrily. "Now, please leave me alone. I'm an honest man and I don't want to talk to the likes of you. I hate sneaks."

'Belikov fidgeted nervously and hastily put his coat on. Horror was written all over his face. This was the first time *anyone* had been so rude to him.

'"You're entitled to say what you like," he said, going out on to the landing. "But I must warn you: it's possible someone has overheard us and in case our conversation is misinterpreted and in case there's trouble, I shall be obliged to report the contents to the Head ... the main points anyway. That is my duty."

'"Report it? Go ahead and report it then!"

'Kovalenko grabbed him by the collar from behind and pushed him. Belikov slid down the stairs, his galoshes thudding as he fell. The stairs were steep and high, but he safely reached the bottom, got up and felt his nose to see if his glasses were intact. But just as he was sliding down, in had come Barbara, with two young ladies. They stood at the bottom and watched him: this was the end. He would rather have broken his neck or both legs than become such a laughing-stock, I do believe. Now it would be all over town, and the Head and the governors would get to hear ... oh, *now* there would be trouble – there'd be a new cartoon and he would finish up having to resign ...

'Barbara recognized him when he was on his feet, and when she saw his ridiculous expression, his crumpled coat, his galoshes, she didn't understand what had happened – she thought he had fallen down the stairs accidentally – she couldn't stop herself breaking into fits of loud laughter that could be heard all over the house.

'And these echoing peals of laughter marked the end of everything: of the courtship and Belikov's earthly existence. He couldn't hear what Barbara was saying, he saw nothing. As soon as he got home he removed her portrait from the table. Then he lay down, never to rise again.

'Three days later Afanasy came and asked me if we should send for the doctor, as "something was wrong with the master". I went to see Belikov. He was lying in his curtained bed, with a blanket over him and he didn't speak. He just replied "yes" or "no" to any question, saying nothing else. While he lay there, Afanasy (looking gloomy, frowning and sighing deeply) fussed round him, reeking of vodka.

'A month later Belikov died. All of us went to the funeral – that is, everyone from the two schools and the theological college. Then, as he lay in his coffin, his face looked gentle and pleasant – even cheerful – just as if he were rejoicing that at last he had found a container from which he would never emerge. Yes, he had achieved his ideal! The weather had turned wet and miserable – in his honour it seemed – and we all wore galoshes and carried umbrellas. Barbara was with us and she burst into tears when the coffin was lowered. I've noticed that Ukrainian women can only cry or laugh, there's no happy medium.

'I must confess burying a man like Belikov was a great pleasure. On the way back from the cemetery we all assumed modest, pious expressions, no one wanted to betray the pleasure he felt. It was the same feeling we had long, long ago when our parents went out and we would run round the garden for an hour or so, revelling in perfect freedom. Freedom, oh freedom! Doesn't the slightest hint, the faintest hope of its possibility lend wings to the soul?

'We were all in an excellent mood when we returned from the cemetery. However, hardly a week passed and we were in the same old rut again. Life was just as harsh, tiring and senseless, not exactly prohibited by the school rules, but not really allowed either. Things didn't improve. Belikov was indeed dead and buried, but how many of these encapsulated men are still left, and how many are yet to come!'

'Yes, that's just my point!' Ivan Ivanovich said, lighting his pipe.

The teacher came out of the barn. He was short, plump, completely bald, with a black beard that nearly reached his waist. He had two dogs with him.

'Just look at that moon!' he said, looking up.

It was already midnight. To his right, the whole village could be clearly seen, with the long road stretching into the distance for about three miles. Everything was buried in a deep, peaceful slumber. Not a sound or movement anywhere and it was hard to believe that nature could be so silent. When you see a broad village street on a moonlit night, its huts, hayricks and sleeping willows, your heart is filled with tranquillity and finds sanctuary from its toil, worries and sorrows in this calm and in the shadows of night. It becomes gentle, sad and beautiful, and it seems that the very stars are looking down on it with love and tenderness, that all evil has vanished from the world and that happiness is everywhere. To the left, at the edge of the village, the open fields began; they could be seen stretching into the distance, right up to the horizon, and over all that vast moonlit expanse there was neither movement nor sound.

'Yes, that's just my point,' Ivan Ivanovich repeated. 'Isn't living in a crowded, stuffy town, writing documents nobody really needs, playing cards, the same as being in some kind of case? And spending our whole lives with idlers, litigants, stupid ladies of leisure, talking and hearing all kinds of rubbish – isn't that living in a case? If you like, I'll tell you another very edifying story.'

'No, it's time we got some sleep,' Burkin said. 'It can wait till tomorrow.'

The two men went into the barn and lay down on the hay. They had only just covered themselves and were dozing off when suddenly they could hear the patter of light footsteps. Someone was walking near the barn. The steps passed, stopped, then came the same patter. The dogs growled.

'That's Mavra,' Burkin said.

The footsteps died away.

'People are such liars,' Ivan Ivanovich said as he turned over, 'and you're called a fool for putting up with their lies. Suffering insults, humiliation, lacking the courage to declare that you're on the side of honest, free people, lying yourself, smiling – all this for a slice of bread, a snug little home of your own, a lousy clerical job not worth a damn! No, I can't live this kind of life any more!'

'Come on, that's another story, Ivan Ivanovich,' the teacher said. 'Let's go to sleep.'

And ten minutes later, Burkin was fast asleep. But Ivan Ivanovich kept tossing and turning, and sighing. Then he got up, went outside again, sat in the doorway and lit his pipe.

Gooseberries

The sky had been overcast with rain clouds since early morning. The weather was mild, and not hot and oppressive as it can be on dull grey days when storm clouds lie over the fields for ages and you wait for rain which never comes. Ivan Ivanovich, the vet, and Burkin, a teacher at the high school, were tired of walking and thought they would never come to the end of the fields. They could just make out the windmills at the village of Mironositskoye in the far distance – a range of hills stretched away to the right and disappeared far beyond it. They both knew that the river was there, with meadows, green willows and farmsteads, and that if they climbed one of the hills they would see yet another vast expanse of fields, telegraph wires and a train resembling a caterpillar in the distance. In fine weather they could see even as far as the town. And now, in calm weather, when the whole of nature had become gentle and dreamy, Ivan Ivanovich and Burkin were filled with love for those open spaces and they both thought what a vast and beautiful country it was.

'Last time we were in Elder Prokofy's barn, you were going to tell me a story,' Burkin said.

'Yes, I wanted to tell you about my brother.'

Ivan Ivanovich heaved a long sigh and lit his pipe before beginning his narrative; but at that moment down came the rain. Five minutes later it was simply teeming. Ivan Ivanovich and Burkin were in two minds as to what they should do. The dogs were already soaked through and stood with their tails drooping, looking at them affectionately.

'We must take shelter,' Burkin said. 'Let's go to Alyokhin's, it's not very far.'

'All right, let's go there.'

They changed direction and went across mown fields, walking

straight on at first, and then bearing right until they came out on the high road. Before long, poplars, a garden, then the red roofs of barns came into view. The river glinted, and then they caught sight of a wide stretch of water and a white bathing-hut. This was Sofino, where Alyokhin lived.

The mill was turning and drowned the noise of the rain. The wall of the dam shook. Wet horses with downcast heads were standing by some carts and peasants went around with sacks on their heads. Everything was damp, muddy and bleak, and the water had a cold, malevolent look. Ivan Ivanovich and Burkin felt wet, dirty and terribly uncomfortable. Their feet were weighed down by mud and when they crossed the dam and walked up to the barns near the manor-house they did not say a word and seemed to be angry with each other.

A winnowing-fan was droning away in one of the barns and dust poured out of the open door. On the threshold stood the master himself, Alyokhin, a man of about forty, tall, stout, with long hair, and he looked more like a professor or an artist than a landowner. He wore a white shirt that hadn't been washed for a very long time, and it was tied round with a piece of rope as a belt. Instead of trousers he was wearing underpants; mud and straw clung to his boots. His nose and eyes were black with dust. He immediately recognized Ivan Ivanovich and Burkin, and was clearly delighted to see them.

'Please come into the house, gentlemen,' he said, smiling, 'I'll be with you in a jiffy.'

It was a large house, with two storeys. Alyokhin lived on the ground floor in the two rooms with vaulted ceilings and small windows where his estate managers used to live. They were simply furnished and smelled of rye bread, cheap vodka and harness. He seldom used the main rooms upstairs, reserving them for guests. Ivan Ivanovich and Burkin were welcomed by the maid, who was such a beautiful young woman that they both stopped and stared at each other.

'You can't imagine how glad I am to see you, gentlemen,' Alyokhin said as he followed them into the hall. 'A real surprise!' Then he turned to the maid and said, 'Pelageya, bring some dry clothes for the gentlemen. I suppose I'd better change too. But I must have a wash first, or you'll think I haven't had one since spring. Would you like to come to the bathing-hut while they get things ready in the house?'

The beautiful Pelageya, who had such a dainty look and gentle face, brought soap and towels, and Alyokhin went off with his guests to the bathing-hut.

'Yes, it's ages since I had a good wash,' he said as he undressed. 'As you can see, it's a nice hut. My father built it, but I never find time these days for a swim.'

He sat on one of the steps and smothered his long hair and neck with soap; the water turned brown.

'Yes, I must confess . . .' Ivan Ivanovich muttered, with a meaningful look at his head.

'Haven't had a wash for ages,' Alyokhin repeated in his embarrassment and soaped himself again; the water turned a dark inky blue.

Ivan Ivanovich came out of the cabin, dived in with a loud splash and swam in the rain, making broad sweeps with his arms and sending out waves with white lilies bobbing about on them. He swam right out to the middle of the reach and dived. A moment later he popped up somewhere else and swam on, continually trying to dive right to the bottom.

'Oh, good God,' he kept saying with great relish. 'Good God . . .'

He reached the mill, said a few words to the peasants, then he turned and floated on his back in the middle with his face under the rain. Burkin and Alyokhin were already dressed and ready to leave, but he kept on swimming and diving.

'Oh, dear God,' he said. 'Oh, God!'

'Now that's enough,' Burkin shouted.

They went back to the house. Only when the lamp in the large upstairs drawing-room was alight and Burkin and Ivan Ivanovich, wearing silk dressing-gowns and warm slippers, were sitting in armchairs and Alyokhin, washed and combed now and with a new frock-coat on, was walking up and down, obviously savouring the warmth, cleanliness, dry clothes and light shoes, while his beautiful Pelageya glided silently over the carpet and gently smiled as she served tea and jam on a tray – only then did Ivan Ivanovich begin his story. It seemed that Burkin and Alyokhin were not the only ones who were listening, but also the ladies (young and old) and the officers, who were looking down calmly and solemnly from their gilt frames on the walls.

'There are two of us brothers,' he began, 'myself – Ivan – and

Nikolay, who's two years younger. I studied to be a vet, while Nikolay worked in the district tax office from the time he was nineteen. Chimsha-Gimalaysky, our father, had served as a private, but when he was promoted to officer we became hereditary gentlemen and owners of a small estate. After he died, this estate was sequestrated to pay off his debts, but despite this we spent our boyhood in the country, free to do what we wanted. Just like any other village children, we stayed out in the fields and woods for days and nights, minded horses, stripped bark, went fishing, and so on . . . As you know very well, anyone who has ever caught a ruff or watched migrating thrushes swarming over his native village on cool clear autumn days can never live in a town afterwards and he'll always hanker after the free and open life until his dying day. My brother was miserable in the tax office. The years passed, but there he stayed, always at the same old desk, copying out the same old documents and obsessed with this longing for the country. And gradually this longing took the form of a definite wish, a dream of buying a nice little estate somewhere in the country, beside a river or a lake.

'He was a kind, gentle man and I was very fond of him, but I could never feel any sympathy for him in this longing to lock himself away in a country house for the rest of his life. They say a man needs only six feet of earth, but surely they must mean a corpse – not a *man*! These days they seem to think that it's very good if our educated classes want to go back to the land and set their hearts on a country estate. But in reality these estates are only that same six feet all over again. To leave the town and all its noise and hubbub, to go and shut yourself away on your little estate – that's no life! It's selfishness, laziness, a peculiar brand of monasticism that achieves nothing. A man needs more than six feet of earth and a little place in the country, he needs the whole wide world, the whole of nature, where there's room for him to display his potential, all the manifold attributes of his free spirit.

'As he sat there in his office, my brother Nikolay dreamed of soup made from his own home-grown cabbages, soup that would fill the whole house with a delicious smell; eating meals on the green grass; sleeping in the sun; sitting on a bench outside the main gates for hours on end and looking at the fields and woods. Booklets on agriculture and words of wisdom from calendars were his joy, his favourite spiritual nourishment. He liked newspapers as well, but he only read property adverts – for so many acres of arable land and meadows, with "house, river, garden, mill, and ponds fed by running springs". And he had visions of garden paths, flowers, fruit, nesting-boxes for starlings, ponds teeming with carp – you know the kind of thing. These visions varied according to the adverts he happened to see, but for some reason, in every single one, there *had* to be gooseberry bushes. "Life in the country has its comforts," he used to say. "You can sit drinking tea on your balcony, while your ducks are swimming in the pond ... it all smells so good and um ... there's your gooseberries growing away!"

'He drew up a plan for his estate and it turned out exactly the same every time: (a) manor-house; (b) servants' quarters; (c) kitchen garden; (d) gooseberry bushes. He lived a frugal life, economizing on food and drink, dressing any-old-how – just like a beggar – and putting every penny he saved straight into the bank. He was terribly mean. It was really painful to look at him, so I used to send him a little money on special occasions. But he would put that in the bank too. Once a man has his mind firmly made up there's nothing you can do about it.

'Years passed and he was transferred to another province. He was now in his forties, still reading newspaper adverts and still saving up. Then I heard that he'd got married. So that he could buy a country estate with gooseberry bushes, he married an ugly old widow, for whom he felt nothing and only because she had a little money tucked away. He made her life miserable too, half-starved her and banked her money into his own account. She'd been married to a postmaster and was used to pies and fruit liqueurs, but with her second husband she didn't even have enough black bread. This kind of life made her wither away, and within three years she'd gone to join her maker. Of course, my brother didn't think that *he* was to blame – not for one minute! Like vodka, money can make a man do the most peculiar things. There was once a merchant living in our town who was on his deathbed. Just before he died, he asked for some honey, stirred it up with all his money and winning lottery tickets, and swallowed the lot to stop anyone else from laying their hands on it. And another time, when I was inspecting cattle at some railway station, a dealer fell under a train and had his leg cut off. We took him to the local casualty department. The blood simply gushed out, a terrible sight, but all he did was ask for his leg back and was only bothered about the twenty roubles he had tucked away in the boot. Scared he might lose them, I dare say!'

'But that's neither here nor there,' Burkin said.

'When his wife died,' Ivan continued, after a pause for thought, 'my brother started looking for an estate. Of course, you can look around for five years and still make the wrong choice and you finish up with something you never even dreamed of. So brother Nikolay bought about three hundred acres, with manor-house, servants' quarters and a park, on a mortgage through an estate agent. But there wasn't any orchard, gooseberries or duck pond. There *was* a river, but the water was always the colour of coffee because of the brickworks on one side of the estate and a bone-ash factory on the other. But my dear Nikolay didn't seem to care. He ordered twenty gooseberry bushes, planted them out and settled down to a landowner's life.

'Last year I visited him, as I wanted to see what was going on. In his letter my brother had called his estate "Chumbaroklov Patch" or "Gimalaysky's". One afternoon I turned up at "Gimalaysky's". It was a hot day. Everywhere there were ditches, fences, hedges, rows of small fir trees and there seemed no way into the yard or anywhere to leave my horse. I went up to the house, only to be welcomed by a fat ginger dog that looked rather like a pig. It wanted to bark, but it was too lazy. Then a barefooted, plump cook – she resembled a pig as well – came out of the kitchen and told me the master was having his after-lunch nap. So I went to my brother's room and there he was sitting up in bed with a blanket over his knees. He'd aged, put on weight and looked very flabby. His cheeks, nose and lips stuck out and I thought any moment he was going to grunt into his blanket, like a pig.

'We embraced and wept for joy, and at the sad thought that once we were young and now both of us were grey, and that our lives were nearly over. He got dressed and led me on a tour of the estate.

' "Well, how's it going?" I asked.

' "All right, thank God. It's a good life."

'No longer was he the poor, timid little clerk of before, but a real squire, a *gentleman*. He felt quite at home, being used to country life by then and he was enjoying himself. He ate a great deal, took proper baths, and he was putting on weight. Already he was suing the district council and both factories, and he got very peeved when the villagers didn't call him "sir". He paid great attention to his spiritual well-being (as a gentleman should) and he couldn't dispense charity nice and quietly, but had to make a great show of it. And what did it all add up to? He doled out bicarbonate of soda or castor oil to his villagers – regardless of what they were suffering from – and on his name-day held a thanksgiving service in the village, supplying vodka in plenty, as he thought this was the right thing to do. Oh, those horrid pints of vodka! Nowadays your fat squire drags his villagers off to court for letting their cattle stray on his land and the very next day (if it's a high holiday) stands them all a few pints of vodka. They'll drink it, shout hurray and fall at his feet in a drunken stupor. Better standards of living, plenty to eat, idleness – all this makes us Russians terribly smug. Back in his office, Nikolay had been too scared even to voice any opinions of his own, but now he was expounding the eternal verities in true ministerial style: "Education is essential, but premature as far as the common people are concerned" or "Corporal punishment, generally speaking, is harmful, but in certain cases it can be useful and irreplaceable". And he'd say, "I know the working classes and how to handle them. They *like* me, I only have to lift my little finger and they'll do *anything* for me."

'And he said all this, mark you, with a clever, good-natured smile. Time after time he'd say "we *gentlemen*" or "speaking as *one of the gentry*". He'd evidently forgotten that our grandfather had been a peasant and our father a common soldier. Even our absolutely ridiculous surname, Chimsha-Gimalaysky, was melodious, distinguished and highly agreeable to his ears now.

'But it's myself I'm concerned with, not him. I'd like to tell you about the change that came over me during the few hours I spent on his estate. Later, when we were having tea, his cook brought us a plateful of gooseberries. They weren't shop gooseberries, but home-grown, the first fruits of the bushes he'd planted. Nikolay laughed and stared at them for a whole minute, with tears in his eyes. He was too deeply moved for words. Then he popped one in his mouth, looked at me like an enraptured child that has finally been given a long-awaited toy and said, "Absolutely delicious!" He ate some greedily and kept repeating, "So tasty, you *must* try one!"

'They were hard and sour, but as Pushkin says: "Uplifting illusion is dearer to us than a host of truths."* This was a happy man whose cherished dreams had clearly come true, who had achieved his life's purpose, had got what he wanted and was happy with his lot – and himself. My thoughts about human happiness, for some peculiar reason, had always been tinged with a certain sadness. But now, seeing this happy man, I was overwhelmed by a feeling of despondency that was close to utter despair. I felt particularly low that night. They made up a bed for me in the room next to my brother's. He was wide awake and I could hear him getting up, going over to the plate and helping himself to one gooseberry at a time. And I thought how many satisfied, happy people really do exist in this world! And what a powerful force they are! Just take a look at this life of ours and you will see the arrogance and idleness of the strong, the ignorance and bestiality of the weak. Everywhere there's unspeakable poverty, overcrowding, degeneracy, drunkenness, hypocrisy and stupid lies . . . And yet peace and quiet reign in every house and street. Out of fifty thousand people you won't find one who is prepared to shout out loud and make a strong protest. We see people buying food in the market, eating during the day, sleeping at night-time, talking nonsense, marrying, growing old and then contentedly carting their dead off to the cemetery. But we don't hear or see those who suffer: the real tragedies of life are enacted somewhere behind the scenes. Everything is calm and peaceful and the only protest comes from statistics – and they can't talk. Figures show that so many went mad, so many bottles of vodka were emptied, so many children died from malnutrition. And clearly this kind of system is what people need. It's obvious that the happy man feels contented only because the unhappy ones bear their burden without saying a word: if it weren't for their silence, happiness would be quite impossible. It's a kind of mass hypnosis. Someone ought to stand with a hammer at the door of every happy contented man, continually banging on it to remind him that there are unhappy people around and that however happy *he* may be at the time, sooner or later life will show him its claws and disaster will overtake him in the form of illness, poverty, bereavement and there will be no one to hear or see him. But

*From the poem 'The Hero' (1830).

there isn't anyone holding a hammer, so our happy man goes his own sweet way and is only gently ruffled by life's trivial cares, as an aspen is ruffled by the breeze. All's well as far as *he's* concerned.

'That night I realized that I too was happy and contented,' Ivan Ivanovich went on, getting to his feet. 'I too had lectured people over dinner – or out hunting – on how to live, on what to believe, on how to handle the common people. And I too had told them that knowledge is a shining lamp, that education is essential, and that plain reading and writing is good enough for the masses, for the moment. Freedom is a blessing, I told them, and we need it like the air we breathe, but we must wait for it patiently.'

Ivan Ivanovich turned to Burkin and said angrily, 'Yes, that's what I used to say and now I'd like to know *what* is it we're waiting for? I'm asking you, *what*? What is it we're trying to prove? I'm told that nothing can be achieved in five minutes, that it takes time for any kind of idea to be realized; it's a gradual process. But who says so? And what is there to prove he's right? You refer to the natural order of things, to the law of cause and effect. But *is* there any law or order in a state of affairs where a lively, thinking person like myself should have to stand by a ditch and wait until it's choked with weeds, or silted up, when I could quite easily, perhaps, leap across it or bridge it? I ask you again, what are we waiting for? Until we have no more strength to live, although we long to and *need* to go on living?

'I left my brother early next morning and ever since then I've found town life unbearable. I'm depressed by peace and quiet, I'm scared of peering through windows, nothing makes me more dejected than the sight of a happy family sitting round the table drinking tea. But I'm old now, no longer fit for the fray, I'm even incapable of hating. I only feel sick at heart, irritable and exasperated. At night my head seems to be on fire with so many thoughts crowding in and I can't get any sleep ... Oh, if only I were young again!'

Ivan paced the room excitedly, repeating, 'If only I were young again!'

Suddenly he went up to Alyokhin and squeezed one hand, then the other. 'Pavel,' he pleaded, 'don't go to sleep or be lulled into complacency! While you're still young, strong and healthy, never stop doing good! Happiness doesn't exist, we don't need any such thing. If life has *any* meaning or purpose, you won't find it in happiness, but in something more rational, in something greater. Doing good!'

Ivan said all this with a pitiful, imploring smile, as though pleading for himself.

Afterwards all three of them sat in armchairs in different parts of the room and said nothing. Ivan Ivanovich's story satisfied neither Burkin nor Alyokhin. It was boring listening to that story about some poor devil of a clerk who ate gooseberries, while those generals and ladies, who seemed to have come to life in the gathering gloom, peered out of their gilt frames. For some reason they would have preferred discussing and hearing about refined people, about ladies. The fact that they were all sitting in a drawing-room where everything – the draped chandeliers, the armchairs, the carpets underfoot – indicated that those same people who were now looking out of their frames had once walked around, sat down and drunk their tea there ... and with beautiful Pelageya moving about here without a sound – all this was better than any story.

Alyokhin was dying to get to bed. That morning he had been up and about very early (before three) working on the farm, and he could hardly keep his eyes open. However, he was frightened he might miss some interesting story if he left now, so he stayed. He didn't even try to fathom if everything that Ivan had just been saying was clever, or even true: he was only too glad that his guests did not discuss oats or hay or tar, but things that had nothing to do with his way of life, and he wanted them to continue ...

'But it's time we got some sleep,' Burkin said, standing up.

'May I wish you all a very good night!'

Alyokhin bade them good night and went down to his room, while his guests stayed upstairs. They had been given the large room with two old, elaborately carved beds and an ivory crucifix in one corner. These wide, cool beds had been made by the beautiful Pelageya and the linen had a pleasant fresh smell.

Ivan Ivanovich undressed without a word and got into bed. Then he muttered, 'Lord have mercy on us sinners!' and pulled the blankets over his head. His pipe, which was lying on a table, smelled strongly of stale tobacco and Burkin was so puzzled as to where the terrible smell was coming from that it was a long time before he fell asleep.

All night long the rain beat against the windows.

Concerning Love

Next day they had delicious pies, crayfish and mutton chops for lunch, and during the meal Nikanor, the cook, came upstairs to inquire what the guests would like for dinner. He was a man of medium height, puffy-faced and with small eyes. He was so close-shaven his whiskers seemed to have been plucked out and not cut off with a razor.

Alyokhin told his guests that the beautiful Pelageya was in love with the cook. However, since he was a drunkard and a brawler, she didn't want to marry him; but she did not object to 'living' with him, as they say. He was a very devout Christian, however, and his religious convictions would not allow him to 'set up house' with her. So he insisted on marriage and would not hear of anything else. He cursed her when he was drunk and even beat her. When he was like this, she would hide upstairs and sob, and then Alyokhin and his servants would not leave the house in case she needed protecting. They began to talk about love.

Alyokhin started: 'What makes people fall in love and why couldn't Pelageya fall for someone else, someone more suited to her mentally and physically, instead of that ugly-mug Nikanor (everyone round here calls him ugly-mug), since *personal* happiness is so important in love? It's a mystery, and you can interpret it which way you like. Only one indisputable truth has been said about love up to now, that it's a "tremendous mystery", and everything else that's been written or said about it has never provided an answer and is just a re-formulation of problems that have always remained unsolved. One theory that might, on the face of it, explain one case, won't explain a dozen others. Therefore, in my opinion, the best way is to treat each case individually, without making generalizations. In doctors' jargon, you have to "isolate" each case.'

'Absolutely true,' Burkin said.

'Decent Russians like ourselves have a passion for problems that have never been solved. Usually, love is poeticized, beautified with roses and nightingales, but we Russians have to flavour it with the "eternal problems" – and we choose the most boring ones at that.

'When I was still studying in Moscow I had a "friend", a dear lady who'd be wondering how much I'd allow her every month and how much a pound of beef was while I held her close. And *we* never stop asking ourselves questions when we love: is it honourable or dishonourable, clever or stupid, how will it all end, and so on. Whether that's a good thing or not, I don't know, but I do know that it cramps your style, doesn't provide any satisfaction and gets on your nerves.'

It looked as if he wanted to tell us a story. It's always the same with people living on their own – they have something that they are only too pleased to get off their chests. Bachelors living in town go to the public baths and restaurants just to talk to someone, and sometimes they tell the bath attendants or waiters some very interesting stories. Out in the country they normally pour out their hearts to their guests. Through the windows we could only see grey skies now and trees dripping with rain – in this kind of weather there was really nowhere to go and nothing else to do except listen to stories.

'I've been living and farming in Sofino for quite a long time now – since I left university, in fact,' Alyokhin began. 'I was never brought up to do physical work and I'm an "armchair" type by inclination. When I first came to this estate they were up to their eyes in debts. But since my father had run up these debts partly through spending so much on my education, I decided to stay and work on the estate until the debts were paid off. That was my decision and I started working here – not without a certain degree of aversion, I must confess. The soil's not very fertile round here, and to avoid farming at a loss you have to rely on serfs or hire farm labourers, which more or less comes to the same thing. Or else you have to run your own estate peasant-style, which means you yourself and all your family have to slave away in the fields. There's no two ways about it. But then I didn't have time for subtleties: I didn't leave a square inch of soil unturned, I rounded up all the peasants and their wives from neighbouring villages and we all worked like mad. I did the ploughing, sowing and reaping myself, which was a terrible bore and it made me screw my face up in disgust, like the starving village cat forced to eat cucumbers in some kitchen garden. I was all aches and pains and I'd fall asleep standing up. From the very beginning I thought that I'd have no trouble at all combining this life of slavery with my cultural activities. All I had to do, so I thought, was keep to some settled routine. So I installed myself in the best rooms up here, had coffee and liqueurs after lunch and dinner, and took the *European Herald* with me to bed. But our parish priest, Father Ivan, turned up and polished off all my liqueurs at one sitting. And the *European Herald* ended up with his daughters, since during the summer, especially when we were harvesting, I never made it to my own bed but had to sleep in a barn, on a sledge, or in a woodman's hut somewhere, so what time was there for reading? Gradually I moved downstairs, had meals with the servants – they were all that was left of my earlier life of luxury – the same servants who had waited on my father and whom I did not have the heart to dismiss.

'In my early years here I was made honorary justice of the peace. This meant occasional trips into town, taking my seat at the sessions and local assizes, and this made a break for me. When you're stuck in a place like this for two or three months at a stretch – especially in the winter – you end up pining for your black frock-coat. I saw frock-coats – and uniforms and tail-coats as well – at the assizes. They were all lawyers, educated men there, people I could talk to. After sleeping on a sledge or eating with the servants it was the height of luxury sitting in an armchair, with clean underwear, light boots, and a watch-chain on your chest!

'They gave me a warm welcome in town and I eagerly made friends. The most significant, and frankly, the most pleasant, of these friendships was with Luganovich, vice-president of the assizes. Both of you know him, he's a most delightful man. Now, all this was about the time of that famous arson case. The questioning went on for two days and we were exhausted. Luganovich took a look at me and said, "Do you know what? Come and have dinner at my place."

'This was right out of the blue, as I didn't know him at all well, only through official business, and I'd never been to his house. I went to my hotel room for a quick change and went off to dinner. Now I had the chance to meet Luganovich's wife, Anna. She was still very young then, not more than twenty-two, and her first child had been born six months before. It's all finished now and it's hard for me to say exactly what it was I found so unusual about her, what attracted me so much, but at the time, over dinner, it was all so clear, without a shadow of doubt: here was a young, beautiful, kind, intelligent, enchanting woman, unlike any I'd met before. Immediately I sensed that she was a kindred spirit, someone I knew already, and that her face, with its warm clever eyes, was just like one I had seen before when I was a little boy, in an album lying on my mother's chest-of-drawers.

'At the trial four Jews had been convicted of arson and conspiracy – in my opinion, on no reasonable grounds at all. I became very heated over dinner, felt bad and I can't remember even now what I said, only that Anna kept shaking her head and telling her husband, "Dmitry, how *can* they do this?"

'Luganovich was a good man, one of those simple, open-hearted people who are firmly convinced that once you have a man in the dock he *must* be guilty, and that a verdict can only be challenged in writing, according to the correct legal procedure, and *never* during dinner or private conversation. "*We* haven't set anything alight," he said softly, "so *we* won't have to stand trial or go to prison."

'Both husband and wife plied me with food and drink. Judging from little details – the way they made coffee together and their mutual understanding that needed no words – I concluded that they were living peacefully and happily, and that they were glad to have a guest. After dinner there were piano duets. When it grew dark I went back to the hotel. All of this was at the beginning of spring. I spent the whole of the following summer in Sofino without emerging once and I was too busy even to think of going into town. But I could not forget that slender, fair-haired woman for one moment. Although I made no conscious effort to think about her, she seemed to cast a faint shadow over me.

'In late autumn there was a charity show in town. I took my seat in the governor's box, where I'd been invited during the interval, and there was Anna sitting next to the governor's wife. Once again I was struck by that irresistible, radiant beauty, by those tender, loving eyes, and once again I felt very close to her.

'We sat side by side, then we went into the foyer where she told me, "You've lost weight. Have you been ill?"

'"Yes, I've rheumatism in my shoulder and I sleep badly when it rains."

'"You look quite exhausted. When you came to dinner in the spring you seemed younger, more cheerful. You were very lively then and said some most interesting things. I was even a little taken with you, I must confess. For some reason I often thought about you during the summer and when I was getting ready for the theatre I had a feeling I might see you today." And she burst out laughing.

'"But now you seem to have no energy," she repeated. "It ages you."

'Next day I had lunch with the Luganoviches. Afterwards they drove out to their country villa to make arrangements for the winter, and I went with them. I came back to town with them and at midnight I was having tea in those peaceful domestic surroundings, in front of a roaring fire, while the young mother kept slipping out to see if her little girl was sleeping. Afterwards I made a point of visiting the Luganoviches whenever I came to town. We grew used to one another and I usually dropped in unannounced, like one of the family.

'That soft drawling voice I found so attractive would come echoing from one of the far rooms: "Who's there?"

'"It's Mr Pavel," the maid or nanny would reply.

'Then Anna would appear with a worried look and every time she'd ask me the same question, "Why haven't you been to see us? Is anything wrong?"

'The way she looked at me, the delicate, noble hand she offered me, the clothes she wore in the house, her hair-style, her voice and footsteps always made me feel that something new, out of the ordinary and important had happened in my life. We'd have long conversations – and long silences – immersed in our own thoughts. Or she would play the piano for me. If she was out, I'd stay and wait, talk to the nanny, play with the baby, or lie on the sofa in the study and read the papers. When Anna came back I'd meet her in the hall, take her shopping and for some reason I'd always carry it so devotedly and exultantly you'd have thought I was a little boy.

'You know the story about the farmer's wife who had no worries until she went and bought a pig. The Luganoviches had no worries, so they made friends with me. If I was away from town for long, they thought I must be ill or that something had happened to me and they would get terribly worked up. And they were concerned that an educated man like myself, speaking several languages, didn't use his time studying or doing literary work and could live out in the wilds, forever turning round like a squirrel on a wheel and slaving away without a penny to show for it. They sensed that I was deeply unhappy and that if I spoke, laughed or ate, it was only to hide my suffering. Even at cheerful times, when I was in good spirits, I knew they were giving me searching looks. They were particularly touching when I really was in trouble, when some creditor was chasing me, or when I couldn't pay some bill on time. Both of them would stay by the window whispering, and then the husband would come over to me, looking serious, and say, "Pavel, if you're a bit short, my wife and I *beg* you not to think twice about asking us!"

'And his ears would turn red with excitement. Often, after a whispering session at the window, he would come over to me, ears flushed, and say, "My wife and I *beg* you to accept this little gift."

'And he'd give me cuff-links, a cigarette case or a table-lamp. In return, I'd send them some poultry, butter or flowers from the country. They were quite well-off, by the way, both of them. In my younger days I was always borrowing and wasn't too fussy where the money came from, taking it wherever I could get it. But for nothing in the world would I have borrowed from the Luganoviches. The very idea!

'I was unhappy. Whether I was at home, out in the fields, in the barn, I couldn't stop thinking about *her*, and I tried to unravel the mystery of that young, beautiful, clever woman who had married an uninteresting man, who could almost be called old (he was over forty) and had borne his children. And I tried to solve the enigma of that boring, good-natured, simple-minded fellow, with his insufferable common-sense, always crawling up to the local stuffed shirts at balls and soirées, a lifeless, useless man whose submissive, indifferent expression made you think he'd been brought along as an object for sale, a man who believed, however, that he had the right to be happy and to be the father of *her* children. I never gave up trying to understand why she was fated to meet him, and not me, why such a horrible mistake should have to occur in *our* lives.

'Every time I went into town I could tell from her eyes that she had been waiting for me, and she would admit that from the moment she'd got up she'd had some kind of premonition that I would be coming. We had long talks and there were long silences, and we didn't declare our love, but concealed it jealously, timidly, fearing anything that might betray our secret to each other. Although I loved her tenderly, deeply, I reasoned with myself and tried to guess what the consequences would be if we had no strength to combat it. It seemed incredible that my gentle, cheerless love could suddenly rudely disrupt the happy lives of her husband and children – of that whole household in fact, where I was so loved and trusted. Was I acting honourably? She would have gone away with me, but where could I take her? It would have been another matter if my life had been wonderful and eventful – if, for example, I'd been fighting to liberate my country, or if I'd been a famous scholar, actor or artist. But I'd only be taking her away from an ordinary, pedestrian life into one that was just the same, just as prosaic, even more so, perhaps. And just how long would we stay happy? What would become of her if I was taken ill, or died? Or if we simply stopped loving each other?

'And she seemed to have come to the same conclusion. She had been thinking about her husband, her children, and her mother, who loved her husband like a son. If she were to let her feelings get the better of her, then she would have to lie or tell the whole truth, but either alternative would have been equally terrible and distressing for someone in her position. And she was tormented by the question: would her love make me happy, wouldn't she be complicating a life which was difficult enough already, brimful of all kinds of unhappiness? She thought that she was no longer young enough for me and that she wasn't hard-working or energetic enough to start a new life with me. Often she told her husband that I should marry some nice clever girl who would make a good housewife and be a help to me. But immediately she would add that she would have a hard job finding someone answering to that description in *that* town.

'Meanwhile the years passed. Anna already had two children. Whenever I called on the Luganoviches the servants welcomed me with smiles, the children shouted that Uncle Pavel had arrived and clung to my neck. Everyone was glad. They didn't understand what was going on deep down inside me and they thought that I too shared their joy.

All of them considered me a most noble person, and both parents and children felt that the very personification of nobility was walking around the house, and this lent a very special charm to their attitude towards me, as if my being there made their lives purer and finer. I would go to the theatre with Anna – we always used to walk. We would sit side by side in the stalls, shoulders touching, and as I took the opera glasses from her I felt that she was near and dear to me, that she belonged to me, that we couldn't live without each other. But through some strange lack of mutual understanding we would always say goodbye and part like strangers when we left the theatre. In that town they were already saying God knows what about us, but there wasn't one word of truth in it.

'Later on, Anna visited her mother and sister more often. She started to have fits of depression when she realized her life was unfulfilled, ruined, and she had no desire to see either her husband or the children. She was already having treatment for a nervous disorder.

'We didn't say one word to each other and she seemed strangely irritated with me when other people were around. She'd quarrel with everything I said, and if I was having an argument she would always take the other person's side. If I dropped something she would coldly say, "Congratulations." If I left my opera glasses behind when we went to the theatre she'd say afterwards, "I *knew* that you'd forget them."

'Whether for better or for worse, there's nothing in this life that doesn't come to an end sooner or later. The time to part finally came when Luganovich was made a judge in one of the western provinces. They had to sell the furniture, horses and the villa. When we drove out to the villa and turned round for a last glimpse of the garden and the green roof, everyone felt sad and it was then I realized the time had come to say farewell – and not only to a simple villa. On the advice of her doctor they decided to send Anna to the Crimea, while soon afterwards Luganovich would take the children with him to the western province.

'A large crowd of us went to see Anna off. She had already said goodbye to her husband and children, and the train was about to leave at any moment. I rushed to her compartment to put a basket that she'd almost forgotten on to the luggage-rack. Now it was time to say farewell. When our eyes met we could hold ourselves back no longer.

I embraced her and she pressed her face to my chest and the tears just poured out. As I kissed her face, shoulders and hands that were wet with tears – oh, how miserable we both were! – I declared my love and realized, with a searing pain in my heart, how unnecessary, trivial and illusory everything that had stood in the way of our love had been. I understood that with love, if you start theorizing about it, you must have a nobler, more meaningful starting-point than mere happiness or unhappiness, sin or virtue, as they are commonly understood. Otherwise it's best not to theorize at all.

'I kissed her for the last time, pressed her hand and we parted forever. The train was already moving. I took a seat in the next compartment, which was empty, and cried until the first stop, where I got out and walked back to Sofino.'

While Alyokhin was telling his story the rain had stopped and the sun had come out. Burkin and Ivan Ivanovich went on to the balcony, from which there was a wonderful view of the garden and the river, gleaming like a mirror now in the sunlight. As they admired the view they felt sorry that this man, with those kind, clever eyes, who had just told his story so frankly, was really turning round and round in his huge estate like a squirrel in a cage, showing no interest in academic work or indeed anything that could have made his life more agreeable. And they wondered how sad that woman's face must have been when he said goodbye on the train and kissed her face and shoulders. Both of them had met her in town and in fact Burkin had even known her and thought she was beautiful.

A Case History

A professor received a telegram from the Lyalikov factory asking him to come immediately. All he could decipher in that rambling, muddled telegram was that the daughter of a Mrs Lyalikov, who apparently owned the factory, was ill.

The professor did not go himself, but sent his house-surgeon Korolyov instead. The house-surgeon had to go two stops by train from Moscow, then travel the remaining three miles by road. A coachman wearing a hat with a peacock's feather, who shouted his replies to every question like a soldier – 'No – sir' or 'Yes – sir' – was sent to pick him up at the station in a three-horse carriage. It was a Saturday evening and the sun was setting. Workers thronged the road from the factory to the station and they bowed to the horses as they went by. He was enchanted by the evening, by the estates and villas to each side of him, by the birch trees and an all-pervading atmosphere of tranquillity, when it seemed that the fields, the forest and the sun were preparing to join with the factory workers in their rest on that Saturday evening – and perhaps to offer up prayers as well.

He was born in Moscow, where he had grown up, was a stranger to country life and had never taken any interest in factories or even visited one. But he had read about them, had been invited to the houses of factory owners where he had had a chance to talk to them. Whenever he saw a factory, whether from far off or close by, he always thought that, while everything appeared so calm and peaceful from the outside, inside those walls there was surely nothing but blindly egotistic bosses who were completely and utterly ignorant; boring, unhealthy work for those who slaved away there; and filth, vodka and insects. And now, when those workers respectfully and timidly made way for the carriage, he could see sure signs of filth, drunkenness, nervousness and bewilderment in their faces, in the state of their peaked caps and in the way they walked.

They drove through the factory gates. On both sides he caught glimpses of the workers' cottages, women's faces, washing and blankets laid out on the front steps. 'Look out!' the coachman shouted as he gave full rein to the horses. They reached a wide open square, devoid of grass. Here there were five enormous factory blocks with chimneys, spaced out a little distance from each other, store-houses and wooden huts: everything was covered with a rather strange grey deposit that could have been dust. Miserable little gardens and the managers' houses with their green or red roofs were scattered here and there, like oases in a desert. The coachman suddenly pulled in the reins and the carriage came to a halt outside a house freshly painted grey. There was a small garden with a lilac tree covered in dust, and the yellow porch smelled strongly of new paint.

'This way please, Mr Doctor,' some female voices said in the entrance hall and at the same time he could hear sighing and whispering. 'Please come in, we're worn out with waiting ... it's something shocking ... this way, please.'

Mrs Lyalikov, a plump, elderly lady, was wearing a black silk dress with sleeves in the latest fashion; but her face showed she was a simple, uneducated woman. She glanced anxiously at the doctor and could not bring herself to offer him her hand – she dare not. A thin, middle-aged woman with close-cropped hair, pince-nez, and a brightly coloured floral pattern blouse was standing next to her. The servants called her Miss Christina and Korolyov guessed she was the governess. She was the most educated person in that household, and it was more than likely that she had been entrusted with receiving the doctor, since right away, without wasting any time, she launched into a minute account of the causes of the illness, giving every tiresome little detail, without saying who was ill and what the trouble was.

The doctor and governess sat talking, while the mistress of the house stood expectantly by the door without moving an inch. Korolyov gathered from the conversation that a twenty-year-old girl called Liza was ill. She was Mrs Lyalikov's only daughter and heiress to the estate; she had been ill for a long time and several doctors had treated her. The whole of the previous night she had suffered such violent palpitations that no one in the house could sleep and everyone feared for her life.

'She was always a sickly child, from the time she was a little girl,'

Miss Christina said in a sing-song voice, wiping her lips with her hand from time to time. 'The doctors say it's nerves, but when she was small they drove the scrofula back inside her, so perhaps that's the reason.'

They went to have a look at the patient. She was a large, tall girl, quite grown up, but ugly like her mother, with the same small eyes and a similar wide, oversized lower jaw. Her hair was uncombed and the blankets were drawn right up to her chin. Straight away she struck Korolyov as a miserable, unhappy creature who was being kept warm and well wrapped up because they felt sorry for her and he could not believe that here was the heiress to five huge factory blocks.

'I've come to give you some treatment,' Korolyov began. 'How do you do.' He introduced himself and shook her large, cold, ugly hand. She sat up and told him her story – she was obviously long-used to doctors and did not care about her shoulders and bosom being uncovered.

'I've been having palpitations,' she said. 'I was scared out of my life all night long . . . it was so bad I nearly died. Please give me something!'

'Yes, I will, I will! Now calm down.'

Korolyov examined her and shrugged his shoulders. 'Your heart's perfectly sound, there's nothing wrong. Your nerves aren't too good, but that's normal. I don't think there'll be any more palpitations, try and get some sleep now . . .'

Just then a lamp was brought in. The light made the girl screw her eyes up and suddenly she clutched her head and burst out sobbing. His first impression of a wretched, ugly creature suddenly vanished and Korolyov no longer saw small eyes or an oversized jaw, but a gentle, suffering expression that seemed so rational, so touching. Now she appeared to embody all that was feminine, graceful and natural and he no longer wanted to supply her with sedatives or medical advice, but a few simple, kind words instead. The mother clasped her head and pressed it to her. How much despair and grief was written on that old woman's face! As a true mother she had nurtured her daughter, brought her up, spared no expense and devoted her entire life to her, so that she could learn French, dancing and music, and had engaged a dozen tutors, the best doctors, a governess; and now she could not understand the reason for all those tears, all that suffering, and consequently she was at her wits' end. Her expression was one of guilt, anxiety, despair, as if she had neglected something that was very important, had let things slip, had forgotten to invite someone – but who, that was a mystery.

'Lizanka, what is it now?' she said, pressing her daughter to her. 'My own little darling, tell me what's wrong! Show some pity, please, tell me . . .'

Both wept bitterly. Korolyov sat on the edge of the bed and took Liza's hand. 'Now that's enough. Is it worth crying about?' he said in a kindly voice. 'Surely there's nothing in this world that's worth all these tears. Now, we're going to stop crying, there's no need to . . .' But he thought to himself: 'Time she was married . . .'

'The factory doctor gave her some bromide,' the governess said, 'but it's only made her worse. In my opinion, if it's the heart, there's some drops . . . I forget the name . . . lily of the valley, I think . . .'

And again came a flood of details. She kept interrupting the doctor, didn't let him get a word in and the effort she was making showed in her face – it was as if she had assumed, as the most educated woman in that house, that it was her responsibility to keep talking to the doctor – and only about medicine, of course.

Korolyov began to feel bored. 'I can't see anything very much wrong,' he said to the mother as he left the bedroom. 'If the factory doctor has been treating your daughter, there's no reason why he should stop. Up to now the treatment has been correct and I don't see the need to change doctor. The illness is really so normal, it's nothing serious . . .'

He did not hurry his words as he put his gloves on, but Mrs Lyalikov stood motionless and looked at him with tear-stained eyes.

'The ten o'clock train leaves in half an hour and I don't want to miss it,' he said.

'But can't you stay the night?' she asked and tears flowed down her cheeks again. 'I feel ashamed worrying you like this, but please do us the kindness . . . for God's sake,' she whispered as she glanced round at the door. '*Please* stay the night. She's all I have, my only daughter. She gave me such a fright last night, I still haven't got over it . . . *Please* don't go, for God's sake . . .'

He wanted to tell her that he had a great deal of work to do in Moscow, that his family was waiting for him. He felt depressed at the idea of spending a whole evening and night in a strange house when there was no need for it. But he looked at her face, sighed and silently started taking his gloves off.

All the lamps in the hall and drawing-room had been lit for him. He sat at the grand piano and turned over some pages of music. Then he looked at the portraits on the walls. There were oil paintings in gilt frames: Crimean landscapes, a storm at sea with small craft, a Catholic monk holding a wine glass – they were all dull, over-elaborate, amateurish. Among the portraits there wasn't one handsome, interesting face and all of them had wide cheek-bones and surprised-looking eyes. Lyalikov (Liza's father) had a small forehead, a smug look and a uniform that fitted his large clumsy body like a sack, and he sported the Red Cross with insignia on his chest. The house showed few signs of culture – any touches of luxury were purely accidental – and revealed poverty of ideas; and it looked uncomfortable, just like that uniform. The floors had a nasty gloss (there was something annoying about the chandeliers as well), and for some reason it all reminded you of the story of the merchant who wore a medal round his neck when he had a bath . . .

Whispers came from the hall and he could hear someone softly snoring. Suddenly there were sharp, abrupt metallic sounds from outside – sounds Korolyov had never heard before and which puzzled him now. They aroused a peculiar, unpleasant feeling and as he turned to the music-book again he thought: 'I don't think I could live here, not for anything!'

'Doctor, please come and have something to eat!' the governess called in a hushed voice.

He went off to have supper. The table was large, laden with many kinds of savouries and wines, but only two sat down to eat – himself and Miss Christina. She drank madeira, ate quickly, peered at him through her pince-nez and said, 'The workers are very happy. Every winter in the factory we have amateur dramatics, the workers play the parts themselves; there are lectures with magic-lantern slides, a marvellous canteen and a lot more. They are absolutely devoted to us and when they heard Liza was getting worse they said prayers. They may be illiterate, but they still have feelings.'

'It seems there are no men at all in the house,' Korolyov said.

'None. Mr Lyalikov died eighteen months ago and there's only the three of us. We spend the summers here, but stay on the Polyanka in Moscow during the winter. I've been with them eleven years, I'm one of the family.'

They had sturgeon, fried chicken and stewed fruit; the wines were French and very expensive.

'Please, doctor, don't stand on ceremony,' Miss Christina said, wiping her mouth on her sleeves as she ate. Clearly she was very satisfied with life in that house. 'Please, do eat.'

After supper the doctor was taken to a room where a bed had been made up for him. But he did not feel like sleeping as it was stuffy and the room smelled of paint. He put on his overcoat and went out.

It was cool outside; dawn was already breaking and all five factory blocks with their tall chimneys, the huts and store-houses stood out quite clearly in the moist air. No one was working, as it was a holiday, and all the windows were dark, except in one of the blocks where a stove was burning, turning the windows crimson; now and again flames leapt from the chimney, as well as smoke. Far beyond the factory yard, frogs were croaking and a nightingale was singing.

As he looked at the factory blocks and the wooden huts where the workers slept, he began to think as he had always done when he looked at factories. Even though there were shows for the workers, lantern-slides, factory doctors and various improvements in the standard of living, they were still those same workers he had met earlier that day on the way from the station and they didn't differ at all from those he had known a long time before when he was young, when there were no shows or improvements in factory conditions. As a doctor who had correctly diagnosed chronic incurable diseases whose cause had been unknown, he viewed factories as a puzzle of the same kind, just as vague and just as difficult to explain. He didn't actually think that these improvements were unnecessary but thought they were the same thing as treating an incurable disease.

'Of course, none of it makes sense,' he thought as he glanced at the crimson windows. 'Fifteen hundred or two thousand workers are slaving away, without a break, in unhealthy conditions, producing inferior cotton print, are half-starved and only now and then find relief from this nightmare in the pub. A hundred people supervise their work and the lives of these hundred supervisors are wasted entering fines in the record-book, swearing and being unfair to the workers; only two or three of them – the so-called bosses – enjoy the profits, although they don't do any work themselves and have nothing but contempt for the cheap fabric. But what exactly *are* these profits, how do they use them? Mrs Lyalikov and her daughter are unhappy and it makes me sorry to see them in such a state. Only Miss Christina, that stupid old maid with her pince-nez, gets any pleasure out of life. As I see it, there's five factories turning out cheap cotton print for sale on the Eastern markets just to keep Miss Christina supplied with madeira and sturgeon.'

Suddenly he heard a peculiar noise, just like the one before supper. Someone was banging away on a metal plate not far from one of the blocks, immediately muffling the sound afterwards, so that it came over in brief, indistinct staccato bursts. After about half a minute's silence the abrupt, unpleasant noise started again, this time near one of the other blocks, pitched lower, with a deep booming note. He counted eleven strokes – obviously it was the night watchman beating out the time.

Then he heard a metallic sound near the third block, then from the others, and then from around the huts and beyond the gates. It was as if that monster, the devil himself, who had the bosses and the workers in his grasp, and who was fooling all of them, was making these noises in the silence of the night.

Korolyov walked out to the open fields.

Someone at the gate challenged, 'Who's there?'

'It's just like a prison,' he thought, and didn't reply.

Now he could hear the nightingales and frogs more clearly and he was aware of the May night all around. The sound of a train carried from the station. Somewhere sleepy cocks crowed, but otherwise it was quiet, the world slept peacefully. Out in the fields, not far from the factories, stood a pile of timber and building materials. Korolyov sat on some planks and continued his train of thought: 'Only the governess is happy in this place – and the factory is working for *her* pleasure. But it seems she doesn't carry much weight round here. The important one, for whom everyone is working, is the devil.' And he thought about the devil, in whom he didn't believe, and looked back at two windows where lights were burning. It seemed these were really the crimson eyes of the devil who was looking at him, of that mysterious force responsible for the way the strong treated the weak, for a serious blunder that was impossible to set right. It was nature's law that the strong should oppress the weak, but this could be made easily comprehensible only in newspaper articles or text-books, in that chaos which everyday life seems to be made, in that hotch-potch of trivia of which the intricate relationships between human beings are composed. It was no law, however, but a logical *non sequitur*, when both the strong and the weak fall victim to their own relationships with one another and both are compelled to surrender to some mysterious power standing beyond ordinary life, alien to man. These were Korolyov's thoughts as he sat on the planks and gradually he was overcome by the feeling that this unknown, mysterious power was actually quite close and watching him. Meanwhile the sky in the east grew paler and time passed quickly. The five factory blocks and their chimneys, silhouetted against the grey dawn, with not a soul to be seen – as if everything had died – had a strange look, quite different from day-time. He completely forgot that there were steam engines, electricity, telephones inside those blocks, but for some strange reason he could only think about pile-dwellings, about the iron age and he sensed that some crude mindless power was lurking close by.

Again he heard that metallic tapping.

There were twelve beats. Then it stopped for about half a minute and started again at the other end of the factory yard – but this time the sound was deeper.

'Very nasty!' Korolyov thought.

Then came a staccato tapping from a third place – the sounds were sharp and abrupt and one could almost hear annoyance in them.

The watchman took four minutes to beat out twelve o'clock. Then all was quiet and he had that same feeling again, as if everything was dead.

Korolyov sat there a few minutes longer, then returned to the house, but it was a long time before he went to bed. He could hear whispering from the rooms to either side, and slippers and bare feet shuffling over the floor.

'Surely she's not having another attack?' Korolyov thought.

He left his room and went to see the sick girl. The rooms were already filled with bright daylight and the weak rays of the sun that had filtered through the morning mist played on the wall in the hall. The door to Liza's bedroom was open and she was sitting in an armchair near her bed with a house-coat wrapped around her like a shawl and her hair was uncombed. The blinds were drawn.

'How do you feel?' Korolyov asked.

'All right, thank you.'

He felt her pulse and smoothed back her hair which had fallen down over her forehead.

'So you're not sleeping,' he said. 'It's lovely outside, spring has come. The nightingales are singing and here you are sitting in the dark, brooding.'

She listened and looked straight into his face. Her eyes were sad and clever, and clearly she longed to tell him something.

'Does this happen often?' he asked.

'Yes. I feel bad nearly every night.'

At that moment the watchman beat two o'clock. At those sharp metallic tapping sounds she trembled.

'Does that noise bother you?'

'I'm not sure. Everything here bothers me,' she replied and became thoughtful. 'Everything. I can tell from your voice that you're concerned and the moment I saw you I sensed I could confide in someone like you – about everything.'

'Please do tell me then.'

'I'd like to tell you what *I* think. It seems that I'm not ill, and I'm worried and terrified for that reason, and because things can't possibly change. Even the healthiest man can't help worrying – for example, if there's a burglar lurking beneath his window.' She looked down at her knees with a timid smile and then continued, 'I'm always having medical treatment and of course I'm thankful and I wouldn't say it's all a waste of time. I don't want to talk to doctors, though, but to someone close to me, a friend who would understand me and could convince me whether I'm right or wrong.'

'Don't you have any friends?' Korolyov asked.

'I'm all on my own. There's my mother, and I love her, but I'm still alone. That's how my life has turned out . . . Lonely people read a great deal, but they don't say much and they don't listen. Life is a mystery for them. People like these are mystics and often see the devil when he's not there at all. Lermontov's Tamara was lonely and she saw the devil.'

'Do you read a lot?'

'Yes, a lot. As you can see, my time is my own from morning till night. I read during the day but at night-time my head is empty and instead of thoughts there are dark shadows.'

'Do you see things at night?' Korolyov asked.

'No, but I sense . . .'

She smiled again at the doctor and gave him such a sad, knowing look. He felt that she trusted him, that she wanted to have a heart-to-heart talk and that she thought about things as he did. But she did not speak and perhaps she was waiting for him.

He knew what he should say to her. There was no doubt in his mind that she should give up those five factory blocks and the million roubles – assuming she had that much – as soon as possible, and that devil who watched her at night. Quite obviously she thought the same and was only waiting for someone she trusted to confirm it.

But he did not know how to put it into words. How could he? One is reluctant to ask convicted persons the reason for their conviction, and in the same way it's awkward asking very wealthy people why they are so rich, why they put their wealth to such bad use, why they don't give it away, even when they can see that it's the reason for their unhappiness. Any discussions on the subject usually turn out to be inhibited, embarrassed and overlong.

'How can I tell her?' Korolyov wondered. 'And *should* I?'

And he told her what he wanted to – not straight out but in a rather roundabout way.

'You're unhappy being a factory owner and a rich heiress, you don't believe in your own rights, and now you can't sleep. Of course this is better than being contented, sleeping soundly and thinking all's well with the world. Your insomnia is something *honourable*: whatever you may think, it's a good sign. In actual fact the conversation we're having now would be unthinkable for our parents. They never discussed things at night, but slept soundly. But our generation sleeps badly, we become weary and feel we can find the answers to everything, whether we're right or wrong. The problem whether they are right or wrong will already have been solved for our children or grandchildren. They will see things more clearly than us. Life will be good in fifty years' time and it's a pity we shan't live till then. It would have been interesting to see.'

'What will our children and grandchildren do?' Liza asked.

'I don't know . . . probably abandon everything and go away somewhere.'

'Where?'

'Where? . . . Anywhere they like,' Korolyov said, laughing. 'There's no shortage of places for a good, clever man.'

He looked at his watch.

'The sun's up already,' he said. 'It's time you got some sleep. Undress and have a good rest now.'

As he shook her hand he added, 'I'm very glad I met you. You're a wonderful, interesting person. Good night!'

He went to his room and climbed into bed.

Next morning, when the carriage was brought round, everyone went on to the front steps to say goodbye. Liza was dressed in her Sunday best, in a white dress, with a flower in her hair; she looked pale, lifeless. She glanced at him sadly and knowingly, as she had the day before, smiled, and her tone of voice suggested she wished to tell him (and him alone) something quite special and important. The larks were singing and the church bells rang out. The factory windows shone cheerfully and, as he drove across the yard and then along the road to the station, Korolyov had forgotten all about factory workers, pile-dwellings, the devil, and was thinking of the time – perhaps not far away – when life would be just as radiant and joyful as that calm Sunday morning. And he thought how pleasant it was riding in a fine troika that spring morning and warming himself in the sun.

In the Gully

I

The village of Ukleyevo lay in a hollow, so that only the church belfry and the chimneys of calico-printing works could be seen from the main road and the railway station. When travellers asked its name they were told, 'It's that place where the lay-reader ate all the caviare at a funeral.'

Once, during a wake at Kostyukov the manufacturer's house, an elderly lay-reader had spotted some unpressed caviare among the savouries and immediately started gobbling it up. People nudged him, tugged his sleeve, but he seemed to be paralysed from the sheer enjoyment of it, which made him oblivious of everything, and he just continued eating, regardless. He scoffed the whole lot – and it was a four-pound jar! All this had happened many years ago and the lay-reader was long since dead, but the story of the caviare was still fresh in everyone's mind. Whether it was because life there was so wretched or simply that the people could find nothing more exciting to talk about than that trivial little incident of ten years before, it was all you ever heard about Ukleyevo.

Swamp fever was still rife here and even in summer there were slimy patches of mud – especially under fences – which lay in the broad shade of old, overhanging willows. There was always a smell of factory waste, of the acetic acid they used for processing the cotton. The factories – three cotton printing-works and one tannery – were not in the village itself but a short distance away, on the outskirts. They weren't very large and the total workforce didn't amount to much more than four hundred. The waste from the tannery made the water in the small river stink horribly, the meadows were polluted by the effluent, the cattle in the village suffered from anthrax, and so it was ordered to close down. However, although it was *supposed* to be shut, it was kept going on the quiet, with the full approval of the district police inspector and doctor, each receiving ten roubles a month from the owner. There were only two houses worthy of the name in the whole village, built of stone and with iron roofs. One of them was occupied by the council offices, while Grigory Tsybukin, a shopkeeper from Yepifan, lived in the other, which was two storeys high and stood right opposite the church.

Grigory kept a grocery store, but this was only a cover for his secret business in vodka, cattle, hides, grain, pigs – in fact he sold anything that came his way. For example, when there were export orders for peasant women's bonnets (these were made into fashionable hats for ladies), he could earn himself thirty kopeks a pair. He bought trees for sawing-up, lent money on interest, and really the old man could turn his hand to anything. He had two sons. Anisim, the elder, was a police detective and seldom came home. The younger son, Stepan, had gone into the business to help his father. However, they could not expect any real help from him as he was in poor health and deaf as well. His wife, Aksinya, was a beautiful, well-built woman, who wore a hat and carried a parasol when she went to village festivals. She was an early riser, went late to bed and all day long kept rushing round the barn, the cellar or the shop with her skirts tucked up and her bunch of keys jangling. Old Tsybukin would cheer up as he watched her and his eyes would sparkle. At such moments he regretted that she had not married his elder son, but the younger one instead, who besides being deaf couldn't tell the beautiful from the ugly.

The old man always had a strong liking for domestic life and he loved his family more than anything else in the world – especially his elder detective son and his daughter-in-law. No sooner had Aksinya married the deaf son than she began to display an extraordinary head for business; in no time she got to know those who were credit-worthy and those she had to turn down. She always took charge of the keys, not even trusting her own husband with them, and she would click away at her abacus. Like a true peasant, she would look at a horse's teeth first and was always laughing or shouting. Whatever she did or said, it warmed the old man's heart and he would mutter, 'Well done, my daughter-in-law! That's the way, my beautiful girl!'

He had been a widower, but a year after his son's marriage he could bear it no longer and remarried. About twenty miles from Ukleyevo they found him a spinster called Barbara, from a good family. Although she was middle-aged, she still kept her good looks. From the moment she settled into her little room on the first floor, everything in the house became shining bright, as though all the windows had suddenly been fitted with new glass. Ikon lamps were lit, tables covered with snow-white cloths, flowers with little red buds appeared on the window sills and in the front garden, and at mealtimes everyone had his own individual dish instead of eating from a communal bowl. Barbara's warm, fetching smile seemed to infect the whole household. And then something quite out of the ordinary happened – beggars, wanderers and female pilgrims began to call at the house. The plaintive sing-song voices of the Ukleyevo women and the guilty coughing of weak, haggard-looking peasants, sacked from the factory for drunkenness, came from outside, beneath the window-ledges. Barbara gave them money, bread, old clothes and, later on, when she was really settled in, brought them things from the shop. On one occasion the deaf son was most upset when he saw her taking away two small packets of tea.

'Mother's just pinched two packets of tea,' he told his father. 'Who's supposed to be paying for them?'

The old man did not reply, but stood there pondering and twitching his eyebrows; then he went upstairs to his wife. 'Barbara, dear,' he said affectionately, 'if ever you need *anything* from the shop, then help yourself. Take as much as you like, and don't feel guilty.'

Next day the deaf son shouted out to her as he ran across the yard, 'Mother, if you need anything, just *help yourself*!'

There was something fresh, cheerful and gay in her displays of charity, just like those brightly burning ikon lamps and the little red flowers. On the eve of a Fast or on a saint's day festival (they usually took three days to celebrate them) when they used to fob the peasants off with rotten salt beef, which gave off such a revolting stench you could hardly go near the barrel; when they let the drunks pawn their scythes, caps, their wives' scarves; when the factory-hands, their heads reeling from cheap vodka, wallowed in the mud, so that the shamelessness of it all seemed to hang overhead in a thick haze – at these times it came as a relief to think that over there in the house lived a quiet, tidy woman who would have nothing to do with either salt beef or vodka. On such distressing, murky days her acts of charity had the effect of a safety-valve.

Every day at the Tsybukins' was a busy one. Before the sun had even risen, Aksinya puffed and panted as she washed herself in the hall, while the samovar boiled away in the kitchen with an ominous hum. Old Grigory, who looked so neat and small in his long black frock-coat, cotton-print trousers and shining jackboots, would pace up and down the house, tapping his heels like the father-in-law in the popular song. Then they would open the shop. When it was light, the racing drozhky would be brought round to the front door and the old man would pull his large peaked cap right over his ears and jump into it with all the friskiness of a young man. To look at him no one would have guessed that he was already fifty-six. His wife and daughter-in-law used to see him off and on these momentous occasions, when he wore his fine clean frock-coat, when the enormous black stallion that had cost three hundred roubles was hitched to the drozhky, the old man didn't like it if peasants came up to him asking for favours or complaining. He hated them and they disgusted him. If he happened to see one hanging around the gates he would shout furiously, 'What yer standing round here for? Clear off!' If it was a beggar he would yell, 'God'll feed yer!'

While he was away on business his wife, with her dark dress and black apron, would tidy the rooms or help in the kitchen. Aksinya served in the shop and one could hear bottles and coins clinking, the sound of her laughter or of offended customers getting cross. At the same time it was all too plain that the illegal vodka business was already running nice and smoothly. Her deaf husband would sit in the shop with her or walk up and down the street without any hat, hands in pockets, vacantly gazing at the huts or up at the sky. They drank tea six times a day in that house and had four proper meals at the table. In the evening they counted the takings, entered them in the books and then slept soundly.

All three cotton-printing works in Ukleyevo, as well as the owners' homes – the Khrymins' senior, Khrymins' junior and the Kostyukovs' – were on the telephone. The council offices had also been connected, but before long the telephone there was jammed with bugs and cockroaches. The chairman of the district council could barely read or write and began every word in his report with a capital letter; but when the telephone went out of order he remarked, 'Yes, it's going to be tricky without that telephone.'

The Khrymins senior were perpetually suing the Khrymins junior, and the Khrymins junior sometimes quarrelled among themselves and sued each other – then their factory would stand idle for a month or two until they had patched things up: all this provided a source of amusement for the people of Ukleyevo, since each row provoked no end of gossip and malicious talk.

Kostyukov and the Khrymins junior would go out driving on Sundays, running over calves as they tore through Ukleyevo. With her starched petticoats rustling and dressed to kill, Aksinya would stroll up and down the street near the shop; then the Khrymins junior would swoop down and carry her off with them as though they were kidnapping her. Old Tsybukin would drive out to show off his new horse, taking his Barbara with him.

In the evening, when the riding was over and everyone was going to bed, someone would play an expensive-sounding accordion in the Khrymins' junior yard; if the moon was shining, the music stirred and gladdened one's heart and Ukleyevo did not seem such a miserable hole after all.

II

Anisim (the elder son) came home very rarely – only for the principal festivals – but he often sent presents, which he handed to friends from the same village to take back for him, as well as letters written by someone else in a beautiful hand and invariably on good-quality paper, so that they looked like official application forms. They were filled with expressions that Anisim would never have used in conversation, for example: 'My dear Mum and Dad, I'm sending you a pound of herb tea for the *gratification* of your *physical requirements*.' At the foot of each letter the name *Anisim Tsybukin* was scribbled – with a cross-nibbed pen, it seemed – and beneath his signature, in the same beautiful handwriting, would appear the word 'Agent'. These letters were read out loud, several times, and afterwards the old man, deeply moved by them and flushed with excitement, would say, 'There you are, he wouldn't stay at home, wanted to be a scholar instead. Well, if that's what he wants! Each to his own, I say.'

Once, just before Shrovetide, there were torrential rainfalls and sleet. The old man and Barbara went to look out of the window, and lo and behold! – there was Anisim coming from the station on a sledge. This was a complete surprise. When he entered the room, he looked anxious, as though terribly worried by something; he stayed like this for the rest of his visit and he behaved in a rather free-and-easy, off-hand way. He was in no hurry to leave, and it looked as though they had given him the sack. Barbara was glad he had come, eyed him cunningly, sighed and shook her head: 'Don't know what to make of it,' she said. 'The lad's turned twenty-seven and he's still running around like a gay bachelor! Oh, *dear, dear* me!' They could hear her quiet, regular speech – a series of '*dear, dear* me's from the next room. Then she began whispering to the old man and Aksinya, and their faces took on that same cunning, mysterious, conspiratorial expression.

They had decided to marry Anisim off.

'Oh, dear, dear me! Your young brother was married ages ago,' Barbara said, 'but you're still without a mate, just like a cock in the market. What kind of life is that? If you did get married, God willing, you could do as you please, go back to work, while your wife could stay at home and be a help to you. It's a wild life you're leading, my boy, I can see you've really gone off the rails. Oh, dear, dear me, you lot from the town bring nothing but trouble!'

When a Tsybukin married, he could take the prettiest girl, as they were all very wealthy, and they found a pretty one for Anisim too. As for him, he was insignificant and uninteresting: while he was short and had a poorly built, unhealthy-looking body, his cheeks were full and plump – as though he were puffing them out. He never blinked and his eyes had a piercing look. His beard was reddish and straggly, and he was always sticking it in his mouth and biting it when he was deep in thought. Moreover, he was very fond of the bottle – one could tell from his face and the way he walked. But when they told him that a very pretty bride had been found for him, he remarked, 'Well, I'm not exactly a freak. All of us Tsybukins are good-looking, that's for sure.'

The village of Torguyevo lay right next to the town. One half had recently been merged with it, while the other stayed as it was. In the town half there lived a widow, in her own little house. She had a very poor sister, who had to go out to work every day; this sister had a daughter called Lipa, who went out to work as well. Her beauty had long been a talking-point in Torguyevo, but her terrible poverty put everyone off. So they reasoned that perhaps some old man or widower might turn a blind eye to this and would marry her or would 'set her up' in his house – and if that happened the mother would not have to starve. When the local matchmakers told her about Lipa, Barbara drove out to Torguyevo.

After that, an 'inspection'* was arranged (as was proper) at the aunt's house, with snacks and drinks. Lipa wore a new pink dress made especially for the viewing and a crimson ribbon shone like a flame in her hair. She was a thin, pale-faced fragile girl with fine, delicate features and her skin was tanned from working in the open air. Her face bore a perpetual sad, timid smile and her eyes were like a child's – trusting and inquisitive at the same time.

She was young – still a little girl in fact – with scarcely noticeable breasts. However, she was old enough for marriage. In actual fact she was a beauty, and the only objectionable thing about her was her large arms, just like a man's, which she allowed to dangle idly, so that they resembled two huge claws.

'We're not in the least worried that there's no dowry,' the old man told the aunt. 'We took a girl in from a poor family for our son Stepan, and now we can't praise her enough. She's a wonderful help in the house and the business.'

Lipa stood by the door and it seemed she wanted to say, 'You can do what you like with me, I *trust* you,' while her mother, Praskovya, who had to go out charring, was overcome with shyness and shut herself away in the kitchen. Once, when she was still a young girl, a certain merchant (whose floors she used to scrub) suddenly stamped his feet at her in a fit of anger. She was terrified, went numb all over and the shock of it never left her for the rest of her life: her arms and legs were always trembling with fright – and her cheeks as well. From where she sat in the kitchen, she always tried hard to hear what visitors were saying in the next room, kept crossing herself, pressed her fingers

*Old Russian peasant ceremony when the bridegroom and his relatives 'inspected' the prospective bride.

to her forehead and peered at the ikon. A slightly tipsy Anisim would open the kitchen door and breezily inquire, 'What you sitting out here for, my dearest mum? It's so dull without you.' This would make Praskovya turn shy and she would clasp her small, wasted breasts and reply, 'But sir, you really *shouldn't*! I'm only too pleased ... sir!'

After the inspection, the wedding day was fixed. Later on, when he was home, Anisim kept pacing up and down whistling; or something would suddenly spring to mind which made him think hard, look at the floor without moving an inch and stare so hard that it seemed he was trying to bore a hole deep into the earth with his eyes. He didn't show any pleasure at the fact that he was getting married, that it was going to be soon – the week after Easter – nor did he show any inclination to see his bride – all he did was whistle. Obviously he was marrying only because his father and stepmother wanted him to and because that was how things were done in the village: sons got married to have someone to help them in the house. He didn't hurry himself when the time came to leave and his behaviour during this last visit was quite different from the previous one – he was particularly free-and-easy with everyone and kept speaking out of turn.

III

Two dressmakers lived in the village of Shikalovo; they were sisters and belonged to the Flagellant sect. They got the order for the wedding dresses and came over very often for the fittings, when they would sit down for hours drinking tea. For Barbara they made a brown dress, with black lace and tubular glass beads, and Aksinya had a bright green dress, yellow in front and with a train. When they had finished, Tsybukin didn't pay them cash but in things from the shop, and so they went away very down in the mouth, carrying little packets of tallow candles and tins of sardines for which they didn't have any use at all. As soon as they were out of the village and in the fields, they sat down on a little mound and burst into tears.

Anisim turned up just three days before the wedding in a completely new outfit. He wore brilliantly glossy rubber galoshes and instead of a tie had a red lace with tassels hanging from it. A brand-new overcoat was draped over his shoulders like a cloak. After solemnly saying his prayers, he greeted his father and gave him ten silver roubles and ten 50-kopek pieces; he gave Barbara the same, while Aksinya received twenty 25-kopek pieces. The principal charm of these presents was that every single coin was brand-new, as though specially selected, and all of them glinted in the sun. In his effort to appear sober and serious, Anisim tensed his face muscles and puffed his cheeks out; he was reeking of drink.

Most likely he had dashed into every station bar during the journey. Once again there was that same free-and-easy attitude, something strangely exaggerated about his behaviour. After his arrival, Anisim drank tea and ate savouries with his father, while Barbara fingered the bright new roubles and asked him about her friends from the village, now living in the town.

'Everything's okay, thank God, they're all living well,' Anisim said. 'But there was a *certain occurrence* in Ivan Yegorov's *domestic* life: his old woman Sofya passed away. From consumption. The caterers charged them two and a half roubles a head for the *funeral repast* for the *repose of her soul*. There was wine too. Some peasants from our village were there – and they had to pay two and a half roubles for each of them! But they didn't eat a thing. You can't expect yokels to know anything about sauces!'

'Two and a half roubles!' exclaimed the old man, shaking his head.

'Well, what do you expect? It's not like the village. If you drop into a restaurant for a bite, you order this and that, friends come and join you, you have a few drinks and before you know what's happening it's dawn and you've run up a nice little bill of three or four roubles a head. And if Samorodov comes, he likes his coffee and brandy after a meal – and with brandy at sixty kopeks a glass! I ask you!'

'He's all lies,' the old man said delightedly. 'Nothing but lies!'

'These days I'm always with him. He's the same Samorodov who does my letters for me. Writes excellently!'

Anisim turned to Barbara and continued cheerfully, 'If I told you, Mum, what kind of man he is, you'd never believe me. We all call him Mukhtar, as he rather looks like an Armenian – black all over. I can read him like a book, know everything he's up to, like the back of my hand, Mum. He knows it all right and he's behind me the whole time, doesn't leave me alone for one minute. Now we're as thick as thieves. Seems he's scared of me, but he can't do without me. Follows me everywhere. Now, I've very good eyesight, Mum. Just take the old clothes' market. If there's a peasant selling a shirt I say, "Hold on, that's been *stolen*." And as usual I'm always right. It *was* stolen!'

'But how do you know?' Barbara asked.

'I don't *know*, I've just got the eye for it. I didn't know anything about the shirt, but somehow I was drawn to it – it *was* stolen, and that was that. The detectives where I work just say the words, "Look, Anisim's gone shooting woodcock!" That means, "He's gone looking for stolen property." Yes ... *anyone* can steal, but holding on to it's another matter! It's a great big world, but there's no hiding stolen goods!'

'But last week, in the village, the Guntorevs had a ram and two ewes stolen,' Barbara said, sighing. 'Only there was no one to go looking for them, oh, dear, dear me!'

'What? *Of course* you can go looking. It's really very easy.'

The wedding day arrived. Although the weather was cool, it was one of those bright and cheerful days in April. Since early morning, troikas and carriages-and-pairs had been driving round Ukleyevo with bells tinkling and their shaft-bows and horses' manes decorated with gaily coloured ribbons. Disturbed by all this commotion, rooks cawed in the willows and starlings sang incessantly, as hard as they could, so that it seemed they were overjoyed at the Tsybukins' wedding.

Back at the house, the tables were already laden with long fishes, stuffed legs of meat and game-birds, boxes of sprats, different kinds of salted savouries and pickles, and a great quantity of vodka and wine bottles. One could smell the salami and soured lobster. The old man went hopping round the tables clicking his heels and sharpening the knives on each other. Time and again they called out to Barbara to bring them something. Looking quite bewildered and gasping for breath, she would run into the kitchen where Kostyukov's chef and the Khrymins' junior head cook had been slaving away since dawn. Aksinya, with her hair set in curls, wearing just a corset without any dress over it and squeaky new ankle-high boots, dashed round the yard like a whirlwind and all one could catch sight of were bare knees and breasts. It was all very noisy, with swearing and cursing. Passers-by stopped at the wide-open gates and everything indicated that they were preparing for something really special.

'They've gone for the bride!'

Harness bells rang out loud and then died away, far beyond the village ... After two o'clock the villagers came running: they could hear the bells again, the bride was coming! The church was full, chandeliers shone brightly, and the choirboys sang from music-sheets, as the old man Tsybukin had specially requested this. The glare of the candles and the bright dresses dazzled Lipa, and the choirboys' loud voices seemed to beat on her head like hammers; her corset (it was the first time she had ever worn one) and her shoes were pinching her to death; from her expression it seemed she had fainted and was just coming to – she looked around without understanding anything.

Anisim stood there in that same black frock-coat, with a red lace instead of a tie; he was in a very thoughtful mood, kept staring at the same spot and crossed himself hastily whenever the choirboys sang very loud. He felt deeply moved and wanted to cry. He was familiar with this church from early childhood; his late mother had brought him there once to take the sacrament and once he had sung in the choir with the other boys. So he remembered every nook and cranny, every ikon. Now he was being married, because that was the *right* thing to do; but he wasn't thinking about that at all and he seemed to have forgotten it completely. He could not see the ikons for tears and his heart was heavy. He prayed and implored God to make those unavoidable misfortunes that were threatening to shower down on him any day now pass him by somehow, just as storm clouds pass over a village during a drought, without shedding a single drop of rain. So many sins from his past accumulated – so many, in fact, that it was impossible to shrug them off or expiate them now – that even to ask for pardon was ridiculous. But he *did* ask to be forgiven and even sobbed out loud; but everyone ignored him, thinking that he was drunk.

Then a frightened child started crying, '*Please*, Mummy dear, take me away from here!'

'Be quiet over there!' shouted the priest.

On the way back from the church, villagers flocked after the couple. Outside the shop, at the gates and beneath the windows overlooking the yard, there were crowds too. The village women had come to sing in their honour. Hardly had the young couple crossed the threshold than the choirboys (already stationed in the hall with their music-sheets) sang as hard as they could, at the top of their shrill voices. Then the band, specially hired from the town, struck up. Sparkling Don wine was already being served in long glasses and Yelizarov, the jobbing carpenter – a tall lean man whose eyebrows were so bushy they nearly covered his eyes – turned to the young couple and said, 'Anisim – and *you*, my child – love one another, live like good Christians and the Holy Virgin will not forsake you.'

He fell on the old man's shoulder and sobbed. 'Grigory Tsybukin, let us weep, let us weep for joy!' he said in his thin little voice and then he suddenly laughed out loud and continued – this time lowering his voice, 'Oho! Your daughter-in-law's a real smasher. She's got everything in the right place, she's running nice and smooth, no rattling – all the machinery is in tip-top order – and there's plenty of screws.'

He came from around Yegoryevsk, but he had worked in the Ukleyevo factories and local workshops since he was a young boy, and that's where his roots were. For as long as the people had known him, he had always been that same thin, tall old man – and he had always gone by the name of 'Crutchy'. Perhaps as a result of spending over forty years doing nothing else but repairs in factories, he judged everybody and everything solely in terms of soundness: did it need repairing? And even before he sat down at the table, he tested a few chairs to see if they were all right – and he also gave the salmon a poke.

After the sparkling wine, everyone sat down at the table. The wedding-guests talked and moved their chairs. The choirboys sang in the hall, the band played, and at the same time the village women sang out in the yard, their voices all at the same pitch, which produced such a horrible, wild jumble of sounds it made one's head reel. Crutchy fidgeted on his chair, elbowed the people sitting next to him, didn't let them get a word in, and cried and laughed out loud in turn. 'My children! My little *children* ... little children!' he muttered swiftly. 'My dearest Aksinya, my sweet little Barbara, let's all live peacefully together ... my darlings ...'

He never drank very much and now one glass of strong vodka made him tipsy. This revolting brew, concocted from God knows what, made all who drank it so muzzy they felt they had been clubbed. Tongues began to falter.

The clergy was there, factory clerks and their wives, and inn-keepers from other villages. The chairman of the parish council and his clerk, who had been working together for as long as fourteen years now – during the whole course of which they had never signed a single document – and who never let anyone leave the office without first cheating and insulting him, had positioned their fat, well-fed selves next to each other. They had lived on lies for so long, it seemed that even the skin on their faces had taken on a peculiarly criminal complexion all of its own. The clerk's wife, a scraggy woman with a squint, had brought all her children along; just like a bird of prey she looked at the plates out of the corner of her eye and grabbed everything within reach, stuffing it away in her children's pockets and her own.

Lipa sat there like a stone and she looked the same as she did during the service. Not having exchanged a single word with her since their first meeting, Anisim still didn't know what her voice was like.

And now, even though he was sitting right next to her, he still didn't break the silence and drank vodka instead. But when he was drunk, however, he began to speak to his aunt, who was sitting on the other side of the table: 'I've a friend called Samorodov, he's a bit out of the ordinary, respected everywhere and a good talker too. But I can see right through him, Auntie, and he knows it. Will you please join me in toasting Samorodov's health, Auntie dear!'

Barbara went round the table serving the guests; she was worn-out, confused, and clearly pleased that there were so many different dishes and that everything had been done so lavishly – *no one* could criticize her now. The sun had set, but still the dinner went on. Now they no longer knew what they were eating or drinking and it was impossible to catch a word they said. Only now and then, when the band stopped playing for a moment, could one hear – quite distinctly – a peasant woman outside shouting, 'You've sucked us dry, you rotten bastards. You can all go to hell!'

In the evening there was dancing with music. The Khrymins junior arrived with their own drink and during the quadrille one of them held a bottle in each hand and a glass in his mouth, which everyone found highly amusing. Halfway through the quadrille they suddenly started dancing Cossack style. Aksinya flashed round the room, a green blur, and her train set up little gusts of wind. Somebody trod on one of her frills down below and Crutchy shouted, 'Hey, you've torn her skirting-board off! Oh, *children*!'

Aksinya had grey, naïve-looking eyes that seldom blinked and a naïve smile constantly played over her face. There was something snake-like in those unblinking eyes, in that small head and long neck, in that shapely figure. As she surveyed the guests in her green dress with its yellow front, she resembled a viper peering up out of the young spring rye at someone walking past – its body erect and head raised high. The Khrymins took liberties with her and it was glaringly obvious that she had been having an affair with the eldest for a long time now. But the deaf husband didn't notice a thing and he didn't even look at her. He merely sat there with his legs crossed, eating nuts, making such a racket as he cracked them with his teeth that it sounded like pistol shots.

And now old Tsybukin himself strode into the middle of the room and waved his handkerchief – a signal that he wanted to join in the Cossack dancing. A rumble of approval ran through the whole house – and through the crowd outside in the yard as well: 'It's the *old boy himself*. He's going to *dance*!'

In fact, only Barbara did the dancing, while the old man simply fluttered his handkerchief and shuffled his heels. In spite of this, the people out in the yard hung on to one another's back to get a good view through the windows, and they were absolutely delighted: for one brief moment they forgave him everything – his wealth *and* the insults they had suffered.

'That's me boy, Grigory!' someone shouted. 'Come on, have a go! You can still do it! Ha, ha!'

The celebrations finished late – after one o'clock in the morning. Anisim staggered over to the choirboys and the band and tipped all of them a new half-rouble piece. The old man, without tottering, but still hopping on one foot, saw the guests off and told everybody, 'That wedding cost two thousand.'

As they were leaving, the publican from Shikalovo discovered that his fine new coat had been exchanged for an old one. Anisim suddenly flared up and yelled, 'Hold on! I'll find it right away! I know who took it! Just wait a moment!'

He ran out into the street and chased after someone, but they caught him, hauled him back to the house by the arms – he was drunk, red with anger and soaking-wet – bundled him into the room where Auntie had been helping Lipa to undress and locked him in.

IV

Five days passed. When Anisim was ready to leave, he went upstairs to say good-bye to Barbara. All the ikon lamps in her room were burning and there was a strong smell of incense. She was sitting by the window knitting a red woollen sock.

'You didn't stay very long,' she said. 'Got bored, did you? Dear, dear me ... We live well here, we've got plenty of everything, *and* we did the right thing by you and gave you a proper wedding. The old man said it cost two thousand. So I'll come straight to the point. We live in the lap of luxury here, only I find it all a bit boring. And don't we treat the peasants *badly*? It plain makes my heart ache, dear, to think how we treat them. My God! Whether it's horse-dealing, buying, taking on a new workman – we do nothing but cheat ... cheat ... cheat. That butter we sell in the shop has turned rancid and rotten – some people's tar is better! Tell me, why can't we sell decent stuff, eh?'

'It's none of my business, Mum.'

'But we're all going to die one day, aren't we? You really should have a good talk with your father! ...'

'No, *you* should talk to him.'

'Now, enough of that ... I'll say my piece and then he'll tell me – just like you, without beating about the bush – that it's *none of my business*. They'll show you in heaven, they will, whose business it is! God is *just*.'

'Well of course, there's no chance of *that*,' Anisim said, sighing. 'There is no God anyway, Mum. So who's going to tell me what I should do?'

Barbara looked at him in amazement, burst out laughing and clasped her hands together. Her sincere astonishment at what he had just said, together with the way she was looking at him as though he were some kind of crank, deeply embarrassed him.

'Perhaps there is a God, but I don't believe in him,' he said. 'All through the wedding service I didn't feel myself at all. Imagine you just took an egg from underneath a hen while the chick's still cheeping inside it ... Well, my conscience suddenly started cheeping and while we were being married I kept thinking that God did exist! But as soon as I was outside the church it had all gone from my mind! Anyway, how do you expect me to know if there's a God or not? We weren't taught about him, right from the time we were very young, and a young baby can still be sucking his mother's breasts and all they teach him is mind your own business. Dad doesn't believe in God either, does he? You said once that the Guntorevs had some sheep stolen ... *I* found out it was that peasant from Shikalovo. He stole them, but it's Dad who's got the skins! There's religion for you!' Anisim winked and shook his head.

'The chairman of the parish council doesn't believe in God, either,' he went on, 'nor does the clerk, nor the lay-reader. And if they do go to church to keep the Fasts it's only so that people won't go saying nasty things about them – and just *in case* there *is* a Day of Judgement, after all. Now they're all talking as if the end of the world has come, because people have got slack in their ways, don't respect their parents and so on. That's a load of rubbish. Now, the way I see it, Mum, is that all unhappiness comes from people not having a conscience. I can see right through them, Mum, *I* understand. I can see if a man's wearing a stolen shirt or not. Take someone sitting in a pub* – you might think all he's doing is just drinking tea. But tea or no tea, *I* can tell if he's got a conscience. You can go around all day and not find anyone with a conscience, all because people don't know if there's a God or not ... Well, good-bye, Mum, I wish you long life and happiness – and don't think too badly of me.'

Anisim bowed very low. 'Thanks for everything, Mum,' he added. 'You're a real help to the family, a right good woman and I'm very pleased with you.'

Anisim felt deeply moved as he left the room, but he came straight back and said, 'Samorodov's got me mixed up in some deal: it'll make or break me. If the worst should happen, Mum, please comfort my Dad.'

*In the old Russian *traktir* tea as well as alcohol used to be served.

'What are you on about now? Dear, dear me! God is merciful. And *you*, Anisim, should show that wife of yours a little affection or you'll be turning your noses up at each other. You should both smile a bit, really!'

'But she's such a strange one ...' Anisim said with a sigh. 'Doesn't understand anything, never says anything. But she's still very young, I must give her a chance to grow up a little.'

A tall, well-fed white stallion, harnessed to a cabriolet, was already waiting at the front door.

Old Tsybukin came running up, leaped into it with the energy of a young man and grasped the reins. Anisim exchanged kisses with Barbara, Aksinya and his brother. Lipa was standing at the front door as well, quite still, and her eyes were turned to one side, as though she had not come to see him off at all but just happened to have turned up for some mysterious reason. Anisim went over to her, barely touched her cheek with his lips and said, 'Good-bye.' She didn't look at him and she smiled very strangely. Her face was trembling and everyone felt somewhat sorry for her. Anisim also leaped in and sat there with hands on hips, so convinced he was of his good looks.

As they drove up out of the gully, Anisim kept looking back at the village. It was a fine warm day. For the first time that year, cattle had been led out to graze and young girls and women were walking round the herd in their holiday dresses. A brown bull bellowed, rejoicing in its freedom, and pawed the earth with its front hoofs. Larks were singing everywhere – on the ground and high up above. Anisim glanced back at the graceful church, which had recently been white-washed, and he remembered that he had prayed there five days ago. And he looked back at the school, with its green roof, at the river where he once swam or tried to catch fish, and his heart thrilled with joy. He wanted a wall suddenly to rise up out of the ground to block his path, so that he could remain there, with only the past.

They went into the station bar and drank a glass of sherry. The old man started fumbling about in his pocket for his purse.

'Drinks on me,' Anisim said.

The old man clapped him affectionately on the shoulder and winked at the barman, as though wanting to say, 'See what a son I've got!'

'Anisim, you should really stay here with us and help in the business,' he said. 'You'd be priceless! I'd load you with money, from head to foot, dear boy!'

The sherry had a sourish taste and smelled of sealing-wax, but they both drank another glass.

When the old man got back from the station, he did not recognize his younger daughter-in-law any more. The moment her husband left, Lipa changed completely and became bright and cheerful. In her bare feet, with her sleeves tucked right up to her shoulders, she washed the staircase in the hall and sang in a thin, silvery voice. And when she carried the huge tub full of dirty water outside and looked at the sun with that childish smile of hers, she was like a skylark herself.

An old workman, who was passing the front door, shook his head and wheezed, 'Oh yes, Grigory, that's a fine daughter-in-law God's blessed you with. No ordernery girl, but a real treasure!'

V

On 8 July (a Friday), 'Crutchy' Yelizarov and Lipa were coming back from their pilgrimage to the village of Kazansk, where the Festival of Our Lady of Kazan had been celebrated. Lipa's mother, Praskovya, lagged a long way behind, as she was in poor health and short of breath. It was late afternoon.

As he listened to Lipa, Crutchy kept making startled 'oohs' and 'ahs'.

'I just love jam, Mr Yelizarov!' Lipa said. 'I like to sit in a little corner, all on my own and just drink tea with jam in it. Or if Barbara drinks a cup with me, she tells me things that I find really touching. They've piles of jam, four jars in all, and they say, "Eat up, Lipa, don't be shy." '

'Aah! Four jars!'

'They live very well and give you white rolls with your tea and as much beef as you want. Yes, they live well, only it's a bit scary there, Yelizarov, ooh, so *scary*!'

'What's scary, dear?' Crutchy asked, as he looked back to see how far behind Praskovya was.

'To begin with, as soon as the wedding was over, I got scared of Anisim. He'd done nothing nasty to me, but I had the shivers all over, in every bone, every time he came near. At night I couldn't sleep a wink and I kept shaking all over and prayed to God. But now it's Aksinya I'm frightened of, Mr Yelizarov. She's all right really, always smiling. It's only when she looks out of the window, her eyes get so angry, all green and burning – just like a sheep in its shed. Those young Khrymins are always leading her astray. "Your old man's got a bit of land at Butyokhino, more than a hundred acres," they tell her. "There's sand and water, so you could build a brickworks there, Aksinya, we'll go halves." Bricks are nearly twenty roubles a thousand now, could be a good thing. So yesterday Aksinya goes and tells the old man, "I want to start a brickworks at Butyokhino, I'll be in charge myself." She smiled when she said this, but Mr Tsybukin gave her a blank look and didn't seem at all pleased. So he says, "While I'm alive, I'm not going to start dividing everything up, we must do everything together." But she looked daggers at him and ground her teeth ... then we had pancakes, but *she* wouldn't touch them!'

'A–ah!' Crutchy said in amazement. 'Wouldn't touch 'em!'

'And you should just see the way she sleeps!' Lipa continued. 'She'll doze off for half an hour, then all of a sudden she'll jump up and start running round to see if the peasants have started a fire or stolen anything ... It's *terrible* being with her, Mr Yelizarov! Those Khrymin sons didn't go to bed after the wedding, but went straight off to town to bring the law on each other. And they say it's all Aksinya's doing. Two of the brothers promised to build her the brickyard, which made the third one mad. As the mill was shut down then for a month, my Uncle Prokhor had no work and had to go begging for scraps round people's backyards. So I said, "Look, Uncle, until it's open again, why don't you go and do some ploughing or woodchopping, why bring shame on yourself like this!" So he said, "Lost the 'abit of farm work I 'ave, can't do nothing, Lipa dear." '

They stopped by a young aspen grove for a rest and to wait until Praskovya caught them up. Yelizarov had been a jobbing carpenter for some time but, as he didn't have a horse, he used to go round the entire district on foot and all he took with him was a little bag of bread and onions. He took long strides, swinging his arms, and it was hard to keep up with him.

A boundary post stood at the entrance to the grove and Yelizarov tested it with his hands to see if it was sound. Then along came

Praskovya, gasping for breath. Her wrinkled, perpetually anxious face beamed with happiness. That same day she had gone to church, like the others, and then she went along to the fair and had a drink of pear kvass.* This was so unusual for her that now she even felt – for the first time in her life – she was really enjoying herself. After they had rested, all three of them started off again together. The sun had already set and its rays pierced the leaves and shone on the tree-trunks. They could hear loud shouting ahead – the girls of Ukleyevo had been out a long time before them but had stopped there in the grove, most probably to pick mushrooms.

'Hey, me g–irls,' Yelizarov shouted. 'Hey, me beauties!'

He was answered by laughter.

'Crutchy's coming! *Crutchy*, you silly old fogey!'

And their echoing voices sounded like laughter as well. Now the grove was behind them. They could already see the tops of factory chimneys and the glittering cross on the belfry. This was the village, the same one where 'the lay-reader ate all the caviare at a funeral'.

Now they were almost home and had only to go down into that great gully. Lipa and Praskovya, who had been walking barefoot, sat down on the grass to put their shoes on and the carpenter sat down beside them. From high up, Ukleyevo looked pretty and peaceful with its willows and white church, its little river – a view spoiled only by the factory chimneys which had been painted a nasty dark grey: they had used cheap paint to save money. On the slope on the far side they could see rye lying in stooks and sheaves, scattered all over the place as if blown around in a storm; some of the rye lay in freshly cut swathes. The oats were ready as well and shone like mother-of-pearl in the sun. It was the height of harvest-time, but that day was a rest day. The following morning, a Saturday, they would be gathering in the rye and hay, and then they would rest again on the Sunday. Every day distant thunder rumbled; it was close and humid, and rain seemed to be in the air. As they looked at the fields, the villagers only thought about one thing – that, God willing, they would get the harvesting done in time – and they felt cheerful, gay and anxious all at once.

'Reapers cost money these days,' Praskovya exclaimed. 'One rouble forty a day!'

*A fermented drink made from malt, rye or different kinds of fruit.

Meanwhile more and more people kept pouring in from the fair at Kazansk. Peasant women, factory-hands wearing new caps, beggars, children . . . A cart would rumble past in a cloud of dust, with an unsold horse (which seemed very pleased at the fact) trotting along behind it; then came an obstinate cow, which was being dragged along by the horns; then another cart rolled past, full of drunken peasants who let their legs dangle over the sides. One old woman came past with a boy who wore a large hat and big boots; he was exhausted by the heat and the weight of the boots, which didn't let him bend his knees, but in spite of this he kept blowing his toy trumpet for all he was worth. Even after they had reached the bottom of the gully and turned down the main street, the trumpet could still be heard.

'Those factory owners ain't themselves at all,' Yelizarov said. 'Something shocking, it is! Kostyukov got mad at me. He says, "That's a lot of wood you've used for the cornices." "How come?" I says, "only as much as was needed, Mr Kostyukov. I don't eat them planks with me porridge." "*What?*" he says, "how dare you, you blockhead, you riff-raff!" Then he starts shouting away, "Don't forget, I made a contractor out of you." "So what?" I replies. "Before I was a carpenter, I still 'ad me cup of tea every day." And he replies, "You're crooks, the whole lot of you . . ." I says nothing and thinks to meself, "Oho! I may be a crook in this world, but you'll be doing the swindling in the *next*." Next day he changes his tune: "Now don't get mad at what I said. If I went a bit too far, it's only because I belong to the merchants' guild, which means I'm your *superior* and you shouldn't answer back." So I says to him, "Okay, you're a big noise in the merchants' guild, and I'm only a carpenter. But Saint Joseph was a carpenter as well. Our work is honest and is pleasing to God. But if you think you're superior, then that's all right by me, Mr Kostyukov." After this – I mean after our talk – I starts thinking to meself, "Who *is* superior, really? A big merchant or a carpenter?" Well, of course, it must be the carpenter, children!'

Crutchy pondered for a moment and went on, 'That's how things are. It's those what work and doesn't give in what's superior.'

The sun had set and a thick, milk-white mist was rising over the river, the fences and the clearings near the factories. And now with darkness swiftly advancing and lights twinkling down below, when that mist seemed to be hiding a bottomless abyss, Lipa and her mother, who were born beggars and were resigned to stay beggars for the rest of their lives, surrendering everything except their own frightened souls to others – perhaps even *they* imagined, for one fleeting moment, that they mattered in that vast mysterious universe, where countless lives were being lived out, and that they had a certain strength and were better than someone else. They felt good sitting up there, high above the village and they smiled happily, forgetting that eventually they would have to go back down again.

At last they arrived home. Reapers were sitting on the ground by the gates close to the shop. The Ukleyevo peasants usually refused to do any work for Tsybukin and farm-hands had to be taken on from other villages; and now, in the darkness, it seemed that everyone sitting there had a long black beard. The shop was open and through the doorway one could see the deaf brother playing draughts with a boy. The reapers sang so softly it was hard to hear anything; when they weren't singing, they would start shouting out loud for yesterday's wages. But they were deliberately not paid, to stop them leaving before the next day. Old Tsybukin, wearing a waistcoat, without any frock-coat, was sitting drinking tea with Aksinya on the front-door steps under a birch tree. A lamp was burning on the table. 'Grandpa!' one of the reapers called out teasingly from the other side of the gates. 'Grandpa, at least pay us half!'

Immediately there was laughter and then the singing continued, still barely audible . . . Crutchy joined them for tea.

'Well, I mean to say, there we were at the fair,' he began. 'Having a great time, children, God be praised, when something nasty happened. Sashka, the blacksmith, bought some tobacco, and paid the man half a rouble.' Crutchy took a look round and continued. 'But it was a *bad* one.' He was trying to keep his voice down to a whisper, but only managed to produce a hoarse, muffled sound which everyone could hear. 'Yes, it was forged all right. So the man asked, "Where did you get it?" And Sashka says, "Anisim Tsybukin gave me it when I was enjoying meself at his wedding . . ." So they calls the policeman, who takes him away . . . You'd better watch out, Grigory, in case anybody gets to hear . . .'

Again came that teasing voice from behind the gates: 'Gra–and–pa!' Then all was quiet.

'Ah, me dear children,' Crutchy muttered rapidly as he got up – he was feeling very drowsy – 'thanks for the tea and sugar. Time for bed. I'm all mouldering, me timbers is rotting away. Ha, ha, ha!'

As he left, he said, 'It must be time for me to die!' and he burst out sobbing.

Old Tsybukin did not finish his tea, but still sat there thinking. From his expression it seemed he was listening to Crutchy's footsteps, although he was well down the street by then.

'That blacksmith, Sashka, was lying, perhaps,' Aksinya said, reading his thoughts.

He went into the house and emerged with a small packet, and when he undid it, brand-new roubles glinted. He picked one up, bit it and threw it on to the tray. Then he threw another ...

'No doubt about it, they're forged,' he murmured and gave Aksinya a bewildered look. 'They're the same as those Anisim gave away at the wedding.'

Then he thrust the packet into her hands and whispered, 'Take them, go on, take them and throw them down the well, blast 'em. And don't say a thing, in case there's trouble. Clear the samovar away and put the lamps out ...'

As they sat in the shed, Lipa and Praskovya saw the lights go out, one by one. Only upstairs, in Barbara's room, were there some red and blue ikon lamps still burning and their glow imparted a feeling of peace, contentment and blissful ignorance. Praskovya just could not get used to the idea of her daughter being married to a rich man and when she came to visit them she would cower in the hall and smile pleadingly – then they would send her some tea and sugar. It was the same with Lipa, and as soon as her husband went away she did not sleep in her own bed any more, but anywhere she could – in the kitchen or the barn; every day she scrubbed the floor or did the laundry and she felt she was being used as a charwoman. Now that they were back from their pilgrimage they drank tea in the kitchen with the cook, then went into the shed and lay down between the sledge and the wall. It was dark there and smelled of horse-collars. All around the house lights went out and then they could hear the deaf brother locking the shop and the reapers settling down to sleep in the open. A long way off, at the Khrymin sons' house, someone was playing that expensive accordion . . . Praskovya and Lipa began to doze off.

When someone's footsteps woke them up everything was bright in the moonlight. Aksinya stood at the entrance to the shed with bedclothes in her arms. 'It's cooler out here, I think,' she murmured. Then she came in and lay down, almost on the threshold; she was bathed in moonlight from head to foot. She could not sleep and breathed heavily, tossed and turned from the heat, and threw off most of the bedclothes. How proud and beautiful she looked in the magical moonlight. A few moments passed and those footsteps could be heard again. The white figure of the old man appeared in the doorway.

'Aksinya,' he called. 'Are you here?'

'Well!' she answered angrily.

'Yesterday I told you to throw that money down the well. Did you?'

'What do you take me for, throwing good money into the water!'

'Oh, my God!' the old man muttered in terror and amazement. 'You're a real troublemaker . . . Oh, God in heaven . . .'

He wrung his hands and went away mumbling something under his breath. A few moments later Aksinya sat down and heaved a deep sigh of annoyance. Then she got up, bundled her bedclothes together and went outside.

'Mother, why did you let me marry into *this* family!' Lipa said.

'People have to get married, my dear daughter. It's not for us to say.'

And a feeling of inconsolable grief threatened to overwhelm them. At the same time they thought that someone was looking down on them from the very heights of heaven, out of the deep blue sky where the stars were, and that he could see everything that was happening in Ukleyevo and was watching over them. However much evil existed in the world, the night was still calm and beautiful, and there was, and always would be, truth in God's universe, a truth that was just as calm and beautiful. The whole earth was only waiting to merge with that truth, just as the moonlight blended into the night.

Both of them were soothed by these thoughts and they fell asleep, snuggling up close to each other.

VI

The news of Anisim's arrest for forging and passing counterfeit money had reached the village a long time ago. Months went by – more than half of the year: the long winter was past, spring arrived and everyone in the house and village was now used to the idea that Anisim was in prison. Whenever they passed the shop or the house at night-time they would be reminded of this. And the sound of the church bells, for some reason, also reminded them that Anisim was in prison awaiting trial.

A deep shadow seemed to be overhanging the yard. The house had grown dirty, the roof was rusty and the green paint on the heavy iron-bound shop door was peeling off and had become discoloured – or, as the deaf brother put it, had gone 'all scabby'. And old Tsybukin himself seemed to have turned a dark colour. For a long time now he hadn't trimmed his beard or his hair, which gave him a shaggy look, and no longer did he leap perkily into his carriage or shout, 'God'll feed yer!' to beggars. His strength was failing and everything he did showed it. The villagers were not so scared of him any longer and the local constable sent in a report about what was going on in the shop – although he still received his share of the money. Tsybukin was summoned three times to the town to stand trial for the secret dealing in spirits; but the case was always postponed because witnesses kept failing to turn up, and all this was sheer torture for the old man.

He frequently visited his son, hired lawyers, submitted appeals, and donated banners to churches. He bought the governor of Anisim's prison a silver glass-holder enamelled with the words: 'Moderation in all things', together with a long spoon.

'There's no one to help us, no one we can turn to,' Barbara said. 'Oh, dear, dear me ... We should ask one of those gents to write to those what's in charge ... If only they could let him out before the trial! It's wicked tormenting a young lad like that!'

Although she was very distressed, Barbara had put on weight, her skin was whiter, and as before she lit the ikon lamps in her room and made sure everything in the house was spotless, serving guests with jam and apple flans. The deaf brother and Aksinya worked in the shop. They had started a new business – the brickyard at Butyokhino – and

Aksinya travelled out there nearly every day in a springless carriage. She drove herself and if she happened to pass friends on the way she would crane her neck, like a snake in the young rye, and give them a naïve and enigmatic smile. Meanwhile Lipa spent the whole time playing with her baby, who was born before Lent. It was a little boy, a skinny, pathetic, tiny thing, and it seemed strange that he could cry and could see, that he was a human being and even had a name – Nikifor. As he lay in his cradle, Lipa would walk over to the door, curtsey and say, 'Hello, Nikifor Tsybukin.' She would dash over and kiss him, and then go back to the door, curtsey again and repeat, 'Hello, Nikifor Tsybukin!' He would kick his little red legs up in the air and his cries mingled with laughter – just like Yelizarov the carpenter.

Finally the day of the trial was fixed and the old man left five days before it was due to start. Later they heard that some peasants from the village had been hauled in as witnesses. An old workman was summoned as well and off he went.

The trial started on a Thursday, but Sunday came and still the old man had not returned, and there was no news at all. Late on the Tuesday afternoon, Barbara was sitting at the open window listening out for the old man. In the next room Lipa was playing with her baby, tossing him up in the air and catching him in her arms.

'You're going to be such a big man, oh so big!' she told him in raptures. 'You'll be a farm worker and we'll go out to work together in the fields. We'll go out to work!'

'Well, well,' Barbara said in a very offended voice. 'What kind of work do you think you're going to do, you stupid cow. *He's* going to be a merchant like us! . . .'

Lipa began to sing softly, but soon stopped and told the child again, 'You're going to grow up into such a big, big man! You'll be a farm worker, we'll go out to work together!'

'Oh, so it's all arranged then!'

Lipa stopped in the doorway with Nikifor in her arms and asked, 'Mummy dear, why do I love him so much?' Then she continued in a trembling voice, and her eyes glistened with tears, 'Why do I feel so sorry for him? Who is he? *What* is he, after all? He's as light as a feather or a crumb, but I love him, just like a real human being. He's quite helpless, can't say anything, but I can always tell what he wants from his dear little eyes.'

Barbara listened hard: in the distance she could make out the sound of the evening train drawing into the station. Was the old man on it? She no longer heard or understood what Lipa was saying, nor did she notice how the minutes ticked by: all she did was shake all over – not with fear but intense curiosity. She saw a cartful of peasants quickly rumble past: these were witnesses returning from the station. As the cart went by, the old workman leapt out and came into the yard, where she could hear people welcoming and questioning him.

'All rights and property taken away,' he said in a loud voice, 'and six years' hard labour in Siberia.'

They saw Aksinya coming out of the shop by the back door. She had just been selling some paraffin and she was holding the bottle in one hand and a funnel in the other. Some silver coins stuck out of her mouth.

'Where's Father?' she lisped.

'Still at the station,' the workman replied. 'Said 'e'll be along when it's a bit darker.'

When the news about Anisim's sentence to hard labour reached the yard, the cook started wailing in the kitchen, like someone lamenting the dead – she thought that the occasion called for it – 'Oh, Anisim Tsybukin, why have you left us, our very dearest . . .'

This frightened the dogs and they started barking. Barbara ran over to the window in a fit of despair and screamed out to the cook as hard as she could, 'Sto–op it, Stepanida, sto–op it! For Christ's sake, don't torture us!'

They forgot to put the samovar on and in fact they couldn't concentrate on anything. Only Lipa had no idea what had happened and she just carried on nursing her baby.

When the old man got back from the station, they did not ask him a thing. He greeted them and then wandered from room to room without saying a word. He didn't have any supper.

'We've no one to turn to . . .' Barbara said when she was alone with the old man. 'I asked you to go and see if any of them gents could do anything, but you wouldn't listen. We should have appealed . . .'

'But I *did* try,' the old man replied, waving his arm. 'As soon as they sentenced Anisim I went up to the gent what was defending him and he said, "There's nothing I can do, it's too late." Anisim says it's too late, as well. But the moment I got out of that courtroom I made a deal with a lawyer and gave him a little something in advance . . . I'll wait and see for another week, then I'll go and have another try. It's all in the hands of God.'

The old man silently wandered around the house, and then came back and told Barbara, 'I must be sickening for something. My head's going round and round, everything's all jumbled up.'

He shut the door so that Lipa couldn't hear and continued in a soft voice, 'There's trouble with that money. You remember the first week after Easter, just before the wedding, Anisim brought me some new roubles and half roubles? I hid one of the packets but somehow or other the others got mixed up with my own money . . . Now when Uncle Dmitry, God rest his soul, was alive, he always went to Moscow or the Crimea to buy goods. He had a wife and once when he was away she started larking around with another man. She had six children. When he'd a drop or two he used to laugh. "Just can't sort 'em out," he says, "which ones are mine and which aren't." Now, I can't make out what money's real and what's forged. Looks like it's all forged.'

'Well, for heaven's sake now!'

'I goes and buys my ticket at the station, hands over three roubles and I starts thinking they're forged. Scared the living daylights out of me. That's why I'm feeling so bad.'

'Look, we're all in the hands of God,' Barbara murmured, shaking her head. 'That's something you should be thinking of, Grigory. Who knows what may happen, you're not young any more. Once you're dead and gone, they'll do your grandson an injury. Oh, I'm so frightened they'll do something to Nikifor! You might as well say he's got no father, and his mother's so young and stupid . . . You ought to put something by for him – at least some land. Yes, what about Butyokhino? Think about it!'

Barbara kept on trying to persuade him, adding, 'He's a pretty boy, it's such a shame. Now, there's no point in waiting, just go tomorrow and sign the papers.'

'Yes, I'd forgotten about my little grandson,' Tsybukin said. 'I must go and see him. You say there's nothing wrong with him? Well then, may he grow up healthy – God willing!'

He opened the door and curled his finger, beckoning Lipa over to him. She went up to him with the baby in her arms.

'Now Lipa, dear, you only have to tell me if there's anything you need,' he said. 'You can have whatever you like to eat, we won't grudge you anything. You must keep your strength up.' He made the sign of the cross over the baby. 'And look after my grandson. I haven't got a son any more, just a grandson.' Tears streamed down his cheeks. He sobbed and left the room. Soon afterwards he went to bed and fell into a deep sleep – after seven sleepless nights.

VII

The old man made a short trip into town. Someone had told Aksinya that he had gone to see a solicitor to make his will and that Butyokhino (where she was running the brickworks) had been left to his grandson Nikifor. She learned this one morning when the old man and Barbara were sitting by the front door, drinking tea in the shade of the birch tree. Aksinya locked the front and back doors to the shop, collected as many keys as she could find and flung them at the old man's feet.

'I'm not working for the likes of you any more,' she shouted and suddenly burst out sobbing. 'Seems I'm your charwoman, not your daughter-in-law any more! Everyone's laughing at me and says, "Just look what a fine worker the Tsybukins have found for themselves!" But you didn't take me in as a housemaid. I'm not a beggar or a common slut, I have a mother and father.'

Without wiping her tears away, she glared at the old man; her eyes were brimming over with tears, had an evil look and squinted angrily. She shouted so hard her face and neck were red and taut from the effort. 'I'm not going to slave for you *any* more, I've worn myself to the bone! I'm expected to work all day long in the shop and sneak out for vodka at night, while you go and give land away to a convict's wife and her little devil. She's the lady of the house round here and I'm her slave. So give that convict's wife the lot and may she choke! *I'm* going home. Find yourself another fool, you damned bastard!'

The old man had never used bad language or punished his children and he just could not imagine one of his own family speaking rudely to him or being disrespectful. And now he was scared out of his wits. He rushed into the house and hid behind a cupboard. Barbara was so petrified she just could not stand up and she waved her arms in the air as though shooing a bee away.

'Oh, what's going on?' she muttered in horror. 'What's she shouting like that for? Oh, dear, dear me . . . The people will hear, please, please be quiet!'

'You've given Butyokhino to a convict's bird,' Aksinya went on shouting. 'Well, you can give her the whole lot, I don't want anything from you! You can all go to hell! You're a gang of crooks, all of you. I've seen enough now and I've had just about enough! You're just like bandits, you've robbed the old and the young, anyone who comes near! *Who* sold vodka without a licence! And what about the forged coins? You've stuffed your money-boxes full of them and now you don't need me any more!'

By now a crowd had gathered outside the wide-open gates and was staring into the yard.

'Let them look!' Aksinya screamed. 'I'll disgrace the lot of you. I'll make you burn with shame! You'll come grovelling!'

She called out to her deaf husband, 'Hey, Stepan, let's go home – and *this minute*! We'll go back to my mother and father, I don't want to live with convicts. Get ready!'

Washing was hanging on the line in the yard. She tore her skirts and blouses off (they were still damp) and threw them into her deaf husband's arms. Then, in a blind fury, she rushed round all the clothes-lines and tore everything down, other people's washing as well, hurled it on the ground and trampled all over it.

'Good God, stop her!' Barbara groaned. 'Who does she think she is? Let her have Butyokhino, let her have it, for Christ's sake!'

The people standing by the gates said, 'What a wo–oman, what a woman! She's really blown her top. It's shocking!'

Aksinya dashed into the kitchen, where they were doing laundry. Lipa was working there on her own, and the cook had gone down to the river to rinse some clothes. Clouds of steam rose from the tub and the cauldron by the stove, and the kitchen was dark and stuffy in the thick haze. A pile of dirty clothes lay on the floor and Nikifor was lying on a bench right next to it, so that he would not hurt himself if he fell off. He was kicking his little red legs up. Just as Aksinya came in, Lipa pulled her blouse out of the pile, put it in the tub and reached out for the large ladle of boiling water on the table.

'Give that to me!' Aksinya said, looking at her hatefully. Then she pulled the blouse out of the tub. 'Don't touch my things! You're a convict's wife and it's time you knew your place and who you *really* are!'

Lipa was stunned, looked at her and did not seem to understand. But when she suddenly saw how Aksinya was looking at her and the baby, she *did* understand and she went numb all over.

'You've taken my land, so take *that*!'

And she grabbed the ladle with the boiling water and poured it over Nikifor. A scream rang out, the like of which had never been heard in Ukleyevo and it was hard to believe it came from such a frail little creature as Lipa. Suddenly all was quiet outside. Without so much as a word, Aksinya went back into the house, with that same naïve smile on her face . . . All that time the deaf husband had been walking round the yard with an armful of washing and without hurrying or saying a word he started hanging it up to dry again. And not until the cook came back from the river did anyone dare to go and see what had happened in the kitchen.

VIII

Nikifor was taken to the local hospital, where he died towards evening. Lipa did not wait for the others to come and fetch her and she wrapped the body in a blanket and started walking home.

The hospital, which had just been built, with large windows, stood high up on a hill. It was flooded in the light of the setting sun and seemed to be burning inside. At the bottom of the hill was a small village. Lipa walked on down and sat by a pond before she reached it. A woman had brought her horse there for watering, but it would not drink.

'What do you want, then?' she was asking in a soft, bewildered voice. 'What else?'

A boy in a red shirt was sitting at the water's edge washing his father's boots. Apart from them, there wasn't a soul to be seen, either in the village or on the hillside.

'Won't drink, then?' Lipa said, looking at the horse.

But at that moment the woman and the boy with the boots went away and then the place was completely deserted. The sun lay down to rest under a blanket of purple and gold brocade, and long red and lilac clouds stretching right across the sky were watching over it. From somewhere far off came the mournful, indistinct cry of a bittern, sounding just like a cow locked up in a shed. Every spring this mysterious bird's song could be heard, but no one knew what it was or where it lived. Up by the hospital, in the bushes by the pond, beyond the village and in the fields all around, nightingales poured forth their song. A cuckoo seemed to be adding up someone's age, kept losing count and starting again. In the pond, frogs croaked angrily to each other, almost bursting their lungs and one could even make out something sounding like 'That's what you are! That's what you are!' What a noise! It seemed that all these creatures were singing and crying out loud on purpose, so that no one could sleep on that spring evening, and so that everything – even the angry frogs – should treasure and savour every minute of it. After all, we only live once!

A silver crescent moon shone in the sky and there were innumerable stars. Lipa could not remember how long she had been sitting by the pond, but when she got up and went on her way everyone in the village had already gone to bed and there wasn't a light to be seen. It was probably another eight miles back to the house, but all her strength had gone and she had no idea how she was going to get back. The moon shed its light first in front of her, then to the right, and that same cuckoo (its voice had grown hoarse by now) was still crying and its teasing laughter seemed to be saying, 'Oh, look out, you'll lose your way!' Lipa hurried along and her shawl fell off and was lost. She looked at the sky and wondered where her child's soul might be at that moment: was it following her or was it floating high up in the heavens, near the stars, and had forgotten its mother? How lonely it is at night out in the open fields, with all that singing, when you cannot sing yourself, amidst all those never-ending cries of joy when you can feel no joy yourself . . . when the moon, as lonely as you are, looks down from on high, indifferent to everything, whether it is spring or winter, whether people live or die ... when the heart is heavy with grief it is hard to be alone. If only Praskovya, her mother, or Crutchy, or the cook, or any of the peasants were with her now!

'Boo–oo!' cried the bittern, 'boo–oo!'

Then suddenly she heard a man's voice, quite distinctly.

'Get those horses harnessed, Vavila.'

Right ahead of her to one side of the road was a bonfire. The flames had died down and there remained only smouldering embers. She could hear a horse munching and then she made out two carts in the darkness, one laden with a barrel and the other, which was slightly lower, with two sacks; and she saw the shapes of two men. One of them was leading the horse to be harnessed, while the other stood motionless by the fire with his hands behind his back. A dog growled near one of the carts. The man who was leading the horse stopped and said, 'Sounds like someone's coming.' The other one shouted at the dog, 'Sharik, be quiet!'

From the voice she could tell it was an old man. Lipa stopped and said, 'God be with you!'

The old man went up to her and after some hesitation said, 'Hello!'

'Your dog doesn't bite, does he, Grandpa?'

'Don't worry, he won't touch you.'

'I've just come from the hospital,' Lipa said after a short silence. 'My little boy's just died there, I'm taking him home.'

The old man must have found this news unpleasant, as he moved away and said hurriedly, 'Don't worry, dear, it's God's will.' Then he turned to his companion and said, 'Stop dawdling, lad. Come on, look lively!'

'Can't find the shaft,' the boy replied. 'T'aint 'ere.'

'You're a dead loss, Vavila!'

The old man picked up a smouldering ember and blew on it; in its light she could distinguish his nose and eyes. When they at last managed to find the shaft he went over to Lipa holding the burning wood and looked at her. His face was full of compassion and tenderness.

'Well, you're a mother,' he said. 'Every mother feels sorry for her child.'

With these words he sighed and shook his head. Vavila threw something on to the fire, stamped on it and suddenly there was nothing but darkness again. Everything disappeared and once more all Lipa could see were those same fields, the starlit sky; the birds were still making a noise, keeping each other awake, and Lipa thought she could hear a corncrake crying from the very spot where the bonfire had been. But a minute later she could see the carts again, the old man and the tall figure of Vavila. The carts creaked as they moved out on to the road.

'Are you *holy* men?' Lipa asked the old man.

'No, we're from Firsanovo.'

'When you looked at me just now, it made my heart go soft all over. And that boy's so well-behaved. That's why I thought you were holy men.'

'Got far to go?'

'Ukleyevo.'

'Get in, we'll take you as far as Kuzmyonki. From there you go straight on and we turn left.'

Vavila sat in the cart with the barrel, while the old man and Lipa climbed into the other. They moved at walking-pace, with Vavila leading the way.

'My little boy suffered all day long,' Lipa said. 'He'd look at me with his little eyes and say nothing – he wanted to tell me something, but couldn't. God in heaven, Holy Virgin! I just fell on the floor with grieving. Then I'd get up and fall down by his bed. Can you tell me, Grandpa, why little children have to suffer so before dying? When a grown-up man or a woman suffers, their sins are forgiven them. But why should a little child who's never sinned suffer so? Why?'

'*Who* knows!?' the old man answered.

They drove on in silence, for half an hour.

'We can't always know the whys and wherefores,' the old man said. 'A bird's got two wings, not four, just because two's enough to fly with. In the same way, man isn't meant to know everything, only half or a quarter. He just knows enough to get him through life.'

'Grandpa, I'd feel better walking now. My heart's pounding.'

'Don't be sad, just sit where you are.'

The old man yawned, then made the sign of the cross before his mouth.

'Don't be sad ...' he repeated, 'your troubles aren't so terrible

It's a long life, and you'll go through good and bad, all kinds of things.'

He looked around him, then back, and went on, 'Mother Russia is so great! I've travelled all over it and I've seen everything, mark my words, dear. There's good to come, and bad. I've gone as a foot-messenger to Siberia, I've been on the Amur, in the Altay. I settled in Siberia, ploughed me own land. Then I pined for Mother Russia and came back to the village where I was born. Came back on foot, we did. I remember, I was on a ferry once, not an ounce of flesh on me, all in rags, no shoes on me feet, frozen stiff, sucking away at a crust, when a gent what was crossing on the same ferry – if he's passed on, then God rest his soul – looks at me with pity in his eyes, and the tears just flowed. Then he says, "Your beard is black – and your life'll be the same too ..." When I got back I didn't 'ave 'ouse nor 'ome, as the saying goes. I did 'ave a wife but she stayed behind in Siberia and she's buried there. So I goes and works as a farm-hand. And what next? I'll tell you what – there was good and there was bad times. And now I don't want to die, me dear, I'd like to hang on for another twenty years. That means I must 'ave 'ad more good times than bad! Oh, Mother Russia is so big!' Once again he looked around as he said this.

'Grandpa,' Lipa asked, 'when someone dies, how long does the soul wander over the earth?'

'Well, who can say! Let's ask Vavila, he's been to school. Teach 'em everything these days.' The old man shouted, 'Vavila!'

'What?'

'Vavila, when someone dies, how long does the soul wander over the earth?'

Vavila made the horse stop first and then replied, 'Nine days. When my uncle Kirilla died, his soul lived on in our hut for thirteen days.'

'But how do you know?'

'There was a knocking in the stove for thirteen days.'

'All right. Let's be on our way now,' the old man said, clearly not believing one word of it.

Near Kuzmyonki the carts turned off on to the main road, while Lipa went straight on. Already it was getting light. As she went down into the gully, the huts and church at Ukleyevo were hidden by mist. It was cold and she thought she could hear the same cuckoo calling.

Lipa was home before the cattle had been taken out to graze. Everyone was still sleeping. She sat on the front steps and waited. The first to come out was the old man. One look told him everything and for quite a while he couldn't say one word but just made a smacking noise with his lips.

'Oh, Lipa,' he said, 'you didn't look after my grandson ...'

They woke Barbara up. She wrung her hands, burst out sobbing and immediately started laying the baby out.

'And he was the loveliest little boy ...' she muttered again and again. 'Oh, dear, dear me ... Her one and only child and still she couldn't look after it, the stupid girl!'

Prayers were said in the morning and evening. Next day the child was buried, and after the funeral the guests and clergy ate a great deal and with such enormous appetites it seemed they hadn't eaten for a long, long time. Lipa served them food at the table and the priest held up his fork with a pickled mushroom on the end of it and told her, 'Don't grieve for your child, for *theirs is the kingdom of heaven*.'

Only when everyone had left did Lipa fully realize that Nikifor was gone, would never come back and she began to sob. She didn't know which room to go into to have a good cry, since she felt that after her child's death there was no longer any place for her in that house, that she was no longer needed, that no one wanted her; and the others felt the same as well.

'Well, now, what's all this wailing for?' Aksinya suddenly shouted, as she appeared in the doorway. For the funeral she had specially put on a new dress and she had powdered her face. 'Shut up!'

Lipa wanted to stop but she just couldn't and sobbed even louder.

'Did you hear!' Aksinya screamed and stamped her feet furiously. '*Who* d'ye think you are, then? Clear off, and don't ever set foot in this house again, you convict's bird! Clear off!'

'Now now ... come on ...' the old man said fussily, 'calm down, Aksinya, dear, *please* ... It's very understandable she's crying ... she's lost her baby ...'

'*Understandable* ...' Aksinya said, mimicking him. 'She can stay the night then, but I want her *out* by the morning.' Again she mimicked him and said, '*Understandable!*', laughed and went off to the shop.

Early next morning Lipa went home to her mother at Torguyevo.

IX

These days the roof and the door of the shop are painted freshly and shine like new. Cheerful-looking geraniums are blossoming in their window-boxes as they used to do, and what happened three years ago at the Tsybukins' is almost forgotten.

Old Grigory Tsybukin is still looked upon as the master, but in fact Aksinya is in charge of everything. She does the buying and selling, and nothing is done without her permission. The brickyard is prospering – since bricks are needed for the railway, the price has risen to twenty-four roubles a thousand. Women and girls cart the bricks to the station, load the wagons and get twenty-five kopeks for it.

Aksinya has gone into partnership with the Khrymins and the factory now bears the name: KHRYMIN SONS & CO. They have opened a pub near the station and it's there, not at the factory, that the expensive accordion is played now. Among the regulars are the postmaster, who has also started a business of his own, and the stationmaster. The Khrymin sons gave the deaf husband a gold watch, and he takes it out of his pocket every now and then and holds it to his ear.

There is talk in the village that Aksinya is very powerful now. And one can see this when she drives to the factory in the mornings, looking pretty and happy (she still has that same naïve smile), and starts giving orders. Whether at home, in the village or in the factory, everyone is afraid of her. When she drops in at the post-office, the postmaster leaps to his feet and says, 'Please, do take a seat, Mrs Tsybukin!'

Once, when a rather elderly landowner, who was a bit of a dandy and wore a fine silk coat and high lacquered boots, was selling her a horse, he was so carried away that he sold her the horse at whatever price she wanted. He held her hand for a long time as he gazed into her gay, cunning, naïve eyes and told her, 'I would do *anything* to please a woman like you, Mrs Tsybukin. Just tell me when we can meet again, without anyone disturbing us.'

'Whenever you like!'

Since then the elderly dandy has been driving to the shop almost every day for some beer, which is plain revolting and has the bitter taste of wormwood. But the landowner just shakes his head and drinks it up.

Old Tsybukin doesn't have anything to do with the business now. He doesn't handle money any more, as he just can't distinguish counterfeit coins from good ones, but he never says a word to anyone about this failing of his. He's become rather forgetful and if no one gives him food, then he doesn't ask for any – indeed, all the others are used to eating without him and Barbara often says, 'My old man went to bed yesterday again without a bite to eat.'

And she says this from force of habit, as though she could not care less.

For some odd reason, the old man wears a heavy coat whether it's winter or summer and he stays indoors only when it's very hot. Well wrapped up in his fur coat, with the collar up, he strolls round the village, along the road to the station, or else he'll sit on a bench by the church gates all day long. He'll just stay there without budging. People greet him as they walk past, but he ignores them, as he dislikes peasants as much as ever. If they ask him a question he'll give them an intelligent, polite but curt reply. There's talk in the village that his daughter-in-law has thrown him out of his own house and refuses him food, so that he has to rely on charity. Some of the villagers are glad, others feel sorry for him.

Barbara is even fatter now and she looks paler too. She still does her good deeds and Aksinya keeps out of her way. There's so much jam that they can't get through it all before the next crop of berries is ready. It crystallizes and Barbara is almost reduced to tears, not knowing what to do with it. And they have almost forgotten all about Anisim. A letter did come from him once, written in verse, on a large sheet of paper – just like an official appeal and in that same lovely handwriting. Clearly, his friend Samorodov was doing time in the same prison. Beneath the verses there was one line, in ugly writing that was almost impossible to decipher: 'I'm always ill in this place, it's terrible, please help me, for the love of Christ.'

One fine autumn day, in the late afternoon, old Tsybukin was sitting near the church gates, his collar turned up so high that only his nose and the peak of his cap were visible. At the other end of the long bench Yelizarov, the carpenter, was sitting next to Yakov, the school caretaker, a toothless old man of seventy, and they were having a chat.

'Children should see that old people have enough to eat – *honour thy father and thy mother*,' Yakov was saying with great annoyance. 'But as for *her*, that daughter-in-law, she threw her father-in-law out of 'is own 'ouse. The old man has nothing to eat or drink – and where can 'e go? 'Asn't eaten nothing for three days.'

'Three days!' Crutchy exclaimed.

'Yes, all 'e does is just sit and say nothing. He's very weak now. Why should we keep quiet about it? She should be sent for trial – they wouldn't let her off so lightly in court!'

'*Who* did they let off lightly in court?' Crutchy asked, not catching what the other had said.

'What?'

'His old girl's all right, a real worker. In their kind of business you can't get far without hard work . . . not without a bit of fiddling, I mean . . .'

'Thrown out of his own 'ouse,' Yakov said as irritably as before. 'You earns money to buy your own 'ouse, then you have to clear out. She's a right one, eh? A real pest!'

Tsybukin listened and didn't move an inch.

'What does it matter if it's your own house or someone else's, as long as it's warm and the women don't start squabbling,' Crutchy said and burst out laughing. 'When I was a young lad, I 'ad a real soft spot for my Nastasya. Quiet little woman she was. She kept on telling me, "Yelizarov, buy a house, buy a house! Buy a house!" When she was dying, she still kept saying, "Yelizarov, buy a nice fast drozhky, so's we won't have to walk." But all I ever bought her was gingerbread, nothing else.'

'That deaf husband of 'ers is an idiot,' Yakov went on, as though he hadn't been listening. 'A real clot, like a goose. Expect *him* to understand anything? You can bash a goose on the 'ead with a stick but it won't understand.'

Crutchy got up to make his way back to the factory. So did Yakov, and they both set off together, still chatting away. When they had gone about fifty paces, old Tsybukin stood up and shuffled off after them, stepping very gingerly, as though walking on slippery ice.

The village had already sunk deep into the dusk and the sun was shining now only on the highest stretch of the road, which twisted down the slope like a snake. Old women and their children were returning from the forest and they carried baskets full of coral milk-cap and agaric mushrooms. Women and young girls crowded back from the station where they had been loading bricks on to wagons and their noses and cheeks – just below the eyes – were caked with the red dust. They sang as they came. Lipa walked on in front of everybody and her thin voice broke into overflowing song as she looked up at the sky, and it was as if she were celebrating some victory and rejoicing that the day, thank God, was at an end, and that now she could rest. Her mother, Praskovya, was in the crowd, carrying her little bundle in her hand and – as always – gasping for breath.

'Good evening, Yelizarov!' Lipa said when she saw Crutchy. 'Hello, my poppet!'

'Good evening, darling Lipa,' Crutchy joyfully replied. 'My dear women and girlies, be nice to the rich carpenter! Oho, my dear little children, my children,' (he started sobbing) 'my darlings!'

The women could hear Crutchy and Yakov talking as they walked away. Immediately they had disappeared, old Tsybukin came towards the crowd and everything went quiet. Lipa and Praskovya were lagging a little way behind the others and when the old man caught them up Lipa made a deep curtsey and said, 'Good evening, Mr Tsybukin!'

And the mother curtseyed as well. The old man stopped and looked at them without saying a word. His lips were trembling and his eyes full of tears. Lipa took a piece of buckwheat pie out of her mother's bundle and handed it to him. He took it and started eating.

Now the sun had completely set and its light was gone even from the high stretch of road. It became dark and cool. Lipa and Praskovya continued on their way and kept crossing themselves for a long time afterwards.

Anna Round the Neck

I

Nothing was served after the wedding, not even light snacks. The bride and groom drank a glass of champagne, changed and drove off to the station. Instead of celebrating with a gay ball and supper, instead of music and dancing, they were going to a monastery a hundred and sixty miles away. Many of the guests approved, as Modeste Alekseyevich was a high-ranking official, wasn't so young any more, and a noisy reception might appear out of place. And in any case it's boring having music when a fifty-two-year-old civil servant marries a girl barely turned eighteen. Moreover, the guests said that a highly principled man like Modeste Alekseyevich must have organized the monastery trip to make it quite clear to his young wife that even in marriage he gave pride of place to religion and morality.

A crowd of office colleagues and relatives went to see them off and stood at the station, glasses in hand, waiting to cheer when the train left. Peter Leontyevich, the bride's father, in top-hat and schoolmaster's tail-coat, already drunk and looking very pale, kept going up to the window of the carriage with a champagne glass and pleading with his daughter, 'Annie dear! Anne! I'd like to say just *one* word!'

Anne leant out of the window and he whispered some incomprehensible words, smothering her with alcohol fumes as he blew into her ear and made the sign of the cross over her face, bosom and hands. His breath came in short gasps and tears glistened in his eyes. Anne's schoolboy brothers, Peter and Andrew, tugged at his tail-coat from behind and whispered in embarrassment, 'That's enough, Papa, please stop!'

When the train started Anne saw her father running after them, staggering and spilling his wine. His face looked so pathetic, kind, guilty. 'Hoo–ooray!' he shouted.

The couple were alone now. Modeste looked round the compartment, put the luggage on the rack and sat smiling opposite his wife. He was a civil servant of medium height, rather round and plump, and very well fed. He had long side-whiskers (but no moustache) and his round clean-shaven pointed chin looked like a heel. The most striking feature in that face was the absence of a moustache, with a freshly-shaven bare patch instead, which gradually merged into two fat cheeks that wobbled like jellies. He had a dignified bearing, rather sluggish movements and gentle manners.

'At this moment in time I cannot but recall a certain event,' he said, smiling. 'When Kosorotov received the Order of St Anne, second class, five years ago, he called on His Excellency to thank him. His Excellency used the following expression: "So now you've got three Annes, one in your buttonhole and two round your neck." I should explain that Kosorotov's wife had just come back to him – she was an irritable, empty-headed woman called Anne. I hope when *I* receive the Order of St Anne, second class, His Excellency will have no cause to make the same comment.'

His tiny eyes filled with a smile and Anne smiled too, disturbed at the thought that any moment this man might kiss her with his fat moist lips – and she wouldn't be able to say no. The smooth movements of his plump body frightened her and she felt terrified, disgusted.

He stood up and without hurrying took off the ribbon from round his neck, his tail-coat and waistcoat and put his dressing-gown on.

'That's better,' he said as he sat beside her.

She recalled the excruciating wedding service when she had thought that the priest, the guests and everyone in the church were looking at her sadly, asking themselves *why* an attractive girl like her was marrying an elderly, boring man. Earlier that morning she had felt delighted that everything had turned out so well, but during the service – and as she sat in the train now – she felt guilty, cheated and foolish. It was all very well having a rich husband, but she still didn't have any money. The wedding dress hadn't been paid for and that morning she could tell by the look on her father's and brothers' faces – when they had seen her off – that they didn't have a kopek between them. Would they have anything to eat that evening? Or the next? For some reason she began to think that her father and brothers would go hungry now she had gone, and would be sitting at home grieving as they had done the first evening after they had buried Mother.

'Oh, I'm *so* unhappy!' she thought. 'Why am I so unhappy?'

With the clumsiness one might expect from a respectable man who had no experience of women, Modeste kept touching her waist and patting her shoulder, but she could only think about money, about her mother and her death, after which her father, an art master at the high school, had taken to drink, so that they really began to feel the pinch. The boys had no boots or galoshes, the father was always in court, and the bailiffs came and put a distraint on the furniture. What a disgrace that had been! Anne had to look after her drunken father, darn her brothers' socks and go shopping. Whenever she was complimented on her looks, her youth and refined manners, she felt the whole world could see her cheap hat and the patches in her shoes which she had stained with ink. And there were tears at night and the nagging, unsettling thought that any day Father might be dismissed for drinking, that the blow would be too much for him and that he would die too. But some ladies – friends of the family – got busy and tried to find a husband for her. And in no time this Modeste Alekseyevich turned up, a man who was neither young nor good-looking, but he did have money – about a hundred thousand in the bank and a family estate which he let to a tenant. He was a gentleman of high principles, on good terms with His Excellency, and he only had to lift a finger to get a note from him for the headmaster or even the education committee and Peter Leontyevich would not lose his job.

While she was brooding over these details, a sudden burst of music and sound of voices came through the window. The train had reached a halt along the line. Two people in the crowd on the other side of the platform had struck up a lively tune on an accordion and a cheap squeaky violin, while from beyond the tall birches, poplars and moonlit country villas came the sound of a military band: most probably there was a dance at one of the villas. The resident holiday-makers and the day-trippers from town, who had come to enjoy the fine weather and fresh air, were strolling along the platform. Artynov was there – he owned all the holiday area and he was a rich, tall, stout man, with dark brown hair, bulging eyes and a face like an Armenian's. He was wearing a very strange outfit – an open-necked shirt, high boots with spurs and a black cloak that hung down from his shoulders and touched the ground like the train of a dress. Following him were two wolf-hounds with sharp, lowered muzzles.

Although the tears still glistened in Anne's eyes, now she forgot all about her mother, money and her wedding, and she smiled cheerfully as she shook familiar schoolboys' and officers' hands with a quick: 'Hello! How are you?'

She went out on to the small platform at the end of the carriage and stood in the moonlight, so that they could all have a full view of her in her magnificent new dress and hat.

'Why are we stopping here?' she asked.

'It's a loop-line,' came the answer. 'They're waiting for the mail train to pass through.'

Noticing that Artynov was looking at her, she blinked coquettishly and started speaking out loud in French – the beautiful sound of her own voice, the music from the band, the moon's reflection in the pond, the fact that she had claimed Artynov's close attention (he was a notorious ladies' man and society darling, and was giving her hungry, inquisitive looks) – all of this, combined with the general mood of festivity, brought a surge of joy to her heart. When the train moved off and her officer friends had given her a farewell salute, she was already humming a polka, which the military band, roaring away somewhere behind the trees, sent flying after her. She returned to her compartment feeling that the stop at that country station had proved beyond doubt that now she could not fail to be happy, in spite of everything.

The couple spent two days at the monastery, then returned to town to live in the flat provided by the authorities. When Modeste had gone off to work, Anne would play the piano or cry with boredom, or lie down on the couch and read novels or look at fashion magazines. Modeste would eat a large dinner and talk about politics, appointments, transfers and decorations, about hard work not hurting anyone, about family life being a duty and not a pleasure; and he maintained that if one took care of the kopeks, the roubles would look after themselves and that religion and morality were the most important things in life.

'Every man should have responsibilities,' he would say, clenching his knife in his fist like a sword.

Anne would become so frightened, listening to all this, that she couldn't eat and she would usually leave the table hungry. Her husband would normally have a rest after dinner and snore loudly, while she went off to see her family. Her father and brothers would give her strange looks as though – just before she arrived – they had been condemning her for marrying that terrible bore, a man she didn't love, for his money. For them the rustle of her dress, the bracelets she wore, the way she looked like a fine lady now, were inhibiting and insulting. They were embarrassed by her visits and they just did not know what to talk about. She would sit down and join them in cabbage soup, porridge, or potatoes fried in mutton fat reeking of candle-grease. Peter Leontyevich's hand would shake as he filled his glass from the decanter and drink rapidly and greedily, and with obvious disgust; then he would take a second, then a third. Peter and Andrew, skinny, pale-faced boys with large eyes, would take the decanter away and exclaim in despair, 'You mustn't, Papa ... you've had enough.'

And Anne would grow anxious as well and she would plead with him to stop. This made him flare up, bang his fist on the table and shout, 'I *won't* be told what to do! Street urchins! And *you* little slut! I'll kick you out, the lot of you!'

But his weak, kind voice gave no one cause for alarm. After dinner he would usually smarten himself up: pale-faced, with his chin cut from shaving, craning his thin neck, he would stand a whole half-hour in front of the mirror trying to make himself look smart, combing his hair, twirling his black moustache, sprinkling himself with perfume or tying a bow-tie. Then he would put on his gloves and top-hat and go out to do some private coaching. If it was a holiday, he would stay at home and paint or play the harmonium, making it grunt and groan. He tried to squeeze beautiful melodies out of it, humming a bass accompaniment or losing his temper with the boys: 'Savages! Wretches! You've ruined it!'

In the evenings Anne's husband would play cards with colleagues who lived in the same government block. Their wives used to come along with them. They were ugly, tastelessly dressed, terribly coarse, and they filled the flat with malicious scandal-mongering that was as ugly and vulgar as themselves. Sometimes Modeste would take Anne to the theatre. In the intervals he made sure she kept close by him and would walk along the corridors and around the foyer holding her arm. After exchanging bows with someone he would whisper quickly, 'A senior government official,' or 'He's got money ... has his own house ...'

Anne would long for something sweet as they passed the bar. She loved chocolate and apple pie, but she didn't have any money and was too shy to ask her husband. He would take a pear, press it and ask hesitantly, 'How much?'

'Twenty-five kopeks.'

'Well, really!' he would say, replacing it.

As it was awkward leaving the bar without buying anything, he would ask for some soda-water and finish a whole bottle off himself, which made his eyes water. At these moments Anne hated him.

Another time he would suddenly turn bright red and hurriedly say, 'Bow to that old lady.'

'But I don't know her.'

'It doesn't matter, she's the wife of the manager of the local revenue office. Bow, I'm telling you,' he would growl insistently. 'Your head won't fall off!'

So Anne would bow and her head didn't fall off. But it was an ordeal, just the same. She did everything her husband wanted and was furious with herself for letting him make such an absolute fool of her. She had married him for his money and now she was worse off than before. Her father, at least, used to give her twenty-kopek pieces, but now she didn't get anything. She could not bring herself to take any money when he wasn't there or ask for some, as she was frightened of her husband, frightened to death, in fact.

She felt that she had *always* had this fear of him. When she was a child, she invariably thought of the headmaster of the local high school as a most awe-inspiring, terrifying force, advancing on her like a storm-cloud or a railway engine that was about to run her over. Another such power – always a subject for discussion in the family and whom they feared as well – was His Excellency. And there were about a dozen lesser fry, including stern, smooth-shaven, unmerciful schoolmasters; and finally, along had come that Modeste Alekseyevich, a man of high principles, who even looked like the headmaster. In her imagination all these forces merged together and took the form of an enormous, terrifying polar bear, advancing on the weak and on those who had gone astray – like her father – and she was too scared to protest, would force herself to smile and pretend to be pleased when they roughly caressed her or dirtied her with their embraces.

Once – and only once – Peter Leontyevich dared to ask if he could borrow fifty-five roubles to settle a particularly nasty debt, but what an ordeal it was! 'All right, I'll let you have it,' Modeste said, after a moment's deliberation, 'but I'm warning you. That's all the help you'll get from me until you stop drinking. This weakness is quite disgraceful for a man in government service. I must remind you of the universally recognized fact that this vice has been the ruin of many able men who, had they only been able to control themselves, might eventually have come to occupy high positions.'

And there followed rambling periods, one after the other: 'in so far as' or 'if we take *that* as a starting-point' or 'in view of the aforesaid', all of which humiliated poor Peter Leontyevich and made him die for a drink.

The boys, who usually had holes in their boots and worn-out trousers when they visited Anne, were also subjected to these lectures.

'*Every* man should have responsibilities,' Modeste would tell them. But he didn't give them any money. However, he presented Anne with rings, bracelets and brooches, and told her that they should be kept for a rainy day. Often he would unlock her chest of drawers to check if anything was missing.

II

Meanwhile winter had set in. Long before Christmas it was announced in the local paper that the usual winter ball would 'take place' on 29 December at the Assembly Rooms. Every evening after cards, Modeste Alekseyevich would get excited and have whispering sessions with civil servants' wives while he anxiously glanced at Anne. Then he would pace from corner to corner for a long time, deep in thought. Finally, late one evening, he stopped in front of Anne and said, 'You must get a dress for the ball. Do you understand? But first consult Marya Grigoryevna and Natalya Kuzminishna.'

And he gave her a hundred roubles, which she took. But when it came to ordering the dress she wouldn't consult anyone, talked only to her father and tried to visualize how her mother would have dressed for the ball. Her mother had always dressed in the latest fashion and had taken great pains with Anne, making sure she was dressed elegantly, like a doll, and taught her to speak French and dance an excellent mazurka (before her marriage she had been a governess for five years). Like her mother, she knew how to turn an old dress into a new one, wash her gloves with benzine, hire jewels and – just like her mother – flutter her eyelids, roll her 'r's, strike beautiful poses, go into raptures when the occasion called for it, or look sad and mysterious. She had her dark hair and eyes and nervous temperament from her mother and the habit of making herself look pretty the whole time from her father.

When Modeste Alekseyevich came into her room half an hour before they left for the ball to tie his St Anne ribbon round his neck in front of the full-length mirror, he was enchanted by her beauty and the glitter of her new gossamer-like dress, and he smugly combed his whiskers and said, 'What a beauty I've got . . . really! Just look at you, my dearest Anne!' His voice suddenly became solemn as he went on, 'I've made you happy and tonight you can make *me* happy. Introduce yourself to His Excellency's wife, I beg you! For heaven's sake! She can help me get a senior position!'

They drove off to the ball and arrived at the Assembly Rooms; at the entrance there was a porter. The hall was full of clothes-racks, scurrying footmen and ladies in low-necked dresses shielding themselves from the draught with their fans. The place smelt of soldiers and gas lights. As Anne went up the staircase on her husband's arm she heard music and caught a glimpse of herself in an enormous mirror lit by many lamps. Then the joy welled up in her heart and she felt she would be happy – as she had been on that moonlit night at the railway halt. She bore herself proudly, confidently feeling for the first time that she was no longer a little girl, but a lady now, copying her late mother's walk and manner. And – for the first time in her life – she felt rich and free. She didn't feel at all tied down having her husband with her: she had already instinctively guessed that the company of an elderly husband didn't in the least lower her in anyone's eyes. On the contrary, it stamped her with that tantalizing mysteriousness adored by men. The orchestra was already roaring away and dancing had started in the large ballroom. After that government flat, Anne felt overcome in a world of light, colour, music and noise, and she glanced around the ballroom thinking how wonderful it all was. At once she picked out all the people in the crowd she had met at parties or on walks – officers, teachers, lawyers, civil servants, landowners, His Excellency, Artynov, society ladies in their very best dresses with plunging necklines – some beautiful and others ugly – already in position at the stands and stalls of the charity bazaar in aid of the poor. A huge officer with epaulettes (she had met him in the Old Kiev Road when she was a schoolgirl and couldn't remember his name now) seemed to loom up out of thin air and invited her to the waltz. She flew from her husband and felt she was sailing in a boat during a violent storm – while her husband remained behind on the distant shore. She danced the waltz, polka and quadrille with fire and enthusiasm, moving from one partner to the other, intoxicated by the music and the noise, mixing Russian with French, rolling her 'r's, laughing, without a thought for her husband or indeed anyone or anything. She had scored a success with the men – there was no doubt about that – and it wasn't really surprising. Breathless with excitement, she feverishly pressed her fan between her hands and wanted to drink. Her father, in a crumpled tail-coat that smelt of benzine, went up to her with a plate of pink ice-cream.

'You look enchanting,' he said, eyeing her delightedly, 'and I've never felt as sorry as I do now that you rushed into that marriage . . . Why? I know you did it for us, but . . .' He pulled out a small bundle of notes with trembling hands and added, 'I was paid for a lesson today so I can repay your husband.'

She thrust the plate into his hands as she was grabbed by someone and whirled away from him; over her partner's shoulders she caught a glimpse of her father, who slid over the parquet floor, clasped a lady in his arms and tore around the room with her.

'He's so nice when he's sober!' she thought.

She danced a mazurka with the huge officer again. He moved across the floor very solemnly, ponderously, like a piece of meat in uniform, just turning his shoulder and chest and hardly shifting his feet – he didn't really want to dance at all. But she flitted around him, teasing him with her beauty and her bare neck. Her eyes burnt with desire, her movements were passionate, but her partner grew more and more cool towards her, holding his hand out graciously like a king bestowing a favour.

'Bravo, bravo!' shouted some onlookers.

But gradually he gave in. He was revitalized, very excited and spellbound by her. He became really animated and started moving easily, like a young man, while she merely moved her shoulders with an artful look, as though she were the queen and he the slave. Now she thought everyone was looking at them and dying with envy. The enormous officer hardly had time to thank her when the crowd suddenly parted and the men curiously stiffened up, their arms at their sides. It was all because His Excellency was coming over in his tail-coat – with two stars on his chest. There was no doubt about it, His Excellency was heading for *her*, as he was staring straight at her with a sugary smile on his face – he always did this when he saw a pretty woman.

'Absolutely *delighted*. Really delighted!' he began. 'I'll have to lock your husband up for hiding his treasure for so long. I've a message from my wife,' he continued, offering his hand. 'You must help us ... Hm, yes ... They should award you a prize for beauty as they do in America ... Hm ... My wife is dying to meet you.'

He led her over to a stall, to an old lady whose enormous chin was so out of proportion to the rest of her face it looked as if she had a large stone in her mouth.

'Please come and help us,' she said in a twanging voice. 'Every pretty woman helps us with the charity bazaar and you're the only one who seems content just to have a good time. Why don't you come and help!'

She left and Anne took her place next to a silver samovar and some tea cups. Immediately she did a roaring trade. She wouldn't take less than a rouble for a cup of tea and she made the huge officer drink three cups. Artynov came over – he was a rich man with bulging eyes and who suffered from shortness of breath. He wasn't sporting that peculiar costume which Anne had seen him wearing during the summer, but wore a tail-coat like everyone else. Without taking his eyes off Anne, he drank a glass of champagne, for which he paid a hundred roubles. Then he drank some tea and gave another hundred – all this without saying a word, and breathing like an asthmatic. Anne coaxed her customers and took their money, quite convinced that these people derived only the greatest pleasure from her smiles and glances. Now she realized that *this* was the life she was born for, this noisy, brilliant life of music, laughter, dancing and admirers, and her earlier fears of that force which was bearing down on her, threatening to crush her, seemed quite comical. She was afraid of nobody now and only regretted that her mother was not there with her to share in her success.

Her father, white-faced, but still steady on his feet, came over to her stall and asked for a glass of brandy. Anne blushed, frightened he might make some indecent remark (she was ashamed enough of having such a pale, ordinary father). But he merely drank his brandy, threw ten roubles down from his bundle and solemnly walked away without saying a word. A little later she saw him dancing the *grand rond* with his partner and this time he was staggering and shouting, much to his lady's embarrassment. Anne remembered a ball, about three years before, when he had staggered around and shouted in just the same way, and it had finished with the police hauling him off home to bed; the next day the headmaster threatened him with the sack. How this memory jarred on her now!

When the samovars in the stalls had cooled down and the weary ladies of charity had handed over their takings to the old lady with a stone in her mouth, Artynov led Anne by the arm into the ballroom, where supper was being served for the charity bazaar helpers. Twenty of them sat down to supper, no more, but it was all very noisy. His Excellency proposed a toast: 'It would be appropriate, in this luxurious dining-room, to drink to soup kitchens for the poor, which are the object of today's bazaar.' A brigadier proposed a toast to 'that power to which even artillery must surrender' – and all the men clinked glasses with the ladies. It was all very, very lively!

When Anne had been taken home, it was already growing light and cooks were going to market. Very happy, tipsy, brimming with new impressions and quite exhausted, she undressed, collapsed on to her bed and immediately fell asleep.

After one in the afternoon, she was woken up by her chambermaid who announced that Mr Artynov had come to visit her. She quickly dressed, went into the drawing-room, and before long His Excellency arrived to thank her for helping with the charity bazaar. He gave her a sickly look, moved his lips, kissed her hand, asked permission to call again, and left. She stood in the middle of the drawing-room absolutely astonished, enchanted, hardly believing that this change in her life – such an amazing one – had come so quickly. At that moment her husband came in. And now he stood there with the usual grovelling, cloying, servile expression he assumed in the presence of powerful and distinguished people. Convinced that she could say what she liked now, she told him – with rapture, indignation and contempt – 'Clear off, you fathead!', clearly articulating each syllable.

After that, Anne didn't have a single day to herself, since she joined the others for picnics, outings and theatricals. Every day she came back in the early hours, lay down on the drawing-room floor and gave everyone a most touching account of the gay life she was leading. She needed a great deal of money, but she wasn't afraid of Modeste Alekseyevich any more and spent his money as if it were hers. And she didn't even bother to ask for it or demand it, but simply sent him bills or notes saying: 'Pay bearer two hundred roubles' or 'Pay one hundred roubles immediately.'

At Easter, Modeste Alekseyevich was awarded the Order of St Anne, second class. When he called to express his thanks, His Excellency put his paper to one side and sank deeper into his armchair.

'That means you've three Annes now,' he said, examining his white hands and pink nails, 'one in your buttonhole and two round your neck.'

Modeste Alekseyevich pressed two fingers to his lips to stop himself laughing out loud and said, 'Now all I'm waiting for is a little Vladimir.* Dare I ask His Excellency to be the godfather?' He meant the Order of Vladimir, fourth class, and already pictured himself regaling all and sundry with this brilliantly apt and bold pun, and was about to produce another scintillating witticism along the same lines but His Excellency just nodded and plunged into his paper again . . .

Most of the time Anne went riding in a troika, hunting with Artynov, took part in one-act plays, dined out, and visited her family less and less. Peter Leontyevich began to drink more than ever, all his money had gone and they had to sell the harmonium to settle his debts.

*Vladimir, also a decoration.

The boys wouldn't let him out in the street on his own and kept following him in case he fell down. And whenever they met Anne on the Old Kiev Road, riding in a coach and pair with a side horse, Artynov sitting on the box instead of a coachman, Peter Leontyevich would doff his top-hat and start shouting. But then Peter and Andrew would hold him by the arms and plead with him, 'Please stop it, Papa. Please ...'